Ab

Kerry Gibb lives in Surrey, England with her husband, four sons, and an abundance of pets, including her three cocker spaniel dogs. She started her writing career as a children's author when she grabbed the hearts and laughter of children with her It's A Kid's Life series. One day, a mum of one of her readers got in touch to say, 'please write one for us mums'. So that's exactly what she did! Kayla's Girls is Kerry's debut novel for adults, written from the heart to win the hearts of mums everywhere.

'Kerry Gibb is such a talented writer. She now has two fans in this house - first my son, and now me!' – Jo Double

'Reading this book was like having a hug from a friend!' - Gemma Stanton

'As a mum, the characters were so relatable. I had tears of sadness one minute and tears of laughter the next!' – Vicki Hannay

Published by Packman Publishing.

First edition published in Great Britain 2021.

A CIP catalogue record for this title is available from the British Library.

ISBN - 978-0-9934937-5-1

This novel is fiction. The names, characters and incidents portrayed in it are at times inspired by real people but mostly from the author's imagination. Any other resemblance to actual persons, events or localities is entirely coincidental.

To Sandra

KAYLA'S GIRLS

KERRY GIBB

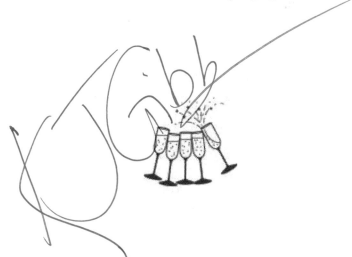

VIP Readers

Head over to kerrygibb.com to join my **VIP** readers
club which gives you access to exclusive insights and
all my latest book news!

This book is dedicated to all the women who have come into my life for a reason, a season, or a lifetime, and to those I am yet to meet...

Chapter 1

I felt my shoulders physically relax as the smooth liquid glided over my tongue. Content in my own company, I pondered the etiquette of the 'Prosecco school mums'. Mirroring the effervescence from their glass that they held in their hands like an accessory to a uniform, they confidently glided their way through the social dynamics of motherhood. Sometimes they could get away with a gin. This allowed them entrance to the 'classy mum crew'. Compliment it with a slimline tonic and they'd nailed the 'fit and sophisticated mum' look. Not that I had much first-hand experience as part of a mummy clique. I was more of a lone ranger, friends with all the mums but no-one in particular. It wasn't intentional, I'd just never been welcomed into the inner circle by anyone. My limited history of a mum's night out consisted of a Christmas get together last year, where I spent the night mingling with imposter syndrome as I sipped my obligatory glass of bubbles.

In that nightly hour of peace that I got at home when everyone else had gone to bed, a glass of full-bodied red wine was exactly what the doctor ordered. I cradled my glass in my hand and closed my eyes, rubbing my left eyebrow with my fingertips. I knew that I should go to bed, but I needed this hour of sanctuary with no-one demanding of me. It was essential for my sanity.

The solitary air was accentuated by the five empty chairs that accompanied me at the kitchen table. Freshly wiped down to remove sticky fingerprints and smatterings of ketchup, the white faux-leather enjoyed its brief moment of elegance before succumbing once again to the chaos of breakfast which would take hold less than eight hours from now.

I looked at the notes on my laptop that the agency had sent through. Male… ex-military… loves dogs – I liked this man already. Clicking on his profile picture, I tried to imagine chatting to him over a cup of tea. He had kind, wise eyes and a jawline that showed signs of age but had once been rugged and slightly intimidating. I chuckled to myself as I thought how the first introduction to a client felt like a scroll through Tinder. This gentleman, however, was not proposing a sensual date to me. Eighty-seven-year-old, Michael Lamb, didn't want me for my body. He wanted me for my talent. My ability to pull out the intricate parts of a person's life and weave them together into their most prized possession – their autobiography.

Six months ago, I had stumbled upon a job advert for freelance writers. The appeal had been instant. I loved the idea of creating a book for someone to share with their loved ones. A book revealing details that had been long forgotten until an in-depth chat with one of the company's researchers unearthed them. They asked questions in a way that triggered the most precious memories from people's lives. As a ghost-writer, it was my job to pull these caches together and present them in words that would do people the justice they deserved, and I bloody loved it. I was a firm believer that everyone had a story to tell.

I was far too tired to do Michael justice tonight though. Starting someone's autobiography with them took patience and a clear head. Unfortunately, these were two things that I was lacking at that moment in time. In the subtle glow of my Himalayan salt lamp, I took another sip of wine and stared blankly at my phone, scrolling through the never-ending social media ream. Thankfully, people were starting to realise that posting photos of what they had had for dinner did little to boost their profile. Inspirational quotes were where it was at now.

'Creativity is intelligence having fun,' – Albert Einstein...

'The truth must dazzle gradually, or every man be blind,' – Emily Dickenson...

'If you think you are too small to make a difference, try sleeping with a mosquito,' – Dalai Lama.

Oh, and Sarah, who I vaguely remembered from my first ever job, never failed to disappoint with her man-hating quotes following a rather messy breakup last year. 'If it looks like a dick and acts like a dick, it's probably my ex!' Good one Sarah!

My thumb seemed to have taken on a life of its own as it kept swiping up the screen. Karen was doing a half marathon and ran 7.2km today – woohoo! Rachel's little miracle fed himself for the first time – look at his cute messy face covered in mushed up crap! Oh, and look, Bethany has shared yet another post from a mummy blogger. This one was titled, 'How to discipline your kids without yelling'. No doubt written by a know-it-all mum whose angelic little child had at worst spilled some granola on his high chair and not cleaned it up.

I winced at myself for being so critical. Who was I to judge anyway? I had once briefly blogged about my life as a mum too. Or maybe that in itself did give me the right to be scathing. Raising my glass to my lips, I justified it as mocking myself.

Glancing back at my laptop, I thought back to the first ever post that I had written. Too scared to allow those who knew me into my inner thoughts – and trust me, there were plenty – I had posted it anonymously.

I couldn't believe how easy it had been. Late one night, after everyone was in bed, I had just started writing and couldn't stop. I had had yet another experience of a miserable old lady expressing her sympathy about my ability to only procreate those with a Y chromosome. My little crew were highly adept at coping with such insensitive old biddies though. I had taught them well. I didn't even need to respond on this occasion as on cue, all four of my sons gave her the death stare warning her not to mess with us. All I had to do was smile sweetly with my mouth whilst giving daggers with my eyes. The ability to do this is widely under-valued. Quite the talent, I had to practise long and hard to perfect it.

I had praised my sons for their solidarity and reminded them that having all of them was like winning the lottery to me. The bitterness had stuck with me though, like it always did. Only this time, I didn't just shrug it off. I had written my feelings down for the world to see — they just weren't aware that the feelings belonged to me.

I had doubted at the time that anyone would read it, but something inside me had felt compelled to share it. Maybe it was the fact that I had unconsciously poured myself a second, and then a third glass of wine whilst writing it. Maybe it was the notion that we all seemed to want to write a diary of our lives these days, but instead of keeping it a secret, we wanted others to acknowledge it. Whatever it was that had made me do it, I couldn't resist. I had quickly made an anonymous *Facebook* page and added my first post. Not ready to let the world know how I was feeling, I had stayed incognito and shared it on my own feed with a caption saying, 'Just came across this and thought I'd share.' Hovering over the post button for just a few seconds, I had taken the plunge and clicked down. The 576 so-called *friends* that I had accumulated over the years suddenly had access to my inner most thoughts.

I had gone to bed that night thinking that a few people may read my words of wisdom but mainly feeling a sense of weight lifted off of me. It was like a sort of therapy without the hefty price tag. Some women took up exercise to recalibrate themselves. Others bought clothes that would probably sit untouched in their wardrobe for months, just waiting for that one night out to arise. Me, I took up writing. Little did I know at that point the impact my words would have. I had woken up the following morning to comments of support, likes, and even shares. People had actually respected my words enough to validate them to others.

These days, I rarely wrote anything for the abyss of social media. Life was so busy, and I had more and more autobiographies coming through that I had to lend my ghost-writing skills to. I also felt like it had served its purpose and I didn't need to talk covertly to strangers in the world anymore. So many people shared their life for the fame – and the money if they could get it. I had just wanted to vent. To share my emotions and see if anyone else related. There were times where my desire to write still enticed my over active mind to express itself. Usually, I just kept it for myself now though – like more of a personal diary.

There was one particular piece of writing that I had started last night that wasn't going to stay in my private file, however. Feeling incensed after reading a so-called 'case-study' conducted by an 'academic', I couldn't resist writing my own thoughts in response. Ignoring the pull of social media trying to entice me back to my phone, I opened the file titled, 'Another Knobhead.' I leant forward to pick up where I'd left off, but before my eyes, the horizontal line that appears after you type a letter was shooting blindly across the screen. Line after line after line. My first reaction was that of any sane person – there was obviously a ghost sitting on my lap taking charge of my laptop!

As I leapt to my feet with a shudder, the line stopped moving. A chill went through my body as I concluded that this was obviously proof that a ghost had indeed been sitting on my lap, and my jump upwards had exorcised him back to the grave. Bravely, I sat back down on my chair and leant forward to continue typing. The horizontal line once again started to move across the page. Jerking backwards in my seat, I saw it stop, flashing like it was taunting me. Pondering that I may have been a little rash in my supernatural explanation, I leant forward again to test out another theory. Sure enough, the mystery writer reappeared. Chuckling to myself, I glanced down and saw my boobs resting without a care in the world on the space bar of the keyboard that was attached to the laptop. Freed from the restraints of the bra that had been keeping them pert all day, they had now succumbed to the laws of gravity – and the collateral damage of four babies sucking them dry for years– and had flopped down onto the nearest perch. Taking a sip of my near empty glass, I leant back an inch to direct my over-sized breasts onto the table top instead where they could do no more harm.

Placing my fingers back on the familiar keys, in one succinct paragraph, I finalised my views on the ridiculous parenting article that dressed itself up as an academic case study to give itself credibility…

So, as you can see, mothers of four or more kids are not less stressed than mothers of fewer children. This is just a load of crappy statistical nonsense from Professor Gobshite who has never parented a child in his life. If a mother of four children looks less stressed, it is probably due to the fact that she has dealt with so much crap over the years that she is now operating on a higher plane of existence which she has been driven to by insanity.

Put that in your pipe and smoke it, I thought to myself as I uploaded it to the comments section of the article. Something seemed to click in my brain at this time of night. It was as if my mind could flow freely and let honesty prevail. Taking a final sip from my glass, I acknowledged the fact that this possibly wasn't just attributable to the late hour, and that the wine that had entered my system tonight probably had made my lips just that little bit looser. I re-read *Professor Gobshite* and giggled. My full-bodied red could almost certainly take the credit for that little gem.

Hearing a cry from upstairs, I closed my laptop, knowing that I was about to squash myself up against a cold wall in a toddler bed whilst cuddling my youngest little man back to sleep. Thank goodness I had already put on my cosy, flannel pyjamas before allowing myself an hour of indulgent 'me-time'. Creeping up the stairs so as not to wake the others, I winced at the loud rumble coming from my bedroom. Curling up in a tiny bed was a far more appealing option than tossing and turning next to someone whose snore was as loud as the guttural roar of a rutting stag. Some nights, I would launch myself up into the air so as to shake the bed and then pretend to be asleep as my husband, Jason, jolted awake with a start. I decided to leave him in peace tonight though. Tomorrow was a big day for him as he was starting a new job. The job that had caused us to uproot our family and move house last week. And a new house meant a new school. A feeling of dread came over me as I climbed in next to my son who immediately stopped crying when he felt the safety of my arms enveloping him. Tomorrow morning was going to be tough, and at that moment in time, I had no idea how I would get three of my sons to overcome their nerves and embrace their new start. I had a feeling that bribery could be the only answer!

Chapter 2

I felt like my eyes had only been closed for a few minutes when I awoke to the sound of The Bangles singing 'Manic Monday'. It wasn't just a random choice. After years of hearing my first husband's alarm clock yelling, 'Rodney, Rodney. Get up you plonker!' before playing the *Only Fools and Horses* theme tune, I had realised that the sound you wake up to can have a huge impact on you as a person. Note the word *plonker* in his wake-up call. And note the phrase *first husband*, aka, previous husband, aka, no longer husband!

According to leading psychologists, the music you wake up to should build up gradually, introducing a strong beat with positive lyrics. Think more 'Wake Up' by The Vamps and less 'Everybody Hurts' by REM. I'm not too sure the 'Manic Monday' lyrics technically fall into the category of positive mental attitude, but it worked for me.

Forcing my eyelids open, I took in my surroundings to see which bedroom I was waking up in today. Seeing a bookshelf top heavy with contemporary female protagonists, I was pleasantly surprised to realise that I had in fact found my way back to my own bedroom at some point in the night as Jason's snoring must have subsided. He appeared at my bedside looking very dapper in his crisp white shirt and new black jeans that would fit in perfectly with the smart-casual dress code his new office allowed.

'Wish me luck,' he said, planting a kiss on my forehead. An advertising firm had headhunted him for an Account Manager role a few months back after he made a name for himself in the industry. At thirty-eight-years old, Jason was beginning to show the tell-tale signs that he was heading towards forty. He didn't have the black bags under his eyes like I did – he had his ear plugs to thank for that – but lines were starting to creep around his eyes and onto his forehead. Plus, his hair line was definitely a few millimetres further back than this time last year.

'Good luck,' I replied, mustering up as much enthusiasm in my voice as I could before closing my eyes again.

'Get up, lazy,' he said, whipping the duvet off me. 'You can't be late to school on their first day.'

Groaning, I forced myself to sit up as 'Manic Monday' came to an end. Never had my wake-up song been so fitting. My stomach churned as I thought about the hour I had ahead of me. My eldest son, Ben, had been mortified when Jason and I had told him about our move. I had vivid memories of him standing on the stairs at our old house shouting that he hated us. Apparently, we were the worst parents in the world for making him leave all his friends behind at his last school. I knew that he would adjust. He was only nine-years-old, but being the oldest of four brothers he thought that he was so grown up and didn't appreciate how young he actually was. He had many years of friendships ahead of him. I was sure that he'd soon settle in, but convincing a raging child of this who thinks you've ruined his life is no easy feat. Taking a deep breath, I headed for the bathroom. I needed a quick five-minute shower before I faced the arduous task of getting everyone out of bed.

Tugging off my pyjamas, I stepped under the warm jet of water, relishing in this rare moment of indulgence. I closed my eyes and held my face up allowing the water to flow over it. My sanctuary was short lived, however, as I heard a giggle from the other side of the shower screen. Springing my eyes open, I saw my four-year-old son, Josh, standing there, smirking and pointing at me.

'Why've you got a hairy willy, Mummy? Sammy, come and look, Mummy's got a hairy willy!'

Before I could reply, his younger brother, Samuel, charged into the bathroom, eager to see what his brother was looking at. So much for me thinking I'd have to wake them up. I should have known those two would be full of beans already.

'Boobies!' he shrieked, joining in the laughter.

Attempting to cover my lady bits with one hand and my boobs with the other, I coaxed them out of the bathroom with the temptation of climbing into my bed to watch cartoons. I would regret it when I had to drag them out again for breakfast, but for now it was a quick fix to save my dignity. Before they made it out the door though, we were joined by Ryan, my seven-year-old son.

'Mum doesn't have a willy,' he said, with the tone of a know-it-all big brother. 'She has a badgina.'

I nearly choked on the shower water where my mouth suddenly gaped open.

'A badgina?' I questioned him through the glass that was thankfully beginning to steam up and provide me with a much-needed shield.

'Mrs Bates told us about it at school, last year,' he said matter-of-factly. 'Boys have willies, and girls have badginas. Everyone knows that.'

Before I could correct him that it was actually a vagina, he ran out of the bathroom to join his brothers in my bed. In an effort to avoid any other unwelcome intruders rushing in to point out my body parts, I hurriedly soaped down and stepped out of the shower. Wrapping a towel around myself, I patted down the tendrils of mahogany hair that had escaped the top knot designed to stop my hair getting wet. Glancing in the mirror, I marvelled at how it actually looked quite good. It was one of life's infuriating little conundrums – attempt a sophisticated bun for a classy daytime style and it ended up looking like it should be complimented by a matching velour tracksuit. Bung it up in seconds to keep it dry in the shower, however, and it looked good enough for a red carpet appearance.

Ignoring the pile of boys now in my bed, I perused my school run attire in the wardrobe, deciding whether to go for the blue jeans with the stylish rips in them, the blue jeggings which sagged around my backside but could be nicely covered up by an oversized jumper, or the skinny blue jeans with tummy control that squashed everything nicely into place. Or I could be really adventurous and go for the black jeans. After a second of deliberation, I settled on the jeggings and paired them up with a teal, thigh-length jumper that hid a multitude of sins.

Looking in the mirror, I focused on the dark shadows encroaching around each of my eyes, like a dusky evening sky robbing us of daylight. Nine years of sleepless nights was beginning to catch up with me. I grabbed my Touche-Eclat out of my make-up bag and dabbed it under my eyes. I had no idea who came up with the crazy idea of covering up your least desirable parts by highlighting them, but they were a genius. I didn't care what the science behind it was, if it made me look more human and less like a zombie then that was good enough for me. A dab of powder and a sweep of mascara and I was done. I tugged the hair band out of my top knot which, of course, no longer looked sophisticated, but was now the more familiar messy, frizzy, lopsided bun.

'Two more minutes, boys, and then I want all of you downstairs for breakfast.'

Six identical, deep blue eyes continued to stare at the television screen, ignoring me. Sighing, I walked out of the bedroom, knowing that they had no intention of doing as I had asked. I wandered into my eldest son Ben's bedroom. He could literally sleep through a booming thunder storm. Snuggled up next to him was our dog, Obi, whose tail started thumping on the duvet when he saw me. Crawling out from under Ben's arm, he hopped off the bed and came over to rub himself against my legs.

'Hello, boy,' I said as I stroked him behind his floppy golden ears. Jason hadn't been keen on dogs before we got Obi. In fact, he hadn't exactly agreed to us getting him. After seeing an advert for some cocker spaniel puppies, I took Sammy and Josh to see them whilst Ben and Ryan were at school one day. There were seven puppies in total, all as cute as each other. I fell in love with each and every one of them immediately, but it was Obi who chose us. As Sammy and Josh peered excitedly over the puppy pen, this gorgeous bundle of golden fluff with ears that were too big for his tiny body rushed straight over and gave each of them a big lick on their little noses. That was the moment that I knew there was no going back. I took a photo of the pup that we were destined to give a forever home to and sent it to Jason with a caption saying, 'Hello Daddy.' After initially giving me a hard time for going behind his back, he gave in. The night that we brought Obi home, he fell in love with him

15

just as much as the rest of us.

'Morning, Big Ben.'

'I've told you not to call me that,' he replied grumpily as he stirred awake.

'Ok, sorry, I won't do it again.'

Moaning, he pulled the duvet over his head. If he was like this at nine, I dreaded to think what he would be like as a teenager. The thought filled me with terror.

'Come on,' I said, whipping the duvet off of him. 'Get some clothes on and then come down for breakfast.' Trying to tempt him, I added, 'I'm making pancakes.'

That got his attention.

'Really?' he asked. 'But it's a school day.'

'A very *special* school day. And a special day requires a special breakfast.'

I knew what I was doing. The next few hours were going to be excruciating. If the promise of pancakes eased things and helped placate my difficult crew then pancakes it was.

'Ok,' said Ben, not able to resist.

He climbed out of bed and pulled on his dressing gown. Not quite the *clothes* I was hoping for but we'd work up to that. Breakfast first, and then I would tackle the trauma of getting them into their new school uniforms. I shouted the magic word as I walked down the stairs and miraculously everyone could suddenly hear again. Ryan and Josh barged each other out of the way as they raced downstairs, shouting that they both wanted the first pancake. Ben followed closely behind with

Samuel on his back. I smiled as I saw them. Being a mum of four boys had its trials and tribulations but seeing them like that reminded me how lucky I was.

As I started prepping the pancake mixture, my phone buzzed with a text from my friend, Beckie.

Good luck today babe! Watch out for the mean mum clique! Love ya x

As my best friend from university, we had shared many memories never to be mentioned again, but our lives now looked completely different. Whereas I had spent the past nine years doing my bit for the future male population, Beckie had become an expert in her field of specialism as a forensic scientist. Our day-to-day lives were so far removed from each other that we had undoubtedly drifted apart somewhat over the years, but our friendship had just about maintained a historical bond through the power of text. I would educate her in the dynamics of the yummy mummy, the slummy mummy, and the earth mummy, and she would educate me in the best technique to lift DNA from a murder scene. Beckie remembering that the boys were starting a new school today meant a lot to me.

Thanks, hun, I text back. **I'll steer clear of all possible suspects wearing resting bitch faces.**

Chapter 3

I looked at the boys sitting there in silence in their unfamiliar surroundings. A school that was the same, yet different. Messages of positivity posted on the walls. A board with photos of smiling teachers on it. A collage of pictures promoting environmentally friendly behaviours designed by the eco-warrior team. All so similar to their last school, yet it felt a million miles away right then. Our cheeks, flushed from the cold outside, were now tinged warm in contrast as the uncomfortable heat from the radiator behind us warmed the school against the bitter January wind.

My legs started to cramp up under the weight of Josh and Samuel who had insisted on sitting on my lap together. It had been a trying morning. The pancakes had helped to lift spirits, but the inevitable drama of getting them all dressed and out of the house had been challenging to say the least. Thanks to the invention of bribery, my children were now going to gorge on a mass array of chocolate delights after school – but we were here. Three smartly dressed boys in their fresh new uniforms, and one stubborn two-year-old dressed in a Spiderman onesie. To the rest of the world, it looked like he had thought long and hard about his costume for the day and was ready to spin webs and catch the bad guys. To me, he was one less person to worry about getting dressed as he had slept in it, last night.

Emotions of guilt were springing out of me in all directions. I felt the burn of tears starting to prick my eyes as I thought about how hard this was for the boys. They all looked so scared sitting there. I blinked, discretely tipping my head back to divert the flood that was threatening to tip over the point of no return. Mustering up my 'everything is alright' mum smile, I reached out for Ben and Ryan's hands. Sitting either side of me whilst their younger brothers balanced precariously on my lap, they allowed me to give their hands a little reassuring squeeze.

We had been told not to arrive until 9.30am which I was very thankful for. Missing out on the manic rush as everyone bustled their kids in before the gates closed was a welcome relief. We all glanced up as we heard footsteps walking towards us and smelt a faint waft of perfume coming down the corridor. Realising that it was a teacher, Josh turned towards me and buried his head in my chest, his face white as a sheet.

'Good morning,' said the teacher in a bright, cheery

voice.

'I'm Mrs Ramsbottom, the Year-Five teacher.'

Samuel started giggling and whispered, 'She daid bottom!' to Josh. Ignoring the sniggers coming from my tribe, I convinced myself that maybe she hadn't noticed and tried to mimic her cheeriness.

'Hi, I'm Amber Clayton, and this is Ben.'

Wrestling Josh and Samuel off of my lap, I stood up to greet her and put my arm protectively around Ben's shoulders as he stood up next to me. He attempted to muster up a smile, trying to be brave for Josh's sake who was now hooked around my right leg like a koala hanging onto a branch for dear life. Ben's lips may have been smiling but his eyes told another story. He suddenly looked like the little boy I had dropped off for his first day at school five years earlier, terrified to be leaving his mummy. Risking a telling off from him later for embarrassing him, I gave him a big hug and kissed him on his head. 'Have a good day, Ben, I'll see you soon.' Saying a brief 'bye' and giving Samuel a little stroke on his head, he walked over to his new teacher.

'Everyone's so excited about meeting you, Ben,' I heard her say as they headed off down the corridor. 'And I've buddied you up with a lovely boy called Tommy.'

Ryan looked up at me hopefully as we sat back down.

'Do you think I'll get a buddy too?'

'I'm sure of it,' I reassured him, hoping that I was right. Out of all of them, he was probably the least worried about starting at a new school. As long as he found someone to play football with, he would be happy. He had crammed his new football that he got for his birthday into his school bag, presuming that he could play it at break-time like at his last school. Seconds later, another teacher appeared to whisk Ryan away. I was over the moon to see that it was a man and then slightly less over the moon to realise that I was probably old enough to be his mother. There was nothing like your children being taught by a teacher who was also young enough to be your child to make you feel old. I was pleased for Ryan though. Their last school had been inundated by females. It would do him good to have a male teacher for a change. Squirming as I hugged him a little too tightly, he promptly followed his new teacher off down the long corridor, leaving just me, Samuel, and my little koala.

'Sweetheart, why don't you come back and sit on my lap,' I said gently. My leg was starting to go numb where he was gripping it so tightly. Scrambling back onto my lap, he looked at me with his deep blue eyes that mirrored mine. It was the one trait of mine that all four boys had. His lower lip wobbled as his eyes glistened with tears.

'Can we go home now, Mummy, I don't want to go to school. I want to come home. I promise I'll be good. I'll play with Sammy all day, and you can teach me counting and letters and stuff.'

I choked back my own tears, knowing that I had to be strong. Why couldn't we have lived in Switzerland? They didn't go to school until they were six, and even then, they mostly played outdoors all the time. Josh had only started school a few months ago, and now here he was having to go through it all over again. I felt like the worst mother in the world. Damn Jason for getting himself headhunted and making us move.

'I wish you could, honey, I really do, but you can't come home. Your teacher would be so disappointed if we left. She's been looking forward to meeting you.'

'Give her Sammy instead,' he suggested, looking hopeful.

Samuel just continued to shoot imaginary webs out of his fingertips, oblivious to the suggestion his brother had just made.

'I think she may notice that he's a little bit too young for school, I'm afraid.'

Josh let out a big sigh as I shot his idea down in flames. He buried his head in my chest again, and his little body started shaking as he gently sobbed. My cleavage felt damp as his tears trickled down… or it could have been his snotty nose wiping against me I realised with a squirm.

I bent my head down and kissed the top of his soft hair. He smelled of my shampoo where I had forced him to let me wash it, last night, much to his annoyance. He had only agreed to let me do it if I used the same shampoo on him that I hide away for myself. Maybe it subconsciously made him feel closer to me because of the smell. As an idea popped into my head, I opened the zip on my handbag and rummaged around for a pen, finding a blue biro in amongst discarded sweet wrappers and broken LEGO figures.

'Hey, give me your hand, I've got an idea.'

Keeping his head buried, Josh reluctantly held out his left hand. Resting it on my own so that his palm was facing upwards, I carefully started to draw on it.

'Hey, that tickles,' he said, lifting his head up to see what I was doing.

'No peeking,' I said. 'It's not quite finished.'

The distraction caused Josh to momentarily forget his tears.

'Ok, now I'm going to draw something on my hand, and after three, we're going to turn our hands over to see them. Ok? But no peeking until I've finished.'

I hurriedly drew the same thing on my hand, conscious that it wouldn't be long before his teacher appeared from the abyss too.

'Right,' I said once I'd finished. 'After three we're going to both turn our hands over. Ready? One, two, three.'

As our palms turned over, they revealed a tiny heart drawn on each one.

Josh looked at me confused. 'You always tell me not to draw on myself, Mummy.'

'Well, I've made a special exception today. I've drawn us both a little heart so that when we're missing each other we can look at our hands and remember how much we love each other, and that we'll be together again later.'

Josh smiled as I breathed a sigh of relief. He gently traced the outside of the heart with his fingernail.

'Where my tart?' asked Samuel, not wanting to be left

out.

'Ok,' I said. 'Josh, do you want to draw the heart on Sammy?'

Josh didn't need asking twice. It wasn't every day he was given permission to draw on his little brother. I wondered if this was a good time to tell Josh about how Ben and Ryan had once drawn a moustache on him with permanent marker pen when he was a baby, but before I had a chance to decide, we were joined by Josh's new teacher. I hadn't even noticed her wander over.

'Hi, you must be Josh,' she said, squatting down so that she was on his level.

In a matter of seconds, I decided that I liked her already. She had a calm, nurturing way about her which was exactly what Josh needed today. Josh ignored her and carried on drawing on his brother's hand.

'Hi,' I said glazing over his lack of response. 'I'm Amber Clayton.'

'Lovely to meet you. I'm Miss Knight. That looks fun, Josh. We're going to be doing some drawing today too. We're even going to be letting you draw on the ground outside with chalk. How does that sound?'

I could see she'd got Josh's attention. He loved doing creative things. His stubborn side was not an easy one to win over though. He shook his head, keeping his eyes transfixed on Samuel's hand.

Miss Knight and I met each other's eyes with a knowing look. She understood – thank goodness she understood. She knew that Josh was pulling on every heartstring I had left.

'Do you know what else I have in my classroom, Josh? I also have a pet hamster called Tilly.'

She had said the magic word. Josh loved animals. He stopped drawing on Samuel for a second and looked up.

'I want a hamster but Mum won't let me have one.'

'Well, maybe you could come with me and have a cuddle with Tilly before you meet all your new friends,' said my new favourite teacher in the world ever!

Josh liked the sound of that. He looked over at me warily, torn between resisting the dictatorship of going to school and succumbing to it in his desire to stroke a cute little hamster. I smiled at him and took his hand in mine.

'You're going to be just fine,' I said, fighting back the lump in my throat. 'Just imagine how jealous your brothers are going to be when they hear how you have a pet hamster in your classroom. Now go quickly with your lovely teacher before Tilly gets tired and needs a little nap.'

Josh took his teachers outstretched hand and with a final little kiss to his soft head, he was gone.

'Right, I guess it's just you and me then,' I said to Samuel, glancing down at him. Inspired by our impromptu drawing on skin session, he had pulled up one of the legs of his onesie and scribbled big blue lines all over it when I wasn't looking.

'Samuel!' I exclaimed.

'What?' he asked innocently.

'Never mind,' I said, taking the pen off him. I was

hardly in a position to lecture him given that I had started it. I smiled as I rubbed my index finger over the heart on my other hand. I felt overwhelmed with emotion and knew there was only one thing for it. In times like these, the only thing to do was eat cake... lots and lots of chocolate cake.

Chapter 4

Picking Samuel up in my arms and hugging him just that little bit tighter than usual, we walked out of the door. I felt numb as I imagined my three other sons sitting there, scared in their new surroundings. As we reached the bright yellow front gates, I spotted another mum running towards me with a toddler in a pushchair and a little boy in his school uniform, balancing on the buggy board. Given how late she obviously was, I expected her to have the look of a mum who was feeling the strain. The look that other mums came to recognise in one another as their paths crossed on the school run. I smiled at her as I held the gate open, allowing her to share a moment of mum solidarity as she rushed past. I had perfected the 'mum smile' on the morning dash over the years. The smile that says 'I've got everything under control' to the casual observer whilst only allowing true friends who look deeper into your eyes to see the inner struggle faced. But the smile that she returned was warm and genuine and showed no signs of this. Her little boy was even giggling as he jumped off of the buggy board after enjoying his mad race to school that made him feel like he was the leader on a track.

Setting Samuel down on the ground, I grabbed his tiny hand in mine to start the short walk home, marvelling at how a mum who was that late to school could appear so calm. If I was running late, which happened frequently, it would be due to a mysteriously vanishing shoe, or a milky breakfast being spilt. Whatever the reason, I always felt the fuse of patience getting shorter and shorter as the positive vibe that I had committed to starting the day with was replaced with inner voices telling me that I was failing where all other mums seemed to be nailing it. I would put a mask of smiles on my face as we would charge to school against the flow of smug mothers of girls who had time to French plait their hair as well as styling their own. On mornings like these, I felt not only like I was swimming against the tide, but like I was also climbing the frigging waterfall. The contradiction of loving being a mum coupled with the doubt over whether I was doing it right may have eased over the years, but it would never fully subside. We had taken about five steps outside the school gates when Samuel stopped to pick a snail up off the ground.

'Look, Mummy, de nail likes me. He's come out to day, Hi!'

His innocent mispronunciation was exactly what I needed at that moment in time. A reminder that I still had a little one in the nest for a few years before I lost him to the school system like his brothers.

'He does like you,' I replied as I looked at the slimy body bravely poking out of its shell. 'Let's put him in the bush over here so no-one steps on him.'

Just as we were deliberating over which leaf on the overgrown holly bush that was invading the path would be suitable – apparently the first five that I had suggested weren't good enough for *Mr Nail* – the mum we had seen moments before appeared next to us with her pushchair.

'Hi,' she said, smiling at us. 'I don't think I've seen you here before. I'm Kayla.'

Having successfully deposited her son at school, Kayla looked even more relaxed than she had before. Friendly, hazel-coloured eyes met mine as she swept her long fringe out of her eyes. Her shoulder length blond hair was scraped back into a pony tail which may have been neatly arranged when she had first tied a band around it, but now had wisps of hair straining out at the edges where the wind had caught it in her mad dash.

'Hi, I'm Amber. I just dropped my sons off for their first day.'

I tried to hide how hard I was finding it, but Kayla must have picked up on the big intake of breath at the end of the sentence.

'That's tough,' she said sympathetically. 'Are you walking this way?'

It turned out that Kayla lived just a few roads along from me. After the fourth time that Samuel stopped us all to inspect yet another insect on the ground, Kayla offered him a ride on her buggy board. You would have thought he'd just been told he was allowed to go on his first ever roller-coaster ride by the excitement etched on his face. Not needing to be asked twice, Samuel hopped on, shouting, 'faster, faster' as we picked up the pace.

'I don't suppose you've got time for a quick cuppa, do you?' Kayla asked, pausing as we reached her road first.

I glanced at Samuel who was gripping tightly to the pushchair handles whilst keeping his feet firmly clamped on the board beneath him. Part of me wanted to just curl up at home with Sammy on my lap, and let him watch *Fireman Sam* on repeat whilst I ate my own body weight in chocolate cake and argued with Jason in my head about our terrible decision to move house. I could even take a brief break from comfort eating and fake arguing to write a diary entry about my latest bout of mum guilt. I must have hesitated a little too long as Kayla suddenly looked embarrassed and laughed awkwardly.

'Don't worry if you have plans. The house is a right tip anyway.'

'That would be great,' I reassured her, pushing aside my mopey thoughts. 'And don't worry about the house being a mess. I'd be more worried if it looked immaculate at this time of day.'

Samuel looked up at me, grinning as he realised that our invitation had just won him a longer roller-coaster ride. Even if it was just another thirty seconds.

As Kayla opened her front door, I felt relieved that she had invited me to her house and not the other way around. If she thought this was a mess, she would have thought that my house had fallen victim to a burglary whilst I was on the school run.

Having extracted a reluctant Samuel from the excitement of his thrill ride, I quickly removed his shoes before he could charge off upstairs in them in search of his next bit of entertainment from this unexpected adventure.

'I want to dress up like Samuel,' said Kayla's little girl, Eden, who was now free from her pushchair straps. 'Where's my dress-up, Mummy?'

'That a good idea. It's in the play room. Why don't you show Samuel all your toys whilst I make his mummy a cup of tea?'

'Come on, Sammy,' Eden said, using the cute version of his name like all his brothers did. She grabbed him by the hand and guided him through the house. He followed her like an obedient puppy at the mere mention of the word *toy*. Life was so easy when you were two!

'Right, let's get the kettle on,' said Kayla.

Joining her in the kitchen, I snuck a look around on my way. The house had a warmth to it that oozed of the fact that a family lived there. Smiling baby photos on the walls, toys scattered around, piles of clothes that hadn't quite made it to the bedrooms after surviving to see the other side of the never-ending washing pile. It reminded me of my own house, only slightly less messy given that Kayla had half of the number of children creating a constant tornado.

The worktop showed signs of toast crumbs and had bowls of cereal that had been discarded after breakfast only to let the residue crust on the sides. There was even an open margarine tub with a LEGO figure sticking into the soft mush. This was definitely a house that I felt at home in.

Rescuing the LEGO from the marge, Kayla flicked the kettle on, asking me if I wanted a tea or coffee.

'A tea would be great, please.'

A slightly uncomfortable silence hung in the air as Kayla busied herself making the drinks. I never had been good with just riding those out.

'So, tough morning getting to school, hey?' I said, referring to her late arrival.

'Just the usual,' she replied as she put a tea-bag in a mug. 'Finn hates school so he does everything possible to delay it. Today, he decided to play hide and seek with Eden just as we were about to leave. I literally couldn't find him. He only came out in the end as I pretended to give Eden some sweets and he didn't want to miss out.'

'Nice tactics,' I said, thinking I'd have to remember that one in case I had to use it one day. 'So, after all that, how did you manage to look so calm and in control when I saw you rushing into school?'

Kayla smiled as she handed me a steaming mug.

'Because what's the worst that can happen? I could get

mad and stress myself out, but being a bit late for school isn't the end of the world. Getting stressed won't change anything. We would still be late so why get upset about something you can't change?'

The words 'Hakuna Matata' popped into my head as I listened to Kayla's philosophical stance on something that had stressed me out for years.

'Besides, you seem pretty calm yourself for someone who has three kids starting a new school today,' she observed.

Years of perfecting my *'everything is ok'* look had obviously paid off. Inside I was a ball of anxiety, but Kayla hadn't realised. Listening to her view on how to handle a stressful morning made me wonder if I should follow suit and act all *Easy McBreezy* too. But whereas I may be able to portray a look of *'I'm nailing this'* on the outside, anyone who took the time to get to know me would realise that my mouth never hides how I'm really feeling. I felt the urge to be completely open with Kayla despite only meeting her less than half an hour ago.

'Honestly, I'm quite the opposite,' I said sighing. 'My morning has been one huge, gigantic struggle. According to my kids, I'm the worst mum in the world for making them move from their old school and leave all their friends behind. And in order to actually get them to go to school this morning I had to promise to do an almighty chocolate run before I pick them up. Oh, and Samuel isn't actually playing Spiderman dress up, but is in fact still in the onesie he slept in last night.'

As if on cue, Samuel suddenly ran into the kitchen at the mention of 'chocolate'. No longer dressed in his Spiderman onesie, he was now looking rather fetching in a princess dress complete with a tiara and a Batman cape.

'Can I have locolate, Mummy?'

'Nice outfit, sweetheart,' I said, trying not to laugh.

'It's Eden's,' he replied innocently. 'Where's the locolate?'

'In the shop. We'll have some when we pick your brothers up.'

Satisfied that he would be getting his *'locolate'* later, Samuel ran back to the playroom before he missed out on anything.

I momentarily wondered if I had shared too much as the thoughts that had been jumbling round my head all morning broke free from their restraints, like dandelion seeds encouraged free by the breath of a child. Kayla bit her bottom lip and looked sheepish for a second.

'Did I mention that I also ate almost an entire bar of Galaxy Caramel chocolate whilst repeating the mantra, 'Inhale, Exhale' over and over again before attempting the school run after the hide and seek incident?'

'Thank God for that,' I exclaimed smiling, thankful that my lack of a filter had encouraged Kayla to be honest rather than make her regret befriending the *new girl*. 'I was secretly impressed with your 'Hakuna Matata' vibe but also slightly scared that you were one of those super mums!'

'Oh my God, no,' she replied, laughing. 'My

philosophy about just accepting my lateness has been weeks in the making, ever since Finn started school. He went in absolutely fine for his first day but then when he realised it was a regular, daily thing, and that Eden got to stay at home with me, he decided to make it as difficult as possible for all of us. After two weeks of tantrums and tears, I realised that keeping calm and patient was the best approach. And seeing as it's not considered acceptable to smoke a spliff on the school run, I have resorted to chocolate and mantras!'

'Mummy, what's a spliff?' asked Eden, appearing from nowhere.

'Mummy, can I have a pif?' asked Samuel, no doubt thinking it was something to either eat or play with.

Kayla and I looked at each other with raised eyebrows, feeling like we had been caught by our parents discussing something forbidden. I thanked my lucky stars that Samuel didn't stand a chance of blending together the *sp* sound needed to drop me in it. I didn't feel as confident about Eden's ability to avoid embarrassing her mum with her new found word though. At just a little under three years of age, her speech was almost as good as mine!

'Good luck with that one,' I said, hiding behind my cup of tea.

'A spliff, sweetheart, is a drink made up of spinach, limes, and figs,' Kayla fibbed, sounding very unconvincing. 'Would you like me to make you both one?'

As tempting as it sounded, Eden and Samuel both

screamed, 'Nooooo!' and scampered back to the playroom, far away from the strange concoction they had just been offered.

'I should have quit at the 'Hakuna Matata vibe' comment and let you think I was the perfect mum, shouldn't I?' Kayla said looking a little worried that I might be judging her dubious sense of humour she had just allowed me to be partial to. 'Just for the record, I don't actually smoke marijuana around the kids. I don't actually smoke it at all. Well, I did try some hash cake at uni once, but that's all. I'm actually quite normal and boring usually. Just a mum who doesn't know when to shut up when she finds the release of talking to another actual adult.'

And that was it. The moment we went from being mums on the school run sharing polite, pleasant conversation to the start of a true friendship.

Chapter 5

Thanks to the unexpected distraction of ending up at Kayla's house, it was time to pick the boys up from school before I knew it. As promised, the pockets of my bulky winter parka bulged with their favourite chocolate bars as I navigated Samuel's pushchair through the unfamiliar school paths towards the canopy outside Josh's classroom.

Huddled underneath it, wrapped up against the cold, were a sea of strange faces. I searched for Kayla as I nervously approached them. We had realised earlier, that her son, Finn, was in the same class as Josh which I was delighted about. I hoped that they would become friends. And if not, then maybe I could encourage it with a few play dates at our house. Josh finished ten minutes earlier than his older brothers and, as luck would have it, Ben and Ryan's classrooms were adjacent to each other, so I could pick all of them up without fear of them thinking I was playing favourites. They were forever arguing over who the favourite child was, no matter how many times I told them that I didn't have favourites. Secretly, I did prefer one over another some days, but that was purely a temporary state of mind based on behaviour, acts of kindness, and whether their competitors had pointed out the fact that an extra line had appeared out of nowhere on my forehead.

Spotting Kayla talking to some of the other mums, I headed over to them, feeling like I was the new girl at school. Another pang of guilt hit me as I imagined how hard it must have been for the boys today.

'Hi, Amber!' called Kayla, welcoming me over.

Mirroring the warm smile that she gave me, I glanced at the two mums standing with her. One of them graced me with the same enthusiasm as Kayla, introducing herself as, 'Maisie's mum', before adding her own name, Shannon, as an after-thought. The other gave me an obligatory, 'Hi', before glancing back down at her phone which obviously had something far more important on it.

'Amber has four boys,' Kayla said to Shannon. 'Three of them just started here, today.'

I braced myself for the shocked face and unoriginal, *four boys, wow, how do you do it?* comments that inevitably followed such an introduction, but they didn't come forth.

'Oh wow, you're so lucky,' Shannon said with no hint of sarcasm whatsoever. 'I would have loved to have four boys. Or even four girls. Or even just one more.' She glanced at Kayla and pulled a comical sad face.

'Never say never,' responded Kayla. 'You could meet the perfect man tomorrow for all you know.'

Suspecting that this was somewhat of a regular conversation between the two of them, I quickly ascertained that Shannon must be a single mum. Before I had a chance to join in, the classroom door swung open and excited little faces came piling out as they spotted their parents in amongst the crowds. The unlucky few whose parents hadn't arrived yet were kept to the side, their faces now etched with concern that they may have been forgotten. I praised myself for ensuring that this was the one thing that I was never late for. I may have a reputation for flying by the seat of my pants and being late on more than one occasion for various things, but when it came to school pick up, I was always on time. Granted, it was at times a case of running at a hundred miles an hour as Samuel happily squealed in the pushchair pretending to be a racing car driver, but I still made it. I couldn't bear the thought of my boys standing there like the few I could see now, wondering why everyone else's mum or dad could make it on time when theirs hadn't. Especially not on their first day at a new school.

Just as I was starting to feel my heart race a touch faster, panicking as to why I hadn't seen Josh yet, his cute little face appeared next to his teacher. He broke into a grin and ran over to me and Samuel. Kneeling down, I wrapped him up in a big hug.

'Hello you, how did your first day go?'

'Ok, did you bring me chocolate?'

Rolling my eyes, I pulled a tube of Smarties out of my pocket. 'As if I'd forget on such an important day.'

Josh flipped open the lid, beaming.

'Where's my locolate?' whined Samuel.

'You don't get any,' smirked Josh. 'Big boys who go to school only.'

I quickly grabbed a packet of chocolate buttons out of my other pocket before the two of them caused a scene in front of all the parents I was yet to become acquainted with.

'Here's yours,' I said, ripping it open for him. And then to placate Josh, I added, 'he needs a bit of chocolate therapy too you know. He's missed you so much all day.'

In truth, he had been so busy playing with Eden that he hadn't given his older brothers a second thought, but Josh didn't need to know that.

'Right, let's go and get your brothers then,' I said as I grabbed hold of the pushchair handles. Saying a quick goodbye to Kayla and Shannon, I made my way round to the other side of the building to wait for Ben and Ryan. The blinds were down in Ryan's classroom, no doubt to block out prying parents, but I could see inside Ben's. I spotted him sitting at a desk next to a boy with a big bush of curly hair on top of his head. Pondering as to whether he inherited the curly hair gene from his mum or his dad, I willed Ben to turn around and look out of the window. My telepathic powers obviously worked as Ben turned around and his eyes met mine. Unable to stop myself, I gave him a big grin and started waving. He didn't wave back so I made my wave a little bigger to help him see it. But instead of acknowledging me, he suddenly looked very interested in something on his desk. He was going to have to up his game there or I'd have to resort to the embarrassing mum tactic I had deployed at his last school. After weeks of him just sauntering off without even saying goodbye, I had threatened to follow him into his classroom one day. He'd thought that I was bluffing which had made me even more determined to do it. So, one day, after he had walked off, unbeknown to him, I had walked straight after him. Just as he had made it to the far side of the classroom, I had poked my head round the door and in my most shrill voice possible had shouted, 'Love you darling, bye!'

In hindsight, it was a bit mean of me and had caused me more hassle than it was worth as Ben refused to talk to me for a week. I'd better not pull a stunt like that again. Especially as he still hated me and Jason for making him move schools. I'd better tread on eggshells for a bit longer yet. So, instead of doing something that might embarrass him more than the sin of waving at him, I pulled a Crunchie bar out of my pocket and started waving that instead.

After successfully collecting Ben and Ryan and bustling our way through the crowds of boisterous children, the five of us ambled home. As we walked along, I asked the boys about their day, eager to hear what they had been up to. Josh seemed happy enough after making a friend called Daniel who he'd played superheroes with. And, as expected, Ryan had managed to impress his classmates with his football skills. Ben, on the other hand, seemed distant and withdrawn from us.

'What about you, Ben?' I asked as he took his last bite of chocolate. 'Was it as bad as you expected or was it ok?'

'I prefer my old school,' he mumbled, refusing to look at me.

He wasn't going to make this easy for me.

'It's going to take a little while to settle in, but you'll get there,' I promised him. 'It's only your first day after all. That boy you were sitting next to looked nice. What's his name?'

'Tommy,' he replied, still not meeting my eyes with his. 'He seems alright, but he was a bit shy.'

'Ok, well I'm sure he'll open up a bit more tomorrow,' I said, feeling racked with guilt. 'Did you do anything interesting in class?'

'Erm, not really. I learnt to say, 'je voudrais une crepe s'il vous plait' in French, and I counted the number of kids who had their pants showing over the tops of their trousers.'

Ryan, Josh, and Samuel giggled at this. I started to give Ben my 'mum look of disappointment' for lowering the tone but stopped myself before it took full effect. If there was ever a time to let a comment like that go, it was now. I knew how tough this was for Ben. Today, called for nice cuddly mum who knew how to bring the treats.

We turned into our road just as the drizzle began to free itself from the murky clouds above. Admiring the bay window that jutted out of the red brickwork, I turned my key in the front door to our brand-new home, and announced, 'Who wants cookies with hot chocolate and marshmallows?' That was sure to cheer up my eldest son.

My phone started ringing as we walked into the house, and my mother-in-law's image flashed up.

'Hi, Sandra,' I said, accepting the video call.

I was greeted with two big nostrils looking up at me where she still hadn't quite mastered the best angle to hold her phone from.

'Hello!' she said in the cheery tone that seemed to appear when the word grandmother entered your repertoire of titles. 'I thought I'd call to see how my lovely grandsons got on at school today. Are they there?'

'Boys, come and say hi to Nan and tell her how school was, today,' I shouted from the kitchen where I had come to make the hot chocolate. When I got no response, I yelled, 'First one here gets extra marshmallows!'.

Suddenly everyone seemed keen to talk to their grandmother as they all barged each other out of the way to get to the kitchen first.

'Alright, you can all have extra marshmallows. Now have a quick chat with Nan whilst I make the hot chocolate.'

I propped my phone up against the fruit bowl on the breakfast bar so the boys could gather round it. Ben picked Samuel up so that he could see too. It never failed to melt my heart when they did things like that. It almost made all the fighting worthwhile.

After getting little more than one-word answers for the next few minutes, Jason's mum realised they weren't in a chatty mood and blew them a kiss down the phone before hanging up. I placed the tempting hot chocolates down in front of the boys and felt content as their eyes lit up at the delicious sight of marshmallows creating a layer above the smooth, soothing liquid hidden underneath. My hot chocolate never failed to bring warmth to the room and break down the barriers that Ben in particular tried to put up at times. Picking up my phone, I sent Sandra a quick text.

Sorry, Sandra. The boys are tired after their first day. I'm sure they'll tell you all about it next time they see you. Speak soon. Xx

As far as mother-in-laws went, I'd got lucky with Jason's mum. She lived far enough away that she couldn't turn up uninvited, and she didn't offer up unwanted advice about how to raise the boys like I had envisaged a mother-in-law would. Not that I'd mind too much if she did as she'd obviously done a sterling job raising a man like Jason. I felt a bit guilty for not calling her back for a proper chat, but right then, all I wanted to do was be with my boys. Even if they did just want me for my hot chocolate making skills. I caught Ben's eye and he smiled at me before quickly remembering that he hated me and

Jason at the moment and looked away again. *Give it time*, I told myself. I tried to remember what it was like to be nine and imagined what it would feel like to believe that your parents had ruined your life. *Yep, I think I would have hated me too!* I made a silent wish that the shy boy who Ben had sat next to would turn out to be an ideal friend for him. Maybe I could do a bit of detective work to find his mum and arrange for him to come over and sample my legendary hot chocolate and marshmallows. That would be sure to make him want to be friends with Ben. On second thoughts, maybe I shouldn't interfere and should give Ben the space to make his own friends. This boy probably had a cupboard full of hot chocolate bombs that would explode with marshmallows as the hot water hit them. I put my jar of Cadbury's powder back in the cupboard, suddenly feeling inadequate against the scenario I had just concocted in my head. Being an overthinker was exhausting at times. Suppressing the tangent my mind was heading down, I joined my boys at the table, taking pleasure in their little hands cradling their steaming mugs. Who needs an extravagant, over-priced hot chocolate bomb when you've got extra mini marshmallows in your arsenal?

Chapter 6

'Tell me all about it then,' I said to Jason. 'Were people friendly? Do they all have their own coffee cups with cheesy slogans on? Are there many women?'

I had finally crawled into bed after an exhausting evening getting the boys settled. After sulking for hours to remind me that I was the worst mother in the world for making him move schools, Ben had eventually decided to talk to me at 9.00pm. Apparently it was the ideal time to discuss the meaning of life and what actually was the point of it. I was beyond shattered!

I reached out for the hand cream that sat nestled on my bedside table in between a tub of Sudocrem and some random LEGO pieces. On second thoughts, I exchanged it for the Sudocrem. My once soft and supple hands were starting to look haggard after years of neglect, and I was sure it wasn't just my imagination that the blue veins were actually popping out above skin level now. I had quickly learnt that the cream I had lovingly spread on my babies' bottoms for years could in fact help with a multitude of sins... chapped hands... outbreaks of spots... ingrowing hairs where you thought it would be a good idea to wax your bikini line yourself. The benefits were endless.

'Everyone was very nice, the coffee cup etiquette is most definitely not a sharing and caring one, and yes, of course, there are some women. I haven't just got a job at *The Masons*, Amber.'

'I know that,' I said, yawning. 'So, are any of them attractive?'

I tried to ask it in a matter-of-fact way, but inside, my heart was racing a little bit. I had never been insecure in my relationships until I had met my first husband, Rob. Thanks to him, I could never let myself fully trust another man again, even one as amazing as Jason.

'I suppose there's a few that aren't bad,' Jason replied absent-mindedly whilst staring at his phone. And then, sensing my frosty silence as my lips pursed together, he quickly added, 'But no-where near as attractive as you of course. Especially with your fresh scent of baby's backside.' Putting down his phone, he picked my right hand up and sniffed it. 'And, why exactly have you just smothered this all over your hands?'

'Just because,' I said, far too tired to explain the countless benefits. 'Night.'

I gave Jason a quick peck on the lips and rolled over,

keen to drift off to sleep after my stressful day. I knew I must be tired when I didn't even make it downstairs for the hour of 'me-time' I loved so much.

I felt my sleepy mind drifting into that bizarre state of limbo where you aren't really awake or asleep. The place where an abstract doorway opens and pumps random thoughts into your head that wouldn't usually be granted access. I pictured Jason sitting at a desk in an office with its cutting edge biophilic design, where his attractive co-workers could poke their heads around the bamboo desk dividers to flirt with him. Even in my semi-conscious state, I could feel the tension of my brow furrowing. Then suddenly, it wasn't Jason at the desk anymore, but Rob. And the attractive co-worker was Miss Knight, Josh's new teacher! Just as I was about to succumb to the weird nightmare that was threatening to have me reaching for my dream analysis book in the morning, I felt Jason's warm breath against my neck. I closed my eyes tighter in a futile attempt to ignore him.

'Jason,' I mumbled, as the annoying puffing persisted to invade my space. 'What are you doing?'

'Fancy a quickie to celebrate my new job?' he asked in a hushed voice.

Hmm, now there was a dilemma I had to take some time to ponder over. Did I close my eyes and let the pure bliss of sleep take over my body, or did I give my husband a 'quickie' that I could predict would be no more than five-minutes of missionary style married sex followed by a satiated, snoring husband whilst I battled to drift off in between each rumble of breath?

'Jason,' I moaned. 'I'm really tired.'

'But we're celebrating,' he persisted. 'It's only ten-thirty. All the kids are asleep for once.' He started reaching around to tug on the elastic of my pyjama bottoms.

'Let's get these sexy flannel pyjamas off and see how you feel then?'

I felt myself relenting. It would be nice to have sex again. I couldn't actually remember when the last time was. Was it on my birthday or Jason's birthday? Oh, I know! It was three weeks ago on Tuesday, after I crept into bed naked at 1am after a night of working on an autobiography for the agency and couldn't find my pyjamas. Jason had jolted awake and thought I was suggesting a bit of late-night romance!

'Ok,' I said, feeling my body respond to Jason's fingertips. I sat up and yanked my pyjama top over my head as Jason pulled my bottoms down before I changed my mind.

'Jesus Christ, Amber,' he exclaimed as he buried his hand in a mass of hair. 'You look like you're auditioning for a 1980's porn movie!'

'Well, if that's how you get your kicks!' I responded, completely unashamed. There were two very valid reasons as to why my lady garden remained wild and untamed. Firstly, the number of times that Jason and I had had sex over the past few months could be counted on one hand thanks to the relentless demands of parenting. As such, I figured that there was no point in putting myself through the pain of waxing when there was a good chance that little hairs would be sprouting back by the time Jason got to appreciate it. Not to mention the unsightly in-growing hairs I would undoubtedly be graced with. And secondly, having four inquisitive little boys in the house who were eager to know what a girl had instead of a willy meant a little extra foliage kept my girly bits well and truly covered up, away from prying eyes.

'Hang on a minute. I think I've got some illuminous pink leg warmers I can stick on to really live the dream for you. How about you grow a Tom Selleck moustache for next time too?' I joked.

Jason was now passed the joking stage, however, as apparently my un-kept lady garden didn't deter him from his animalistic instincts after all.

Hmm, that actually feels quite good, I thought to myself. 'We really should do this more often,' I murmured.

'Do what more often, Mummy?'

I opened my eyes and saw Josh standing next to the bed frowning.

'Daddy, why are you wrestling Mummy? You always say we're not allowed to wrestle on your bed?'

I felt thankful that Jason had gone for the pinning my arms above my head with his hands look rather than the 'reverse cow girl'. That one would have been a lot harder to put the wrestling spin on!

'Ok, I give up, you win,' I said to Jason in an attempt

to play along with Josh's wrestling diagnosis.

Accepting that our moment of intimacy had been rudely interrupted, Jason cautiously rolled off of me, taking care to keep the duvet over both of us. Naked wrestling would be a lot harder to justify when Josh recounted this story to his brothers in the morning, or God forbid, his teachers at school!

'What's the matter, sweetheart?' I asked my second to youngest son. 'Why aren't you asleep?'

'My bum's itchy.'

'Ok,' I said. 'Let's go to the bathroom and see what we can do about that.'

I reached under the covers to retrieve the pyjamas I had carelessly abandoned moments before. *Great*, I thought. I had literally gone from a sexy 1980's porn star temptress to a mum searching my four-year-old's bottom for worms in a matter of seconds.

Chapter 7

After finally managing to get to sleep at about midnight, I miraculously got the boys to school with relatively little drama the following morning, although my heart still weighed heavy as I waved their worried little faces off. Despite having found their feet reasonably well yesterday, they still felt nervous in their unfamiliar surroundings.

I found myself searching the busy crowds of parents for Kayla as I directed Samuel's pushchair towards the front gate. I couldn't face walking with him now that the boys didn't have the luxury of starting later than everyone else. Today, we joined the mad rush of parents as we all swarmed on the school at once. A toddler who stopped every two seconds to inspect tiny insects that others would just trample on really didn't fit into the chaos.

I instantly clocked the mum clique standing in their

little gaggle on the path outside the school. Every school had one. The mums who formed a little circle barricade around themselves to ensure no outsiders were able to infiltrate their morning gossip. This one in particular consisted of the Lycra wearing '*active mums*' complete with perfectly tamed pony tails and Prada sunglasses – which were obviously a complete necessity on a gloomy January morning – no doubt discussing their latest Instagram diet fad guru, and how Camilla from Year-Two's mum had put on a shocking ten-pounds last month.

I turned my attention away from the group before they realised that I was staring at them. Racing down the path towards me was Kayla. I chuckled to myself, placing her in the '*always late*' school gate mum category. Smiling through puffed breath, she charged past me with Finn on the buggy board and made it through the gate just in the nick of time. I slowly started walking home, hoping that Kayla would catch me up. I didn't know her well enough to wait for her yet and didn't want to look desperate. She might have hundreds of other school mum friends for all I knew and may have just taken pity on me yesterday. I cursed my analytical mind and quickened my pace slightly. There was a reason why so many writers shared a common underlying state of intense cogitation. Their written words were an outlet for their thoughts that would otherwise consume them in amongst the basic cognitions that were essential to daily life. Those lacking creativity merely saw the world as it was presented. The creative souls amongst us processed it through its past, its present, its future, and every possibility that could exist in between.

'Amber, wait up,' came a voice from behind me.

Turning round, I saw Kayla, frantically running up the path, trying to catch up with me.

'Hi,' I said, giving her a big smile as I felt relief wash over me that I hadn't imagined the connection we seemed to have the day before.

We fell into sync walking together with Sammy and Eden babbling away to each other from their pushchairs.

'How did the boys get on, yesterday?' Kayla asked.

'Not too bad. Josh and Ryan seemed to settle in well. I'm still a bit worried about Ben, but it's early days.'

'Give it a few weeks,' she said, reassuringly. 'He'll be fine.'

We walked the rest of the way, drifting somewhere in between amiable small talk and the more familiar chat that you only get with someone that you do actually click with.

After saying goodbye to Kayla and Eden at their road, Samuel and I arrived back home just ten minutes after dropping his brothers off. Living so close to their new school was definitely a plus point of our upheaval compared to the arduous twenty-minute drive through traffic to their last school.

'Ok, Sammy, what shall we do, this morning, then? Play-Doh, colouring, LEGO, what do you fancy?'

'Fireman Dam!' shouted Samuel jumping out of his pushchair.

'Ok, *Fireman Sam* it is then,' I said, preparing myself for an hour of rescuing Samuel's teddies from various high up points in the garden. We definitely needed a few more play dates with Kayla and Eden to maintain my sanity.

After lunch, Samuel snuggled down with me on the sofa with his blanket for a nap. As much as I loved spending time with him, I did cherish this hour I still got in the afternoon when he dozed off after a busy morning playing. I knew it wouldn't last much longer given that he would be three on his next birthday. Carefully extracting myself from underneath him, I laid his head down on a cushion and kissed his rosy cheek. Wandering over to the kitchen table, I grabbed my laptop and a packet of chocolate digestives on the way. I flipped the laptop open and searched for the document containing my latest client's life story. Opening up the audio file, I pulled my headphones over my ears and took a bite of my first biscuit. There was something seriously indulgent about the way the chocolate layer broke through the otherwise bland digestive as it melted onto my tongue. The soft, warm tones of Joanna's voice filled my head as I heard her starting the interview with Michael Lamb.

Joanna was a pro, and by far my favourite interviewer at the firm. There was an art to talking to people to get the best out of them, and Joanna was the Picasso of it. People felt instantly relaxed in her presence as her kind eyes looked deep into their souls, connecting with them on a level that would make their most distant memories surface. She had studied Psychology for three years at the University of Sussex and prided herself on her ability to understand the human mind and the social interactions we all engage in. She had a way of asking a question that would encourage the client to elaborate to the extent that would make an SAS interrogator jealous. Maybe I should suggest that to her as an alternative job, should she ever get bored of the firm. I furiously scribbled notes on my pad as I listened to the interview. Michael Lamb certainly was an interesting man. At eighty-seven-years of age, he had undoubtedly lived a full life. After warming him up with the basic facts about where he grew up and safe themes such as his parent's jobs, Joanna effortlessly swept into the emotional substance that makes someone's autobiography such a compelling read. Facts are interesting, but learning about the experiences and feelings of someone is inspiring. Before I knew it, I was reaching for my fifth chocolate digestive as I became totally wrapped up in the story of Michael Lamb. As a young man fighting in the war, he remembered the comradery he had experienced with fellow men, scared of the life they had been thrown into. I felt a lump in my throat as he told Joanna how, out of three brothers, he was the only one to survive. I immediately thought of my own sons and felt the emotion that Michael's mum must have felt seeing her own sons being sent off to fight, only to have one return. It was a gut-wrenching pain that only a mother could feel. The numbness that transcends your body as you feel out of control of the most precious things in your life. I didn't even realise I was crying until a tear dropped onto the pad that I had been making notes on. Someone's autobiography, when written well, had the ability to do that. The ability to provoke emotions in those who read it – happy and sad. And if you could shock someone with some secret information that they never knew about the person, then even better. And that was why I loved my job. Between Joanna and me, we would do Michael Lamb the justice his life deserved and create an autobiography that his family could cherish forever. Nearly an hour later, I regrettably pressed stop on the audio file as I saw Sammy stirring on the sofa. Tonight, would be one night I would definitely be taking my hour of me-time once everyone was in bed. Or technically, me, Joanna, and Michael Lamb time.

Chapter 8

Amber, I need you!

I had literally just stepped inside my front door when the text from Kayla arrived. Two weeks had passed since our first cup of tea together and it was safe to say that any awkwardness had now vanished.

What's wrong? Is it Eden? I replied worried.

No. Mum's coffee morning at Francesca's! Pleeeeeaaaase come with me! Eden is the only child coming and she needs a playmate so I can talk like a proper grown up for an hour!

Urgh, anything but that, I thought to myself. Francesca was the mum who Kayla had introduced me to alongside

Shannon on our first day. The one who could barely manage to peel her eyes away from her phone to greet me. Francesca was *that* mum at school. The mum who talks just a slight octane higher than everyone else. The mum who exasperates over how hard it was to get little Jeremiah out of bed, this morning, as he had gone to sleep at 7.15pm instead of 7pm sharpish. The mum who loves to tell you about her struggles to keep her six-bedroom house clean. The mum who will grace you with saying hello one morning to just blank you the next like you are not worthy of her attention. Every school had one, and this school had Francesca. I tried to think of an excuse that I could give Kayla.

Sorry hun, I'm in the middle of cleaning the floor.

Immediately, I winced at the lameness of my excuse. I may have only known Kayla for two weeks but we had shared enough morning play dates after dropping our older children at school to know that cleaning my house was not number one on my list of priorities.

Ok, I'll give you 10 mins to finish then come and grab you!

Defeated, I text back a simple thumbs up. I looked down at my jeans and baggy top that had sticky finger prints on it already. Rushing upstairs to make myself presentable, I quickly pulled on a jumper that had ochre in it. Francesca would undoubtedly know the must have colour this season. Such an on-trend colour had found its way into my wardrobe purely by chance when I had spotted it in a sale whilst aimlessly scrolling through my phone one night. Little did I know what a trend setter I was. A few months later and ochre was everywhere!

Dashing into the bathroom, I inspected my face in the mirror for stray hairs. Eyebrows, check. Upper lip, check. Tilting my chin upwards at a slight angle, I squinted my eyes, looking sharply for any stray black hairs that had decided to sprout out overnight. I didn't see any straight away but thought it best to double check by gently moving my fingertips around my jaw line. Sure enough, I felt a bristling. Tipping my head upwards to reveal the guilty area, I spotted one lone, but very much there, thick black hair poking out of my chin. Feeling mortified that the inch-long monstrosity must have been hiding there for a full week without my knowledge, I grabbed my tweezers and plucked the bugger out. I could handle the expanding waistline that my post-partum figure had given me. I could even handle the pencil test under my boobs getting easier every year. But throwing hairs onto my chin that quite frankly resemble those of the pubic nature was Mother Nature taking things one step too far!

Satisfied that there were no other embarrassing hairs lurking, I put a little extra highlighter under my eyes to top up this morning's quick effort to look more alive for the school run. I decided to put a dab of lip gloss on too. The *Francesca-mummy-squad* would be sure to have immaculate glossy pouts. A quick twirl of my hair tongs through my hair to give it a little bounce at the end and I was ready. *Almost ready*, I thought to myself. I headed to my bedroom to grab one essential accessory that would finish the look off perfectly. Sunglasses! For my head!

There, I thought to myself, glancing in my bedroom mirror. *The mummy clique look has been perfected.* Now all I had to do was perfect the mummy clique talk. 'Hi ladies, thanks so much for asking me today. I was planning to do some yoga but I can always do that this afternoon. I had a bit too much Prosecco last night, anyway. Hahahaha.'

Yep, nailed it, I complimented myself as I practised.

'Mummy, who you dalking to?' came Samuel's little voice up the stairs.

'No-one, sweetheart. How would you like to take a trip out to play at someone's house with Eden?'

Samuel certainly didn't need asking twice. He had clicked with Eden as well as I had clicked with Kayla. Right on cue, the doorbell rang, announcing their arrival.

'Nice shades,' Kayla said laughing as I opened the front door. 'You do know it's raining, don't you?'

'Purely for aesthetic purposes,' I said. 'Look I even put lip gloss on. I am mummy-clique ready.'

Kayla rolled her eyes, laughing. It hadn't taken us long to realise we shared a very similar sense of humour.

'Floor looks like it dried quickly,' said Kayla, raising her eyebrows as she looked at my perfectly dry and slightly grubby looking hall floor.

'I only got as far as the kitchen floor,' I fibbed as I

grabbed mine and Samuel's coats. 'Let's go.'

Francesca only lived about a ten-minute walk away, but to save us arriving like drowned rats we all jumped into Kayla's car. Samuel found this very exciting as it meant he got to sit in the back with Eden. Adopting the role of entertainer, he started making funny noises to make her laugh. I couldn't help but admire the simplicity of their friendship.

'Did you know in Germany they say, 'It's raining puppies'?' I said to Kayla as the windscreen wipers danced in front of us.

'That's so bizarre,' said Kayla. 'Although I guess it's no weirder than us saying, 'It's raining cats and dogs'.'

'Or the French saying 'It's raining like a pissing cow',' I replied.

'You totally made that up,' said Kayla, laughing.

'I promise I didn't,' I protested. 'Il pleut comme vache qui pisse.'

Kayla laughed again. 'You're so random, Amber. I thought the French said, 'It's raining frogs'.'

'I guess that one is more socially acceptable,' I agreed wondering if my sources – namely the French exchange student that stayed with us when I was twelve – may be slightly questionable.

After just a few minutes of driving, Kayla pulled into the driveway of a large Victorian house. *Of course,* I thought, *Francesca was never going to live in a three-bed-semi, now, was she?*

There were three other cars already in the driveway.

'Who else is coming?' I asked Kayla.

'You, me, Shannon, Francesca obviously, Louisa, and Maddison.'

I relaxed a little when I heard that Shannon and Louisa would be there too. They had both been really friendly to me whenever I had chatted to them at school. I hadn't had a proper chat with Maddison yet though. She usually found her phone more important than getting to know me, just like Francesca.

As Francesca opened the door to us, a scent that undeniably came from a diffuser that originated in a chic boutique, as opposed to my £7.99 bargain from Tesco, filled my nostrils. Crisp clean walls exuded a warmth in a grey that only an interior decorator could perfect. I had attempted a classy grey in my last house that had looked amazing in the magazine that I had glimpsed at the dentist's surgery. In reality however, the only thing missing from it on my walls were the big drops of rain you'd expect to come dripping out at any moment.

'Come in, come in,' exclaimed Francesca as she kissed the air about a foot away from our cheeks. She looked as expensive as her house did, from the way her hair was perfectly shaped to the designer labels oozing out of her meticulous clothes. I absent-mindedly picked at a dog hair that had attached itself to my jumper like it was a magnet for Obi's fur.

'Hi, Francesca,' said Kayla, leading the way.

'Hi,' I said, almost sheepishly, like I was a tagger-on at a party I hadn't really been invited to. It was strange how the vibe of some people just zapped your confidence. Suddenly, I felt like I was fifteen again and I was trying to talk to one of the cool girls at school.

'You've got a lovely house,' I continued. Rule number one to feeling uncertain around new people – if in doubt, admire their home.

'Thank you!' Francesca said with an air of superiority about her. 'You'll have to excuse the mess though. I didn't have time to tidy up after getting the kids to school.'

I looked around me for the mess. Seeing perfectly swept floors and dust free surfaces, I decided that by 'mess', she must mean the cardigan one of her guests had left on the banister as they had walked in. I made a mental note to use the bin bag trick if I ever had to host a 'mum's coffee morning' at my house. It had been a lifesaver in the last house whenever the estate agent had thrown a last-minute viewing on us. I would grab a black bin bag, sweep everything in sight into it and then hide it in the car boot. It had worked a treat! I had even given it a name to inform the boys as to my intentions when they saw their belongings disappearing into what the uninformed eye would see as a one-way trip to the tip. A quick heads up that I was having a 'blean' and their concern would cease.

Kayla led the way in the direction of the voices we could hear chatting away in the kitchen. At least Francesca was going for the informal kitchen get together as opposed to seating us all in her lounge. The temptation to curl my feet up on her sofa would have been far too great whilst Francesca sat properly with her legs crossed as she pretended to be comfortable on the edge of her seat.

'Hello, ladies,' said Kayla as she greeted Shannon, Louisa and Maddison with familiarity. She pulled out the two nearest bar stools, pushing one in my direction. Up until that moment, I had been more than happy with my faux-granite breakfast bar at home. Now, I had what could only be described as breakfast bar island envy. So big was Francesca's kitchen that her breakfast bar sat slap bang in the middle of the room. It was so island like that I had an image flash into my head of palm trees surrounding us and the coffee machine hum became gentle waves breaking on the shore. Francesca's voice brought me back to reality.

'So, what would you like to drink, Kayla and Amber, I have coffee, decaf, green tea, matcha mint, rooibos, liquorice, nettle…'

'Wow, that's a lot of tea,' exclaimed Kayla.

'Did you know there is actually an insect poop tea?' I blurted out.

Oh shit, it had happened again! Why did my mouth always kick into action before my brain filtered itself? Beckie was going to love psychoanalysing this one with me when I text her about it later.

Samuel and Eden giggled. The mums that I barely knew, however, looked at me like Kayla had brought along a blaspheming parrot to their cliquey coffee morning.

'It's one of the most expensive teas in the world actually,' I continued as if someone else was in control of my mouth, forcing me into the socially awkward realm of no return. 'It's made by bugs digesting tea leaves, and then their poop dropping is sifted together and dried into a tea-like substance. It's considered quite the delicacy!'

Jesus Christ, Amber. Stop talking!

Kayla was the first to save me. 'You know, I think I heard something about that on one of those survival-expert shows once. It's totally a thing.'

I smiled at my new friend, thankful for her support in my moment of potential rejection from motherhood society for ever more.

'Oh my God, yes!' agreed Shannon. 'Only knowing those survival experts, they probably sifted their own poop for a nice steamy cuppa!'

Everyone laughed at that and I immediately decided that Shannon could be my new best friend too. Francesca was laughing with her mouth but her eyes actually said, *'talking about shit in my kitchen is totally unacceptable. Please sort yourselves out or you will be kicked out of the sorority, ritual or no ritual!'*

'Sorry to lower the tone, Francesca,' I said, composing myself. 'I'll have a green tea if that's ok.' I knew I was safe with a green tea. I really didn't need the caffeine of a coffee to fuel my over-active mouth. It would taste like an old pond, but no doubt Francesca would add a slice of lemon to it to disguise the putrid stench.

'Coffee for me please, Francesca,' said Kayla. 'Eden, why don't you grab your bag of toys and take Samuel into the room next door to play. Is that ok, Francesca?

'Yes, of course, go on through you two,' said our 'hostess with the mostess'.

'Give me a shout if you need me,' I told Samuel as he hurried off with Eden.

'How are your boys settling in at school, Amber?' asked Louisa.

'A lot better than I expected,' I answered honestly.

'That's great,' Louisa replied, with a genuine smile. 'My daughter, Lottie's, exact words were, *Mum, the new boy is really funny, and all the girls want to marry him!*'

'Oh, that's so sweet. I'll have to tell Ben that when he gets home.'

'No, don't tell him! She'd be mortified if she thought I'd told you that. Well, maybe tell him they think he's funny, but not the marry part!'

'Ok, your secret's safe with me. I do recognise the name Lottie. Ben must have mentioned her to me.'

'Speaking of marriage, did anyone hear the rumour that Mr Sturridge has spilt up with his wife?' announced Maddison.

Everyone gasped as I looked blankly, wondering who Mr Sturridge was.

'How do you know that?' Shannon asked wide-eyed.

'Apparently, Mrs Lacey from the office overheard him talking to Mr Wallace in the staff room, and she told Mrs Clancey, who told Miss Hall. Chloe overheard them whispering in the corridor when she was choosing her new reading book from the library.'

Maddison had a look of smug pride in her eyes as she described her eight-year-old daughter as the modern-day Miss Marple discovering this valuable information.

Shannon spoke directly to me to fill me in on who Mr Sturridge actually was. 'Mr Sturridge is the other Year-Five teacher. Think the stubbled jaw line of Matt Bomer, combined with the hair of Patrick Dempsey, blessed with the patience of a man who can captivate a class of thirty Year-Five kids. In other words, my dream man.'

Whilst I made a mental note to Google, Matt Bomer, Kayla joked, 'Every single man over the age of thirty-five is your dream man.'

'It's alright for you,' retorted Shannon. 'You have the best husband money could buy. Good looking, great with kids, a stable job. What more could you want?'

'I would just settle for a husband who doesn't shag his work experience university student?' said Louisa as Francesca joined us, perching her Gucci clad backside on the last remaining bar stool.

Looking embarrassed by her sudden outburst, Louisa cradled her mug and concentrated very hard on taking a sip of the steaming hot liquid. As she did this, it felt like an entire minute of shocked silence passed, during which I squeezed far too much lemon juice into my green tea from the predictable slice Francesca had placed next to my mug, just moments before. I worried myself slightly that as well as processing the bombshell that Louisa had just dropped, I was also deliberating over whether *work experience university student* was the correct way to word it as it just didn't sound quite right. Maybe *university work experience student* was more grammatically correct? *Maybe pondering pointless things like this is why I'm not often invited to mum's coffee mornings*, I mused.

Maddison was the first to break the silence. 'Please tell me you're not referring to Damien?'

Louisa looked up from her mug with tears threatening to fall and ruin her perfectly executed make-up.

'Yep. I saw a text from her on his phone, last night.'

'What did it say?' asked Kayla, reaching her hand out to put it on top of Louisa's in a show of support.

Louisa took a deep breath and tried to compose herself.

'It said, *'Thank you for yesterday. I learnt so much from you.'* And then she put a winky-face emoji with an avocado emoji, a peach emoji and a coconut emoji.'

'What the hell does that mean?' exclaimed Francesca. 'Bloody millennials and their emojis.'

'It means he slept with her!' said Louisa. She pursed her lips together like she was fastening the seal on a package that was bulging under the strain of what was inside. 'An avocado and a peach emoji mean sex!'

I shifted uncomfortably in my seat, feeling like I was spying on a conversation between close friends who had known each other for years. Louisa obviously hadn't meant to blurt her news out like that, but now she had, there was no going back. If I was being honest with myself, the uneasy feeling I had was also due to the painful memories of my own that Louisa had provoked.

'Are you absolutely sure?' asked Shannon. 'Because I was texting that guy who I met at the gym for two weeks and kept doing that sweat droplet emoji in an attempt to show I was getting fit, when in fact he always interpreted it as me suggesting a quickie in the sauna!'

'I think she's right,' confirmed Kayla. 'I'm sure an avocado is meant to be a penis and then the peach is… well you can guess what the peach is.'

'So, what do all the other vegetables mean then?' asked Maddison, looking intrigued. 'Because I sent my mum one with a hot pepper emoji last week when giving her a recipe, and now I'm worried she's going to reuse it on the old men at bingo and get herself in all kinds of trouble.'

'Can we please get back to the point of what an absolute shit Louisa's husband is!' exclaimed Francesca.

'Has he cheated before?' I asked, and then worried I had over stepped the mark. I may have happened to have been in the room when Louisa divulged her personal life, but that didn't mean she intended for the *new girl* to get involved.

She didn't seem to mind though as she shook her head and looked at me sadly. 'I don't think so, but then again, I don't know now. Maybe I was just stupid and naïve and didn't see it.'

'You're not stupid or naïve,' I said firmly, thinking back to my own situation with Ben's dad all those years ago. 'If it is true, then he's the one who's stupid, not you.'

'So, what do I do now?' asked Louisa, suddenly seeming so vulnerable. She was a far cry from the confident woman I had judged her to be from my first impression of her at the school gates. Like so many other women, she was obviously just great at putting on her school mum mask to present the perfect image of herself.

'Now,' said Shannon, 'we swap these mugs for wine glasses and we find some cake. Tomorrow we will help you decide how to handle this, but right now you need to vent and plot hypothetical revenge theories.'

Francesca quickly gathered together some wine glasses and a bottle of Champagne from the fridge. It felt wrong to drink alcohol when it wasn't even 11am yet, but I didn't want to be rude and refuse the glass as it was handed to me. Presuming Champagne was a normal thirst quencher for Francesca when faced with a friend's problem, I justified it as a show of solidarity for Louisa as I eyed up the chocolate cake that Francesca seemed to have magicked up from one of her luxury kitchen cupboards.

'Don't open your best Champagne, Francesca,' exclaimed Louisa as she saw Francesca about to expertly pop the cork. 'Surely you guys are saving that for a special occasion.'

'Don't worry about it,' Francesca, reassured her dismissively. 'This was delivered by the Ocado driver yesterday. I put it in my online trolley to secure my delivery slot and forgot about it.'

'Isn't that about the third time you have had a lone

bottle of Champagne delivered to your doorstep instead of your weekly shop?' Kayla asked, raising her eyebrows.

'It's actually the fourth,' confessed Francesca. 'But enough about me. Let's talk about what Louisa is going to do now.'

'We could all turn up at his office on mass and catch them at it on his desk,' suggested Maddison.

Everyone frowned at her to show their annoyance at her tactless suggestion. Deciding that I didn't know her well enough to join in the brow furrowing, I attempted a pity smile instead.

'We could cut all of his favourite ties in half,' suggested Kayla, trying to take it down a notch.

'Or put chilli peppers in his pants,' offered Shannon. 'That would give him and Little Miss Pert Cheeks a shock next time they sneak off at work.'

Louisa even managed a strained laugh at that one. At least I think the puff of breath through her nose accompanied by the strange squeak she released was a laugh. Laughing whilst holding back tears never captured someone in their best light. Her appearance suddenly altered though as a lightbulb moment flashed across her face and she started tapping away on her phone.

'What are you doing?' asked Shannon. 'You're not texting Damien, are you?'

'No, just give me a minute,' Louisa replied. 'Francesca, is there somewhere in the house that has better Wi-Fi? I keep losing my signal.'

'The landing upstairs is the best place,' Francesca

replied. 'Feel free to wander up.'

I admired Francesca's confidence that allowed her to direct her friend upstairs with no worry that a pile of dirty washing had been left there out of sight of the guests, or that the bedroom doors leading off the landing might be ajar revealing bedrooms with unmade beds and toys strewn everywhere. There was no doubt in my mind that Francesca's upstairs was as immaculate as her downstairs.

'Do you guys really think Damien would do that to her?' whispered Maddison when Louisa was out of earshot.

Never having met Louisa's husband, I refrained from commenting and became an objective observer in the discussion that played out. I quickly ascertained that Damien was regarded nowhere near as highly as Luke in the husband ranks. Pleasant enough when they had all got together for barbeques with the kids, but prone to boasting about his latest under par score at the golf club or what car he was thinking of getting when his bonus came in at work.

I tried not to be judgemental about someone I'd never even met, but I couldn't help but form an image in my head of a man who ponced about in expensive suits with the scent of *Armani* aftershave wafting after him. At no taller than five-foot-four in his golfing shoes, he would hold eye contact with every woman he met with eyes that were nowhere near as sexy as he perceived them to be in his egotistical mind. His main topic of conversation being a well-rehearsed speech about his penthouse apartment in Marbella, he would struggle to fathom how any woman could resist his charms.

Far from being the objective observer I had set out to be, my subjective interpretation had Damien tried, convicted, and executed in his golfing jumper before he'd even had a chance to shout *'Fore'* to warn those around him of the fall out of his infidelity. Realising that I was in danger of looking like a woman in a trance as I fabricated this version of Damien in my head, or worse still, someone who didn't give a shit about the topic of conversation everyone else was so invested in, I tried hard to focus on what was being said.

'I really don't think he'd cheat on her though,' said Shannon. 'He wouldn't risk losing her and Lottie, surely?'

'He'd be an idiot to risk that,' agreed Francesca.

'Twenty-two percent of men cheat on their partners,' I announced. 'According to statistics anyway.'

'Well, if those stats are right, the chances of one of us being victim to an affair are pretty high,' voiced Kayla.

As everyone looked at each other pondering this, Shannon said, 'Don't worry girls, I'll take one for the team. Maisie's dad can be the twenty-two percent of our men. You're all fine.'

This would have been the perfect moment to stand firm with Shannon and throw Rob into the twenty-two percent category, but before I could share this sensitive information, Louisa walked back into the kitchen looking flushed and slightly erratic in her demeanour.

'What are you all doing this Saturday?' she asked with

wide expectant eyes.

In amongst replies of football club and street dance lessons, Louisa turned her phone around to us to reveal a picture of a boutique hotel with a luxury spa on the outskirts of Guildford. At the bottom of the screen, it read, *Thank you for your booking!* in big bold letters.

'Now that is a great idea,' said Kayla. 'Take yourself off for the day. Get your head straight and then tackle Damien about it. There could be a very good explanation for that text.'

'The booking is for six,' replied Louisa, looking smug. 'I've booked all of us in for the day spa including lunch, two luxury treatments of your choice, and a complimentary dressing gown and slippers. All courtesy of Damien's credit card!'

Chapter 9

Louisa's revelation about her husband brought back memories of my break-up with Rob that hung over me like a black cloud for the rest of the day. The ability to use clouds to describe feelings and phenomena was one of life's graces that I never failed to appreciate. Luckily for me, this particular black cloud did have a silver lining. If it had been any other old relationship, I probably would have forgotten about the person years ago, but our lives would always be connected because of Ben. That was one part of the relationship that I would never regret. I would always be thankful for Ben, no matter what.

'Mum, can I go over to Tommy's after school one day next week?' asked Ben, as we arrived back at the house after school.

'Yes, of course you can,' I replied, feeling relieved that Ben had become friends with a boy in his class, and hoping that he might now drop the *I Hate You* act a little bit.

'He told me he's got this amazing tree house with a TV in it and everything,' said Ben, looking impressed. 'I'm not sure if he's telling the truth or not though.'

'He's probably not lying about it,' I said. 'He may be exaggerating a little about the TV in it though. I'm sure that can't be true.'

'Yeah, probably not. He also said he's got a fridge in it where he keeps loads of cans of lemonade.'

'Your friend has a great imagination. Either that or his parents are millionaires,' I laughed.

Seeing Ben's amused face felt so good after weeks of him giving me the cold shoulder. It was a huge weight off of my mind to think that he might be starting to forgive me for making him move schools. I thought that finding him a new karate club to go to would have helped, but apparently, I'd just ruined that by letting Josh join as well.

As Ben rushed off to his room, I told Ryan, Josh and Samuel that they could all watch a bit of television before dinner. I felt the familiar feeling of mum guilt that I wasn't doing something crafty with them which was such a misplaced conception as they were all happy to be watching cartoons together. I just needed to take a moment and sit with a cup of tea whilst I pulled myself out of my passing slump.

I reminded myself that things weren't always bad with Rob as I wouldn't have married him if they had been. Everything was so simple in the beginning. We had the naïve optimism of those in love, so when Rob had proposed to me, I hadn't hesitated in saying yes. Impulsively, Rob had decided that we should get married straight away. He had wanted to go to an exotic island and say our vows on the beach, just the two of us. It was hardly the big white wedding I had envisaged as a child, but Rob's enthusiasm had been contagious, and his persistence when he wanted something his way had been hard to fight. A month later, we had stood on the white sands of Antigua, just me, Rob, and bartender, Maurice, as our witness, complete with bulging speedos and an impressive amount of curly black chest hair. Our wedding photos truly were one of a kind.

We had happily lived in our bubble of wedded bliss for three months before I hit Rob with the bombshell that I was pregnant. At twenty-six years of age, I had felt more than ready to be a mum. It may not have been planned but it certainly wasn't *not-planned,* and I couldn't have been happier. Rob went along with it, but it was apparent that his level of excitement about the pregnancy was far from what I'd hoped. I had ignored the feelings of doubt though, telling myself that he was just nervous about being a dad and as soon as our little boy or girl arrived, he wouldn't be able to imagine life without them.

When I held Ben in my arms, it had felt like nothing else in the world mattered. But whereas being a parent brought out the best in me, it had brought out the worst in Rob. His egocentric nature couldn't handle my attention being taken by someone else. I began to realise how selfish he had always been and how I'd been blind to it. He wasn't prepared to share me and I could see the resentment he felt towards his son. I had started to dread him coming home from work, wondering how he would react to the fact that Ben might be crying whilst we tried to have dinner together, or that he might take too long to settle at bedtime whilst Rob was waiting for me to watch a movie with him. As the weeks passed, he often arrived home late from work and I had felt relieved, rather than concerned. It was just me and Ben in our little bubble with Rob drifting further and further away. One night, Rob just didn't come home at all. After two days of imagining car crashes and bodies in rivers, I had received a text from him stating what I already knew. He wasn't ready to be a dad. He couldn't handle the stress of it and we would be better off without him. There was one little piece of information that I hadn't seen coming though. He'd met someone else. I remembered the feeling of shock as if it were yesterday. I had later found out that he had met her at work. Whilst I was at home nursing his son, he had been sneaking around with a twenty-two-year-old nymphomaniac every chance he got. I could have text him back a torrent of abuse. I could have turned up at his work, demanding to see the women who had morals so low that she would sleep with another women's husband, and tell her exactly what I thought of her. But I didn't. I was shocked and angry, but after the initial discovery of it hitting me like a freight train, I had felt bizarrely relieved. Never in a million years did I think that

I would feel relieved to hear my husband had been cheating on me, but much to my amazement, I did – relieved that this was closure. There was no going back from this. Me and Rob were done. Ben was my future and I was going to make sure my gorgeous little boy felt nothing but love in our family of two. I didn't hear another word from Rob for ten months.

Taking a final sip of my tea, I took a deep breath in and breathed out all of the negativity that had weighed me down since my morning with the school mums. I had learnt long ago that it was normal for my feelings from my past to overwhelm me at times, and it was ok to take a moment for myself and allow that to happen. It enabled me to then put those feelings back in their box and focus on the positivity around me. The positivity that came in the form of four little boys who drove me to the edge of insanity and then gave me a hug so special that it just melted all the unease away.

Chapter 10

A few days later, I escaped the usual family shenanigans to indulge in the life of a pampered princess at a spa hotel fit for royalty. Jason hadn't batted an eyelid when I had asked him if he could look after the boys for the day. He'd found his old remote-control car, The Bigwig, in a box in the garage so planned to take the boys to Brooklands disused race track to educate them in its power. I don't know who was more excited, him or the boys! The promise of whizzing it around a real race track followed by a trip to McDonald's meant that I was happily waved off by my troop without so much as a, *'miss you Mummy'!*

The heavenly scent of Thai lime and mango diffusers coupled with the relaxing music being piped out of the speakers were doing wonders to rid me off any jealousy I may have felt for not being as exciting as Daddy though. I had felt a little nervous about spending the day with five other women who seemed to know each other so well, but Kayla was the best wing woman any girl could ask for. She and Shannon made me feel like I had been part of their clique for years. Louisa was lovely too, a sentiment largely aided by the fact that she had paid for me to have a day at the spa with them when the closest I'd usually get to a spa day is the steam from the dishwasher hitting me in the face upon being prematurely opened. Maybe it was just as revenge on her cheating husband but it certainly helped pave the way to me feeling accepted. If it had just been the four of us, it would have been perfect. I could have been myself just like I always was with Kayla. Francesca and Maddison still made me feel a little guarded though. I couldn't put my finger on anything in particular. They were both friendly enough now that they graced me with their presence rather than ignoring me in favour of their phones at the school gate. They just had a vibe to them that zapped me of my mojo and made me retreat into my shell a little. Hopefully a day at the spa with them would take us to the next level of friendship where I felt more comfortable with them too. And the first step to breaking down those barriers was the awkward changing room moment where we got ready for the aqua-aerobics session. The changing rooms alone were enough to impress me, and I hadn't even seen the rest of the spa yet. Five separate vanity stations were arranged at discreet points in the L-shaped room. Each had not just its own hairdryer, but its own GHD straighteners too. On a little ledge underneath, sat three bottles of expensive looking moisturiser, one for the face, one for the body, and one for the hands. There was even some Jo Malone Parfum positioned to the right of the expertly polished mirrors. I would have thought some poor lady had forgotten to take her expensive perfume home with her had it not been for the fact that all five vanity stations had one. I was pleased to note that there were individual cubicles rather than a group change. That really would have been far too much like being back at school, worrying that bitchy Natasha with her woman-like figure would point mockingly at your Mark's and Spencer's knickers because you hadn't yet discovered La Senza. I pushed open the door to one and was met with a little dressing table complete with a bouquet of fresh flowers and yet more moisturiser. Jason must have rung ahead and begged them to brainwash me into using something other than Sudocrem on my cracked, ageing hands! Pulling down my trousers, I felt relieved that I had opted for a safe tankini which nicely covered up my backside and my saggy tummy. Plus, the length of the bottoms meant that my embarrassingly overgrown bikini line could be nicely tucked away from view. Francesca would be horrified if she saw a curly black hair escaping down below. She probably had her pubic hair shaped into a heart with diamante dotted around it from her latest vajazzle!

'Are you ready, Amber?' called Kayla, knocking on the door to my cubicle.

I pulled my complimentary dressing gown over my

tankini and opened the door. Kayla was wearing an identical one over her swimsuit. Placing my belongings safely in the nearest locker, we walked around to the pool where the others were already waiting.

'Ready to get your wobbly bits out, ladies,' said Shannon, removing her dressing gown and laying it on the bench next to the pool. She turned her back to us and started twerking her voluptuous backside. I felt envious of her big round buttocks and subconsciously touched my pancake like cheeks in comparison.

Laughing, we all took off our own robes, feeling a little less self-conscious now that Shannon had broken the ice. It wasn't that I hated my body. I had accepted long ago that I would never have the gorgeous flat stomach that twenty-year-old Amber had had. After desperately trying to get back into shape after having Ben, and then falling pregnant again, I had accepted by baby number four that my wobbly tummy was my trophy for pushing four tiny humans out of my body. And on days where I was feeling a little self-judgemental after eating the entire box of chocolates rather than just the few I had intended to, my mantra was *'I would rather have a job as a mum than a job as a bikini model, I would rather have a job as a mum than a job as a bikini model, I would rather have a job as a mum than a job as a bikini model.'*

'Ooh, this is actually really warm,' exclaimed Kayla, dipping her toe into the inviting pool water.

'Well, this is a luxury spa,' said Francesca with a touch of arrogance. 'Did you expect it to be as cold as the lido?'

Following Kayla's lead, we all slowly dipped in. If I closed my eyes I could imagine being in a tropical paradise. *Hmm, palm trees, white sands, monkeys throwing coconuts off trees...* I was snapped out of my daydream by our perky little aqua-aerobics instructor, bobbing up and down on the edge of the pool in her perfectly non-saggy leggings and crop top, as she encouraged the class to get moving under the water.

'Right ladies, let's get those legs moving and feel the burn. Let's start with some jumping jacks.'

I giggled to myself, knowing that a swimming pool was the only place I would dare to attempt a star jump nowadays, and hoped that the concept of a urine detector dye for swimming pools really was a myth invented to scare the common man out of relieving themselves in a public pool.

After an hour of moving our bodies in all sorts of ways that made me thankful that the water hid a multitude of sins, we were ready to spend the rest of our day on a higher plane of relaxation as we soothed our stressed bodies and minds. Each treatment room had the option of joint experiences designed for indulgent couples, so the six of us paired up. After a brief but scary moment of feeling like I was back in PE class at school, hearing the words 'find a partner', I felt Kayla link my arm with hers as we naturally went into our most comfortable pairs – Francesca and Maddison, Shannon and Louisa, and me and Kayla. As the door closed, ensuring our privacy in the softly lit room, the scent of bergamot ascended into my nostrils, creating an aura of calm.

'You don't think Shannon will mind you coming in with me instead of her, do you?' I asked Kayla, speaking through the hole that had been left for me to breathe through as I lay on the massage bed. I imagined a highly unattractive, large red ring forming round my face as I squished it against the material.

'No, not at all,' Kayla said convincingly. 'She's not one of those possessive friend types. Besides, she's probably loving giving Louisa all kinds of advice on how to deal with her cheating husband right now. She is the expert!'

'Did Shannon's husband cheat on her? Is that why she's on her own with Maisie now?'

'Not her husband but her boyfriend of three years. Whilst she was pregnant with Maisie!'

Hearing this made the hairs on my arms stand up in contrast to how they should have reacted to the warm oil being gently rubbed into my back as my Swedish body massage began. I bet the masseuses heard all kinds of gossip in these joint massage rooms.

'What a complete and utter bastard,' I said.

'Yep, he was. Left her at six months pregnant after telling her he wasn't in love with her and she had trapped him by getting pregnant. She hasn't heard from him since. He doesn't even know whether he has a son or a daughter.'

'Wow. That's dreadful. Poor Shannon. And poor Maisie.'

'That's one way of looking at it,' Kayla said matter-of-factly. 'The way Shannon looks at it is they both had a lucky escape. He doesn't deserve to have a child like Maisie. Shannon is an amazing mum, and Maisie knows no different. They have such a close relationship. She was obviously heart-broken when it happened but her philosophy on life is amazing. She is the poster girl for the 'What doesn't kill you, makes you stronger,' slogan!'

'I know exactly what you mean,' I said, thinking how different my life would have been had Ben's dad not left us when he did. I had had a lucky escape too. I wondered if this shared experience would strengthen my friendship with Shannon if we ever spoke about it. I was usually quite guarded about the information I gave other mums about Ben's dad, preferring them just to think that he was Jason's son like his brothers, but Kayla and Shannon had a way of making people open up to them. I chastised myself for momentarily wishing that Rob hadn't ever wanted anything to do with Ben, just like Shannon's ex hadn't with Maisie. As much as I hated him, he was still a part of Ben's life, now he'd finally decided to man up. It wasn't fair on Ben for me to wish otherwise.

'I saw her sitting on her own at an ante-natal class one day', continued Kayla. 'I remember she looked like she was in a complete daze. I asked her if she was ok and she simply replied, 'No, right now I'm not ok, right now I need to eat cake.' So that's what we did. We left the class together when it finished and went to a café to eat chocolate cake. She told me everything that had happened and we chatted every day after that. Sometimes over text message, sometimes on face-time, and then when we both went on maternity leave, often at each other's houses whilst eating cake. The pair of us put on about two stone in those last two months of being pregnant! I reminded her for those first few weeks that it's ok to admit you're not ok sometimes, and that one day she would be ok again but until then I would be there eating cake with her every step of the way.'

'No wonder you're so close,' I said, feeling a pang of jealousy. I wished I had had a close friend like that when Ben's dad had left. I could have done with a Kayla in my life back then.

'I wish I'd known you when Ben was a baby,' I said before I realised the words had left my mouth.

'Don't worry,' Kayla replied. 'We can make up for lost time by eating lots of cake together now.'

I felt a hand close over mine as it rested by my head and knew it was Kayla. She gave it a squeeze that I knew meant she understood. I had briefly mentioned that Jason wasn't Ben's biological dad when Rob had called to discuss picking Ben up one weekend when I had been at Kayla's, but I hadn't elaborated. I knew that I would fill Kayla in on the details one day soon, but with two strangers in the room working the tension out of our muscles whilst pretending not to listen, that day would have to wait until we had a little more privacy.

By lunch time, we all felt well and truly relaxed. Even Louisa, who had every right to be a ball of anxiety after her traumatic discovery, seemed to not have had a care in the world all morning. It felt almost uncomfortable that no-one had addressed the big elephant in the room as to how we had actually all come to be at the spa together that day, and I asked Kayla about it as we walked towards the restaurant to meet the others.

'I did ask her how she when we arrived,' said Kayla, 'but all she would say is, let's just enjoy the morning and I'll tell you all about it at lunch.'

'And she seemed perfectly fine?'

'Yep, almost like it had never happened.'

'Well, I guess we'll find out what's going on now. I hope she hasn't forgiven him and just brushed it under the carpet.'

We spotted the others over in the far corner, looking over the menus. Like us, they were wearing just dressing gowns and slippers, looking completely relaxed after a morning of aqua aerobics, body massages and Galvanic facials. Even the restaurant had an ambience of calm about it with its strategically placed plants purifying the air around us.

'Oh, thank God you're here,' exclaimed Francesca as we took our seats. 'Louisa said she has something to tell us but refused to say anything until you two arrived. She told Shannon whilst they were having their massages.'

Louisa looked a little sheepish. 'Ok, so it's about what I told you about Damien having an affair,' she started.

'What did you say to him when he got home that evening?' Maddison interrupted, desperate for the details.

'Did you confront him straight away?' added Francesca.

Louisa bit her lower lip and looked hesitant. 'Well, I had it all planned,' she said. 'I waited until Lottie had gone to bed, and then gave Damien a big speech about how I wouldn't be taken for a fool. If he wanted to shag some twenty-something university student then good luck to him, but he might not be able to use his credit card to sneak her off to trashy hotels for a while as I had maxed it out on a spa weekend for six and he wasn't invited!'

'So, you didn't ask him if it was true then?' asked Kayla. 'You know, give him a chance to explain.'

That sheepish look flashed over Louisa's face again. 'Um, nope.'

'So, you just when hell for leather, full attack then?' asked Maddison.

'Yep, pretty much a take no prisoners approach,' Louisa confirmed. 'And then he asked me what the fuck I was talking about. So, I said, something along the lines of, 'Don't you try to deny it you arrogant cockwomble'?'

'You actually said cockwomble?' I asked.

'Yep, always wanted to use that one,' Louisa replied.

'But surely it was more of a bastard, wanker, tosser moment, rather than a *cockwomble* moment?' suggested Kayla.

'Probably, but like I said, I'd always wanted to use it and I didn't know when I'd have another chance!' Louisa said, rolling her eyes. 'Anyway, the word I used isn't really the point here.'

'Fair enough. *Cockwomble* it is then,' said Kayla, holding up her hands in acceptance.

'And that was when she got my text!' Shannon butted in.

'Yes, well I heard the text come through at that point but I ignored it as thought I was in full flow ending my marriage. So, I shouted a bit more and told him it was bad enough that he had cheated on me, but to do it with someone young enough to express herself with avocado and peach emojis was just insulting. And then he started laughing, which made me even angrier so I grabbed my phone and stormed off to the bedroom.'

'And that's when she actually *read* my text!' elaborated Shannon.

'Yes,' confirmed Louisa. 'That's when I read your text and realised that the avocado emoji means an actual bloody avocado and isn't some coded picture for male genitalia. That, upon further investigation, would appear to be the aubergine emoji! I confused the avocado with the aubergine, put two and two together and came up with a hundred and fifty!'

I did a rather un-lady like snort into my pomegranate and spinach smoothie at this point as we all burst out in shocked laughter.

'So,' continued Louisa as we all tried to compose ourselves, 'apparently the avocado, peach and coconut emojis were genuinely representing an avocado, a peach, and a coconut, and were referring to an amazing smoothie that Little Miss Pert Cheeks had enjoyed at a quirky beach hut on The Gold Coast in Australia.'

'So, Damien isn't shagging her then?' asked Maddison.

'No, Damien isn't shagging her,' verified Louisa, looking sheepish again.

'But, don't you think it's a bit strange she's sending her boss messages about her favourite smoothie?' Kayla asked tentatively.

'That's what I said to him,' agreed Louisa. 'And it was at that point that he told me he was going to have to tell me something which would completely ruin the surprise, but he would rather that than have his wife thinking he was a cheating scumbag.'

'What surprise?' asked Francesca, looking confused.

'Well, I wanted to tell you all together which is partly why Damien was ok with me going ahead with this spa day with all of you and didn't flip his lid that I made such a mistake and his credit card suffered the punishment. The whipper snapper was recommending her favourite Australian smoothie to him as he has been offered a position in the Australia office. Which means, we are moving to Australia!'

'Oh my God!' exclaimed Kayla. 'That's amazing and dreadful all at the same time.' Her eyes filled with tears as she realised that one of her friends would be moving to the other side of the world.

As everyone digested the unexpected news, we moved closer to Louisa in a big group hug. I strategically positioned myself next to Kayla as still felt like a bit of an outsider, despite their lovely efforts to include me. An image of Ben's face flashed into my head from when I had mentioned to him that I had met Lottie's mum. I'd got the distinct impression that Ben had a bit of a soft spot for Lottie. I hoped he wouldn't be too disappointed to hear that she would be leaving school to move away. The group hug broke up and all of my new friend's eyes looked glassy as we raised a toast with our mixtures of healthy, yet revolting, smoothies.

'Don't get all emotional on me,' laughed Louisa, wiping her own eyes with a tissue. 'It's not going to happen for months yet so don't breathe a word of it to anyone. I don't want to let Lottie know until much nearer the time as she'll only worry about leaving her friends.'

'Absolutely,' voiced Francesca as we all nodded our agreement. 'Mums the word. Now let's go and see if we can squeeze in one more heavenly treatment before we have to leave this haven of tranquillity and let normal life resume.'

Chapter 11

'Cuppa?' asked Kayla as we neared the turning to her road. It had fast become a morning tradition that we either stopped off at Kayla's after dropping the older kids at school or carried on the few minutes further to my house.

'Sorry, I can't today. I need to finish the autobiography I'm working on and get it to my boss.'

Monday morning had brought us back to reality with a bump after our day of indulgence on Saturday.

'Ooh, what's it about this time?' asked Kayla, looking intrigued.

I had previously told her about an autobiography I had written for one of my first assignments. My boss had thrown me in at the deep end with an eighty-year-old lady named Agatha. She had travelled round Europe some twenty years ago following the death of her husband. As well as wanting to experience culture and cuisine, she also went with the intention of experiencing the male delights that each country had to offer! I had managed to keep a straight face as the pre-recorded interview told me about Marius in Paris, and Alessandro in Rome, but as the countries kept growing and climaxed with a spliff induced fling with Daan in Amsterdam, I was left wide-eyed with my pen lying on the floor where I hadn't even noticed I'd dropped it five-minutes earlier. I had to rewind the interview so that I could actually make notes. Agatha was certainly in my top three most entertaining autobiographies to write. I was left wondering whether she had maybe shared a bit too much though when she had described how Nikolas in Helsinki had a manhood twice the size of her late husband, making her realise how she had been conned all those years by a 'tiddly one'!

'It's about a lovely old man called Michael,' I told her.

'And?' she pressed.

'They're not all as juicy as Agatha you know. A lot of people just want to leave a legacy for their family. Everyone has a story to tell. They may not all be shocking and dramatic, but they all deserve telling.'

'You really love what you do, don't you?'

She was right. I did. I would have loved for my grandparents to have both left a story of their life for me to read. I had no doubt that I would write my own for my children. I also had no doubt that I wouldn't be quite so forthcoming with divulging all my secrets like Agatha had!

'Do you want me to take Samuel for the day so you can get it finished?' asked Kayla.

'Oh my God, are you sure?' I replied with wide eyes. 'That would actually be amazing. I'd been feeling guilty that I'd have to sit him in front of the TV for most of the day so that I could focus.'

'Of course,' Kayla smiled. 'Eden would love it.'

Before I could even ask him, Samuel had hopped out of his own buggy and climbed onto the buggy board on the back of Eden's. His face was beaming at the thought of playing with Eden's toys all day.

'That's decided then,' said Kayla ruffling the top of Samuel's hair. 'I'll give him back to you at school pick up.'

I hugged my new friend, feeling blessed. I thanked my lucky stars, not for the first time, that I had bumped into her on that stressful first day of school. I'd always thought having a friend like Beckie in my life was all the support I needed, but with the texts between us becoming fewer and fewer as we were both so caught up in our own lives, Kayla made me realise how important it was to have a friend who was at a similar stage of life as me.

Giving Samuel a kiss on his head, I carried on the short walk home. It felt strange doing it alone without Samuel chattering away. As I walked up the path to my front door, I thought to myself how at home I was starting to feel there. I had been so worried about moving when Jason had told me about his new job, but things seemed to be falling into place. The boys were now happy at their new school, I had a mummy friend, and the house was better than I could have ever imagined thanks to Jason's healthy salary. The stars all seemed to be aligning for us.

'Hello, boy,' I said as Obi bundled into me, hearing my key open the door. I ruffled his head in much the same way that Kayla had done to Samuel moments earlier. Obi looked at me with the puppy dog eyes that he had mastered long ago to get around us. He had even perfected a cute little ear twitch at the same time just to ensure that he sealed the deal.

'Not today I'm afraid, fella,' I said, knowing he was hoping that I was about to grab his lead and take him on a lovely stomp through the woods. 'I've got a very important piece of work to do.'

My phone pinged as I wandered into the kitchen to put the kettle on. It was a message in the group chat that my boss had set up for myself and the other freelance writers that worked on his projects. There were already five unread messages there that I had missed whilst taking the boys to school.

Magda – Someone please give me an inspirational kick up the backside! My creative juices are flowing backwards, upstream, and steering off into a pathetic ephemeral river!

I chuckled to myself. I had only met Magda once in person, but I liked her a lot. She had worked for the company for five years now. Originally from County Cork in Ireland, at fifty-six years old, she had written six novels and co-written fifteen autobiographies, ranging from Z-list celebrities right up to senior politicians. She was a force to be reckoned with and never shy to say what she was thinking. She had made enough money to retire and live a life of luxury, but her love of writing and desire to help other people's stories be told compelled her to work freelance a few days a week for 'Everyone's Story Matters', the company that I had discovered six months ago. We often private messaged each other to vent when our boss displayed his sexist old Etonian persona. I may have absolutely loved my job, but I certainly didn't feel the same about my boss, Edward Pinkerton. The *'me too'* movement was apparently completely lost on Mr Pinkerton as he regularly made his sexist comments and innuendos to myself and the other women on the freelance team. Being interviewed by his lovely second in command, Adele, I didn't actually have the pleasure of meeting him until after I'd ghost written my first autobiography. By then it was too late to walk away from the job. I was absolutely hooked. Given the success of the company, they had taken on five other freelance writers at the same time as me so Adele had arranged a little soiree for us to get to know each other. I had been so nervous at the thought of having to make actual grown-up conversation without having the boys there. It was hard to explain, but after being 'just a mum' for so long, it was like the boys were my comfort blanket when I spoke to someone. If I was feeling a bit lost when meeting someone new, I could cuddle Samuel into me or act distracted as one of the other boys demanded my attention. Without them there, I felt exposed and vulnerable. I needn't have worried though as Adele, Magda and the other freelancers couldn't have been more welcoming. After initially worrying about my lack of experience, I realised that we were made up of all sorts of backgrounds - authors, bloggers, journalists. Apparently, we all had our own qualities that suited us to different clients. Half way through the night, Edward Pinkerton, founder of 'Everyone's Story Matters', graced us with his presence. At forty-seven years old, he had the confidence and charm you'd expect from a successful businessman who had been educated to the highest of standards. He had greeted each of us with a warm handshake. Not just the kind where two hands meet fleetingly whilst one tries to dominate the other, but the kind where their second hand comes over the top of the handshake in a sort of miniature hug. When he said the words, 'Amber Clayton, how lovely to finally meet you,' he had looked intently into my eyes as if he was trying to establish a deep connection with my soul. Twenty-one-year-old Amber may have been naïve to it and gone weak at the knees. Thirty-something-year-old, Amber, with four kids and one dick-head ex-husband however, merely got an image of Doctor McSteamy in her head from when she had binged watched *Grey's Anatomy* the previous year. I had immediately put an invisible wall up between us and made a mental note to decline all invitations to a private editing session in his office. My initial assumption of his character was further confirmed over the next few weeks by a number of emails landing in my inbox that would put up remarkable competition for Bridget Jones's boss, Daniel Cleaver. All they were missing was the, 'P.S like your tits in that top!'

I scrolled through the messages I had missed.

Adele – Inspirational quote of the day for you... 'you can always edit a crap page... you can't edit a blank page with fuck all on it. Get writing!'

Magda – Alright, alright, keep your wig on!

Isaac – Can you lot be quiet, some of us are trying to work.

Magda – We're not in an office, you eejit, just turn your notifications off!

As I poured boiling water on the tea bag that was resting in my favourite mug, I squidged it to induce the strong perfection that a cup of tea deserves and smiled to myself. I loved the connection to my little freelance group. It could get a bit lonely working from home sometimes so we all kept in touch regularly, giving each other support when we needed it but mainly enjoying a bit of banter like you'd expect in a normal office. Isaac was the youngest of our group at a mere twenty-four years old. I felt envious of him that he had discovered his talent for writing at such a young age. His autobiography, *Secrets Every Girl Should Know About Me,* allowed woman an intricate insight into how he made it through three years of university with a string of girlfriends, a job as a naked waiter, and a first-class degree. He had pulled off a publicity stunt at his university a year after he'd left which had the fresher girls flocking to buy his book. Thanks to their love of posting everything on social media, word quickly spread, and before he knew it, Isaac had sold copies to practically every female undergraduate in the country!

Isaac – Chill your beans! I'm just kidding! Here's another motivational quote for you… 'Everyone has a story to share, but only a true writer makes others want to listen.' Feel free to quote me to the masses!

Oh Isaac! His early success had unmistakably left him with a touch of arrogance, but I couldn't help but like him. I'd read a few of the autobiographies he had ghost written for the company and I had to say, the boy had talent. His ability to turn someone else's basic words into a work of art was pure genius. I giggled at his *chill your beans* comment. It was something I could imagine Ben and Ryan saying. Wanting to get involved, I started typing my own message.

Me – Got to get my latest one finished today. Wish me luck!

I winced as I re-read my contribution to the 'banter'. Boring with a capital B! I really needed to up my game. I was out of practise after spending nine years talking to children.

Magda – Good luck

Adele – Good luck

Isaac – Good luck

After totally killing the bants tornado, it was time to get my head down and do Michael's life story justice. Reading through what I had already written, I realised that there wasn't too much adding and editing that needed to be carried out. Joanna had done a great job of drawing the best out of Michael in her interview, thus making my job easy. The minutes flew by as I immersed myself in my client's world as if our words were one. I was just tweaking the last few pages when my phone pinged again and Edward Pinkerton's name flashed up.

Edward - Amber, please confirm you'll have the completed autobiography to me today so that it can go to print.

Me – Absolutely Edward, just putting the finishing touches on it now.

Edward – Great. Why don't you come to my office at 2pm and we can check over it together?

I shuddered as I processed the message. It wasn't the first time I had received one like it. To a normal person, it simply said, *'let's go over your work together so I can check how you're doing.'* To an over-thinking writer such as myself it said, *'come to my office at 2pm so that I can see if my charm works on you like it has other freelance writers in the past who I have been able to sleep with due to my good looks and my power as their boss.'*

Me – Sorry, I can't. I have to pick my boys up from school. I'll send it over and just let me know any changes that need making.

The beauty of being a freelance writer meant that although he felt like the boss, he wasn't technically my boss. I was my boss! He just gave me the work. If I wanted to say no to him, I could and I would. I tunelessly sang a little Aretha Franklin to myself as I typed a message to Magda on my phone.

Me - Mr Prickerton just tried it again! No way is he getting this strong, independent woman in his office for a one on one!

I then hit the microphone button to the right of the screen and recorded myself singing a rendition of 'Respect' complete with an exaggerated American twang. I praised myself on the level of effort I put into the performance and pressed send. That should make Magda smile and give her a little bit of much needed inspiration. It would certainly make up for my boring comment on the group chat earlier. Seeing that the battery was nearly dead, I plugged my phone into its charger and went to the kitchen to make some lunch. I'd been so busy working away that I hadn't even noticed how hungry I was. Opening the cupboard door, I grabbed a chicken and mushroom pot noodle out. I had survived three years of university without so much as touching a pot noodle. Nine years of living in a house of boys and it was game over. I boiled the kettle and poured the hot water over the powdered noodles before waiting the strict two-minutes before adding the soy sauce. Marvelling at my creation, I wandered back to the table and checked my phone to see if Magda had replied. Disappointed to see that she hadn't, I clicked on the group chat instead where a whole load of messages had appeared whilst I was playing MasterChef with my pot noodle. Starting at the latest one I scrolled backwards.

Edward – Too late!

What's too late, I wondered. *I hope someone hasn't missed their deadline.*

Adele – Does anyone know how to delete someone else's messages?!?

That's strange. I hope they didn't take the banter too far and offend each other.

Magda – Amber, read these damn messages quick!

Ooh, I don't want to miss out on the drama. Magda must want me to see them before they get deleted. Juicy!

Isaac – Oh shit! (crying with laughter face followed by wide eyed shocked face!)

Magda – AMBER!!!!

Magda – AMBER, you complete and utter eejit!

I started to get a sinking feeling in my tummy.

Magda – OMG, Amber, delete your message quick! You've sent it to the group chat!

Closing one eye in the hope that it would stop the inevitable, I scrolled up to the message above Magda's. There was my voice, sounding like the start of an *X Factor* bloopers compilation singing my version of 'Respect', complete with a dedication to 'Mr P'. And the message above read clear as day…

Me - Mr Prickerton just tried it again! No way is he getting this strong, independent woman in his office for a one on one!

I was such an idiot! I had sent my message intended for Magda to the group chat by mistake. A group set up by none other than Mr Edward Pinkerton himself! That damn two-minute pot noodle! If it hadn't been for that I would have seen Magda's response and had the chance to delete it. Just when everything was starting to seem like it was all fitting into place, I did something stupid and messed it all up. I put my head in my hands and ran my fingers along my eyebrows. Any other day, I would have pondered how unlucky I was to be the bushy eye-browed girl at school in the nineties when girls today actually drew their eyebrows on to look that big. At that second, however, all I could think about was how I had made a right royal mess up of a job that I absolutely loved.

Chapter 12

Kayla shielded her mouth with her hand in an attempt to disguise the laughter she was trying so hard to suppress.

'Oh Amber, I'm so sorry,' she managed to mumble out. She was trying to be a supportive friend, but the creases around her eyes and her twitching left eyebrow gave her away.

'It's not funny!' I said like a sulky child as I sipped my hot cup of tea.

'What's not funny?' asked Josh, not wanting to miss out on the adult gossip.

'Nothing,' I replied. 'It's the complete opposite of funny.'

Quickly losing interest, Josh ran out into the garden to see what mischief he could get up to with his brothers whilst I was so obviously distracted. Kayla and I were sitting in my kitchen, perched on stools at the breakfast bar. Little rainbows flashed on the walls as the sun caught the silver flecks in the worktops. The sight usually never failed to brighten my mood. The ability of the sun to create such a wonder always amazed me, and whenever I saw the captivating spectrum of colours appear in the sky in front of a dark cloud, I would excitedly call to the boys to come and look. The fact that we now had mini rainbows appearing in our kitchen had sent me into a delirious state of happiness when I had unexpectedly seen them on the day that we had moved in.

Today, however, I was not in a happy, rainbow and unicorn loving kind of place. I pulled my phone out of my handbag and showed the message to Kayla. The message that Mr Edward Pinkerton had sent in reply to the fatal error I had made on the group text earlier that day.

Edward – Please don't worry about coming to my office for a one to one. I would hate for you to feel uncomfortable in my presence, and would like to relieve you of your obligation to freelance for me. I feel your talents are being wasted, and you would be much better off starring in an Aretha Franklin tribute band. I command a little more *'Respect'* from those I allow to work for my company, and you should maybe *'Think'* a little more in future about *'Who's Zoomin'* who when sending a group message. All the best, Edward

'Oh wow, he's good!' remarked Kayla. 'Love the

'Who's Zoomin' who reference – genius.'

I tried to glare at her but it was no good. She was right. You had to give the man credit. He could have been strictly professional and just sent me a simple, 'your services are no longer required' memo. But instead, he chose to use our group chat to shoot me down in flames and have the last word with style and grace.

'Are you ready to laugh at yourself yet, or is it too soon?' Kayla asked hesitantly.

'Too soon!' I replied indignantly, to which Kayla passed across the double chocolate deluxe cookies she had brought round after school when I had briefly filled her in on my predicament when collecting Samuel from her at school pick up. So far, we had managed to sneakily keep the gourmet biscuits to ourselves by enticing the gaggle of children we had between us into the garden with the promise of ice lollies.

'Seriously though, Amber, I am sorry. I know how much you loved that job.'

'I really did. It's so tough finding good, well-paid freelance writing jobs, and I have literally thrown it down the drain. I'm such an idiot!'

'You could look for a job working for a magazine,' suggested Kayla.

'I could,' I agreed. 'It's just there was something so satisfying about writing about people's lives for them. I got such a sense of fulfilment out of it.'

'Then why stop?'

'Erm, because I pissed off the owner of the company

who would now rather have a five-year-old writing for him than me,' I replied, wondering if Kayla had actually been paying attention when I'd told her what had happened.

'That just means you have to stop writing for him. Why not just do it yourself?'

My cup stopped mid-air in my hands as I paused to take in what Kayla had just said.

'He was the one making all the money whilst you were doing all the great writing,' she continued as she realised that she had my attention. 'Why not cut out the middle man and do it yourself?'

'But he's got an established company,' I said, not yet ready to drag out my inner positive self after my recent humiliation. 'Why would people come to me when they can go to him with all his five-star reviews?'

'Because you give the personal touch,' she fired back, gaining momentum with her inspirational idea. 'Because you won't charge the ridiculous prices he charges. Because you will gain recommendation after recommendation when people see how great you are at this.'

'But what about the interviewing part?' I countered. 'I may be great at writing – your words, not mine,' I quickly added so that I didn't come across as arrogant. 'But I've never interviewed anyone in my life.'

'That's the easy part!' exclaimed Kayla. 'Just be nosy! You already know the types of questions they ask as you get sent the interviews to work from. Just mirror those questions and make them your own, and then delve even deeper. And if they aren't being forthcoming, just conduct your interviews over a glass of wine. They'll soon tell you their life story!'

'I don't know Kayla. How would I fit it in around the boys?' I asked, looking for an excuse not to get excited about the idea that was quickly moving from the glum, down on my luck segment of my brain to the part of self-belief and motivation.

'Exactly how you have been this past year,' she replied confidently. 'You just take it on one client at a time and build it from there.' She put her hands on my shoulders and looked me straight in the eye. 'You can do this, Amber.'

I felt the click in my brain. The shift of my Leo - Virgo alter ego that existed thanks to my arrival in this world on the cusp of the two zodiac signs that were so close, yet so different. My unique personality that made me confident and positive one minute, and vulnerable and anxious the next, always adjusting according to the situation and the aura of others. Kayla brought out the best in me as our psyches gelled instantly. People come into your life for a reason, a season, or a lifetime, and in the short time we had known each other, I truly believed that our friendship was the latter.

I smiled at Kayla as I absorbed the entirety of what she had suggested. 'Ok,' I said. 'On one condition. You are my test client that I interview over a glass of wine to practice my interviewing skills.'

Before she could reply, we heard screaming from the garden followed by shouts of, 'Mum, Ben told us he's going to tell you to get us all adopted if we don't leave him alone!'

'I think we'd better move this conversation to the garden,' I said.

'I'm actually amazed we've managed to chat for this long without one of the kids coming to get us,' agreed Kayla as she jumped off her stool to come outside with me. 'Let's just stash the rest of these cookies in the cupboard before the kids see them!'

'Mum, they're so annoying,' moaned Ben storming past me. 'Tommy's coming over in a minute. Please tell them to leave us alone.'

Ben's newfound friendship with Tommy meant that he was fast becoming a permanent fixture in our house after school, and my other three sons seemed to like him as much as Ben did. I made a mental note to ask Kayla about his parents. I hadn't met them yet, and from what Ben had said, they were never around. The only interaction I had had was with the housekeeper when Ben had initially asked to go to Tommy's house and I had felt the need to check in with an adult. As such, my maternal instincts kicked in whenever Tommy was over as I treated him like a fifth son in my already busy household. It was the least I could do given how grateful I was that Ben had found such a good friend after moaning so much about us making him move schools.

Chapter 13

'Muuuuuuum!'

I heard the unmistakeable sound of a child who didn't want to go to school, calling me from upstairs.

'Ryan, please can you keep an eye on your brothers eating their cereal whilst I pop up to Ben?'

I hoped it was just a reluctant, can't be bothered to get out of bed plea, as opposed to a genuine illness. But, then again, it had been unusually cold for the month of March and had even snowed yesterday. Maybe Ben did genuinely have the flu.

'Are you ok, sweetheart?' I asked Ben as I walked into his bedroom, stepping over the various items of clothing scattered over the carpet. 'You look very hot!'

I bent down to brush my lips against his forehead. After many years of childhood bugs, my very own lip thermometer was even more accurate than the expensive ear thermometer in my medicine cupboard. Ben's head felt like it was on fire.

'I don't feel well, Mum,' Ben said in a weak voice. I've been sick as well.' He indicated to his pyjama top that had some congealed sick dripping down it.

'Ok, no school for you today then,' I said, wondering how on earth I was going to manage the school run and Samuel's football class with Ben throwing up everywhere.

'Do you think you're going to be sick again? Or do you think it was just a one off because your temperature's so high?'

'No, I don't think I'm going to be sick again, but I can't go to school. My head hurts too much.'

'Ok, I'll go and grab you some medicine. Stay in bed whilst I drop your brothers at school and then you'll need to come to Samuel's football class with us.'

'Can't he just miss it today?' Ben asked, looking mortified. 'He's only two. It's not like he's training for the World Cup.'

'We can just take a bowl with us in case you're sick, and you can snuggle into me on a bench well away from the other parents whilst we watch. It's only for forty-five minutes. Your medicine should have kicked in by then, and you'll start to feel much better.'

I knew that I wouldn't follow through with it if I got home from the school run and Ben still seemed really unwell. But I had to play my tough-mum card to see how ill he really was. It wouldn't be the first time Ben had feigned illness to get out of going to school. If it was genuine, we'd grab some duvets and have a movie day on the sofa. If I sensed that there may be a slight exaggeration on the sickness front then he would just have to join in with the day I already had planned. It probably was genuine though given that he'd been sick too. I tried to think back to yesterday evening to consider whether Ben may have eaten too much ice-cream after dinner.

Wondering whether I was doing the right thing leaving Ben on his own so that I could drop Ryan and Josh at school, I rushed out the door with Samuel in the pushchair. It was only a short walk, and I could dash back quickly rather than ambling along chatting to Kayla. He would be ten in a few months, and he was quite grown up for his age thanks to being the eldest of four brothers. Telling myself these things didn't prevent me from imagining everything that could go wrong in the short fifteen-minutes that I was gone for though.

I breathed a sigh of relief as Samuel and I made it back in record time, and I found Ben lying on the sofa watching TV with Obi on his lap. He looked a lot better now that the paracetamol had brought his temperature down and he had changed out of his sick-covered pyjama top.

'How are you feeling now, sweetheart?'

'A bit better. I could probably make it to Samuel's football class. You said the other day it makes him tired so he'll want to sleep this afternoon if we go.'

I smiled at my eldest son, realising that he was looking for some quality mother-son time whilst his little brother slept. The sacrifice of being dragged to Samuel's football

115

class was obviously worth it. Every day his friendship with Tommy grew, his hatred of me seemed to lessen a little more. I breathed a sigh of relief, hoping that we were over the worst of getting Ben through the trauma of moving schools. This time next year, he wouldn't even remember how hard it was.

'Cleaning toilets wasn't exactly what I was thinking when I said we'd have the afternoon as just you and me,' Ben said, looking aghast.

By mid-morning, I had realised that Ben certainly didn't seem as ill as he had when he first woke up. My mum-radar was also telling me that he may well have faked it, but I couldn't put my finger on how. I could explain the high temperature by maybe holding his lamp close to his head or pressing a hot flannel on it, but the sick had looked very real.

'It'll only take you five minutes,' I encouraged him. 'I'm teaching you some life skills. I am not going to have sons who think cleaning is woman's work you know.'

'Why doesn't Dad do any cleaning then?' challenged, Ben.

'Exactly my point! I'm teaching you the skills Nan failed to teach your dad.'

Handing Ben the toilet cleaner, I showed him how to squirt it around the rim before scrubbing it clean. There was another reason for my ploy to teach him some life skills. I thought that cleaning the bathroom together would get me his full undivided attention to have a proper mother-son chat as I felt like we hadn't talked properly in ages.

'So, how are you feeling about everything now, Ben? Are you happier at school now you've made friends with Tommy?'

'Yeah, I guess,' he replied. And then he sheepishly mumbled, 'Sorry I was so mad at you and Dad for moving.'

'That's ok,' I said giving him a hug. 'I completely understand. I'm just glad you're alright now.'

Ben and I had always had a special relationship, and it had broken my heart that our decision to move had upset him so much. He had no idea how much I needed the reassurance that he had just given me that everything would be ok. I obviously loved all the boys as much as each other, but Ben and I had that bond of a mother and son who had been on their own at some point. I had met Jason not long after Rob had left, but those months that it was just Ben and I were the unique blend of the most tough but the most precious moments that I'll never forget, and no-one could ever take that away from us. Thinking of this reminded me that Ben would be seeing Rob the following weekend. Since walking back into our lives after ten-months of initial absence, Rob had decided that he was ready to be a father. It would seem that his definition and my definition of being a dad were somewhat different to each other though. To me, a dad was someone who was there for you and loved you unconditionally. Someone who picked you up when you fell off your bike, and told you off when you pushed the boundaries. Someone who made you feel safe in this unpredictable world. Rob's idea of being a dad meant showing up once or twice a month to take his son to the arcade and eat pizza. And that was why Ben called Jason, 'Dad', and Rob was just the sperm donor. I was glad that Ben knew Rob and that they had formed a relationship of sorts, but I would be forever thankful that I had met a man like Jason who loved Ben just as much as his other three sons. The lack of toilet cleaning on his behalf was just a little blip that we could overlook given that my alternative life could have seen me serving a life-long sentence with Rob. I physically shuddered at the thought of what could have been had Rob not left us when he did. It was hard to imagine a time when I had ever loved him now. It was as if the day he had left, I had had a veil lifted from my face and I could finally see through the fog he had created. They say that people show their true selves when under stress and Rob had certainly done that. His true self was selfish. He put himself before his child and I was just grateful that I had realised his true character when I did.

'Did you remember you're seeing Rob next weekend?' I asked Ben.

'Yeah. I expect it will just be the arcade and pizza again,' he replied, rolling his eyes.

'I expect so,' I agreed. 'Does he ever talk to you about stuff?'

'Like what?'

'Like whether he's still living at Nana Collins house?

Or if he's got a job now?'

I knew I was being nosy, but I felt I had a right to know a bit about his life given that I trusted my son over to him for a few hours every month. Rob and I were able to mutter pleasantries to each other now after years of me barely being able to look him in the eye, but we were a far cry from serious discussions such as whether he had accepted the reality of adulthood enough to fend for himself rather than living in his mother's spare bedroom. I had gauged from various sources that the protagonist of his quarter-life-crisis that he had left me and Ben for had been nowhere near as committed to him as he had been to her, and she had moved onto her next victim after just two months. I may or may not have gloated a little when I first heard of this unfortunate turn of events for him!

'Actually, he's got a new girlfriend called Cassie who he's moved in with,' Ben told me.

I felt a slight unexpected twinge in my gut as Ben told me this which surprised me. I certainly didn't have any feelings of love for Rob anymore. Jason was ten times the man that he was. Still, there was an uneasy feeling that had come over me. Quickly psychoanalysing myself, I realised that the feeling was related to Ben, not Rob. The thought that another woman in the figure of a 'mum' might come into his life. I knew that it was irrational and the limited time that Rob spent with Ben meant that it was highly unlikely that this new girlfriend would encroach on my role, but the thought still made me feel a little vulnerable and I hated myself for it. Hearing of Rob with another woman triggered memories of our relationship and how sour it had turned. I might be perfectly happy in the life I now had, but the hurt that Rob had once caused me was like a permanent hidden scar. It had taken me many years of therapy, aka late-night text message sessions with Beckie, to accept that it was ok to be perfectly content now whilst still feeling sad about aspects of my past. To realise that whilst I am glad Rob left when he did, I am still allowed to acknowledge the hard time that I went through. Sadness is a real emotion and suppressing it is like putting too many chocolate chips in your cookie mixture. No matter how much you push those chips into the dough, they will melt away in the oven and seep out the cookie edges as it's heating up.

'Wow, maybe Rob's finally growing up,' I said to Ben, deciding that my nine-year-old son really didn't need to be subjected to my ridiculous cookie dough analogy that Beckie and I had come up with during a wine fuelled text marathon one night. Baking cookies had never felt quite so light-hearted again!

'Maybe,' said Ben. 'He's still more like an uncle than a dad though. Make sure Dad doesn't do anything too fun with the others whilst I'm out with Rob.'

I smiled at Ben. 'That lot don't know what to do with themselves when you're with Rob for the afternoon. It's like one of their limbs is missing.'

I told him this partly because it was true how much

his brothers missed him when he wasn't there and partly because I never wanted him to feel left out and like he was different to them. Jason had four sons and that was that. There was no 'step' in our family, we were just family and Ben knew that.

'So, what's Lottie in your class like then?' I asked picking up on the fact that her name had come up in conversations I had overheard Ben having with Tommy on more than one occasion. Ben's cheeks turned red at the mention of her name.

'She's just a girl who sits behind me,' he replied. 'She's alright.'

I didn't push the conversation but the blushing cheeks warned me that Ben probably wouldn't be too thrilled about the news that Lottie would be moving to Australia in the not-too-distant future.

Chapter 14

'This was such a good idea,' Kayla said as she took a sip from her glass of wine. 'Why have we never done this before?'

'Because, believe it or not, we haven't actually known each other that long,' I replied.

We were sitting at a table in the local pub, which as luck would have it was only a five-minute walk from where we lived. As a typical, charming English country pub, with cosy tables under bevelled wood beams, it had definitely played a part in swaying our decision to buy the house. Jason and I had stopped for lunch here whilst house hunting, and I remembered him breathing in the familiar smell of sloshed beer round the pumps that would have you reaching for ventilation at home but felt so warm and welcoming in a pub. Right now, Kayla and I were seated at the very same table that Jason and I had been sat at when we had discussed the pros and cons of which house to buy. I never imagined back then, that just a few months later, I would be sitting here again with a woman who I considered to be one of my closest friends, embarking on yet another momentous adventure.

It was less than a week since Kayla had suggested that I go it alone with my writing, but it had been all that I could think about. Jason had been completely supportive of the idea, and I didn't hesitate when he said he'd have a boys' night at home with Ben, Josh, Ryan, and Samuel so that we could conduct our practise interview over a glass of wine.

'Was Luke ok about you leaving him with the kids, tonight?' I asked Kayla.

'Absolutely. He always says I should take a break more and do things for myself.'

'Is Luke actually the perfect husband?' I asked, wide-eyed. I'd never met Kayla's husband, but from what she'd said, he seemed quite literally to be a flawless specimen.

'Shannon would say so," Kayla said, laughing "You know, I swear she actually flirts with him sometimes."

'No way!' I exclaimed. 'Don't you say something?'

'Nooooow,' Kayla replied in an exaggerated way as she screwed up her face. She reminded me of Eden having one of her dramatic moments when she was playing with Samuel.

'Shannon's one of my best friends. She's just desperate to find a man like Luke. She's probably just practising her techniques on him, knowing he's too polite to ignore her. And in answer to your question… No, he is far from the perfect husband as we all know that the perfect husband would have the chiselled jawline of Brad

Pitt, the body of a Greek God, and the personality of Woody.'

'The personality of Woody?' I questioned. 'Woody, as in Woody from *Toy Story*?'

'Yep,' she replied, not elaborating any further.

'Because every girl needs a cowboy in her life?' I enquired, raising my eyebrows.

'No,' she said, giggling. 'Although a little bit of cowboy in my life might be nice! It's because he is loyal, intelligent, and passionate.'

'Oh,' I said, grabbing my notebook.

'Hang on a minute, you're not writing that down, are you?' she asked, looking slightly concerned. 'I didn't realise the interview had started yet.'

'Rule number one of interviewing,' I replied, quoting some guidelines I had found on the internet earlier that afternoon. 'Make the client feel like you're just having an informal chat, and then swoop in with your killer questions.' Recounting it out loud, I started writing... 'Her image of an ideal man demonstrates a blend of a lingering desire from her late teenage years when she drooled over a bare-chested man wearing a cowboy hat in *Thelma and Louise*, and a later appreciation of a fictional toy wearing a cowboy hat. Diagnosis is this amazing lady has spent far too much time watching movies with her kids lately and has a secret fetish for cowboy hats, which she herself may not even have been aware of until now.'

'Jesus Christ, Amber!' Kayla exclaimed, nearly choking on her wine. 'Are you a writer or a shrink?'

124

'A writer, and apparently now an absolute master of interviewing techniques too. Now tell me, Ms Kayla, what is your earliest childhood memory?'

'Um, sitting in my buggy under my rain cover listening to the rain.'

'Very cute. Now, when you were a little girl, what job did you want to do?'

'That's easy. A midwife.'

'Really? I can totally see you doing that.'

'Do you think?'

'Absolutely. You've got that lovely calm way about you that would put mums at ease. Not sure I could do it with all that mess that's involved though.' I shuddered as I remembered losing control of my bodily functions whilst pushing the boys out. Being a midwife certainly wasn't for the faint-hearted. Kayla didn't look phased though.

'Yeah, I don't think that would bother me. Knowing that you're helping to bring a tiny human into the world would make it all worthwhile.'

Her eyes had a sincerity to them as she said this, giving away the fact that this wasn't just a dream that she'd had as a young girl, and was in fact a desire that had followed her into adulthood. I wondered how many women put their dream careers on hold when their ovaries started calling to them – never to pursue it further than reminiscing over a childhood fantasy.

'Ok, moving on,' I said in my best interviewer voice, 'Who would you say had the biggest influence on your life and why?'

'Ooh, that's a good one. Can I have a minute to think?'

'Sure, I'll get us another drink whilst you're pondering.'

The near empty bar, given that it was a school night, didn't give Kayla long to mull it over as I returned to the table. Picking my notepad back up, I looked Kayla in the eye. 'So, your biggest influence?' I repeated.

'My sister,' she replied. 'A bit boring, I know, but totally my sister. I looked up to her. I learnt from her mistakes and she gave me great advice when I made my own.'

'That's not boring at all,' I said. 'In fact, the simplicity of it is quite lovely.' I thought of all the times I had said to my boys how lucky they were to have each other. They may not realise it yet, but one day, they would hopefully appreciate each other just like Kayla did her sister. As an only child, I felt jealous of that bond I saw in siblings. I would have given anything to have a brother or sister to share the love of my parents. Whenever my boys accused me of having favourites, I always told them that a mother's love isn't divided when she has more children, it simply expands as she is graced with even more love to share. Taking a sip of wine, I continued my interrogation.

'So, going with the sister theme. What is the naughtiest thing you two did together when you were kids?'

Kayla got a glint in her eye as I triggered a memory. 'Ok, I'll tell you, but promise you won't ever tell my kids!' she said looking guiltily mischievous.

After a length of time that was given away by the substantial number of wine glasses sitting empty on our table, I had ten pages of notes detailing key milestones, passions, opinions, and dreams, as well as a detailed explanation of who Kayla would pick to replace her as a wife for Luke if she ran off with her blended *Brad Pitt/Greek God/Woody* fantasy man. I now felt like I knew teenage-Kayla and reckless early-twenties-Kayla, as well as present day mum-Kayla, and thanks to her, I had a new found confidence in my ability to actually make this work. Now I just needed a website to convince other people that I could do this and market myself out to the world. I felt a tingle in my spine, representing the slight intoxication of my body but mainly a mixture of excitement and fear all rolled into one.

'Just one more question and then we're done,' I said. 'If you could give your thirteen-year-old self and your twenty-one-year-old self some words of wisdom, what would they be.'

'Technically that's two questions,' Kayla chastised.

'Potato Potarto,' I replied, shrugging my shoulders.

'Ok, so I would tell my thirteen-year-old self that the awkward teenage years are just a small part of her life and would soon be a distant memory. Oh, and that Little Miss Bitchy, Clare Wilks, ends up cleaning toilets in the Nags Head and amounts to absolutely nothing which is just what she deserves after telling me I looked like her Uncle Trevor and making everyone call me Trev for a year!'

Kayla sat back with her arms folded, and if she had been five-years-old, I would have said her face said *'so there,'* followed by a big raspberry noise.

'Ooh, harsh,' I said, giggling at the image I had in my head. 'That bitch totally deserved to scrub those toilets.'

Kayla giggled too. 'Sorry, erm not too sure where that came from. Your shrink techniques obviously dredged up a suppressed memory that I needed to deal with.'

'And, your twenty-one-year-old self?' I asked. 'Any words of wisdom?' And, then as an afterthought, 'or suppressed trauma we need to counsel out of you?'

'Erm, let me think… ok here's a good one!'

She cleared her throat as if preparing to make a big speech.

'Young Kayla, I have two very important things to say to you. Firstly, become a vegan if you want to, but don't be a dick about it. And secondly, when Jack looks lovingly into your eyes and tells you that you are the perfect woman and he wishes he had met you when you were both five years older, what he actually means is, *'I'm still an immature prick who wants to shag as many girls as possible before I settle down with one woman who I can convince to have my children.'* It is not the compliment you think it is, and you will find out the hard way about six months from now when you go to surprise him at his flat with just your underwear on under your coat. You will find him wearing even less clothes than you whilst standing on a chopping board so that his pathetic excuse for manhood can reach the parts of the equally naked woman that have no business perching on any kitchen worktop.'

'Oh!' I said, feeling at a loss for words that would be a suitable response to Kayla's very in-depth answer.

'Did I share a little too much?' Kayla asked, taking a sip of wine.

'No, no, that was some great stuff,' I said. 'I expected the typical cliché *Always believe in yourself* type crap, but no, what you gave was way better. Now, just to clarify for my notes, are we talking a basic medium thickness wooden chopping board, or one of those chunky marble ones?'

'Let's embellish it and say a chopping board and a breadbin! He really was lacking in the height department. Why he thought the worktop would work for him, I'll never know!'

Kayla grinned at me as we finished the last of our wine and put our coats on. 'I told you you'd be great at this,' she said.

'Thank you, if it hadn't been for you, I'd still be crying into my cup of tea about my massive cock-up.'

'Don't mention it,' said Kayla wobbling slightly as her head suddenly felt the effects of the wine as she stood up. 'Do you think you're ready to laugh at yourself now about what a truly massive cock-up it was? As I'm not gonna lie Amber, keeping a straight face whenever I think about what you did is actually starting to hurt my cheek bones.'

I don't know if it was the wine, or my excitement over my new project, or the sight of Kayla's face contorted in a very unnaturally ugly way as she tried to suppress her laughter, but thinking of the ultimate epic fail I had

129

committed with my 'boss' suddenly didn't seem so gut-wrenchingly awful anymore. Relief washed over Kayla as she realised that she could finally let out the laughter that she had contained in front of me for days. It was contagious, and in a matter of seconds the two of us were crossing our legs as our pelvic floors threatened to stick two fingers up at the physios who tell you it is possible to regain complete control of your bladder after childbirth!

'You know, I think I now know more about you than friends who I've known since I was about ten,' I said when we finally managed to compose ourselves. 'I think I should interview all new friends that I make from now on.'

'Just make sure it's over a bottle of wine,' Kayla advised. 'I never would have told you about the chopping board incident had I been sober.'

'Very true,' I said. 'I feel like I should be sharing some of my deepest darkest secrets with you now too after that revelation.'

We crossed over the road and gave each other a big hug before heading off in opposite directions back to our houses. I couldn't wait to look over my notes the next day and compare them to the notes that the interviewers from Edward Pinkerton's company used to give me. I made a mental note to invest in a Dictaphone so that I could record everything my future clients divulged. If they were anything as compliant as Kayla, I would get some absolutely golden material to use. People would be hammering down my door to get their autobiographies written. I put my key into my front door feeling a bubble of excitement in my tummy. My little Aretha Franklin moment with Edward Pinkerton could possibly turn out to be the best mess up I had ever made.

Chapter 15

The next few weeks were a whirlwind of being a mum by day and planning my new business by night. One of Jason's work colleagues recommended an amazing website developer called Satellite7, who started work almost immediately for me. Kayla allowed me to share snippets of her interview on there, albeit heavily censored from what she had actually told me, and under the pseudonym of *Janet from Leeds*. My *About* section portrayed the passion I had for turning people's life stories into a work of art through words. My packages were affordable, yet not so cheap as to devalue myself. It looked professional and credible, and as I sat looking at it on my laptop in bed one night, I felt a huge pang of excitement that this was actually happening. My face must have mirrored my thoughts as Jason reached over and took my hand in his.

'You're going to be great at this, Amber. Your love of psychoanalysing everyone you meet coupled with your passion for writing is a winning combination.'

'I don't psychoanalyse everyone I meet,' I replied averting my eyes from my website to look at my husband questioningly.

'Ok, whatever you say,' he said raising his eyebrows.

'I don't!' I repeated indignantly.

'I know about your late-night texting with Beckie. The pair of you think you're the twenty-first century Freudettes.'

'Did you just call me a Freudette?'

'Yes, you know as in Freud — Mr Id, Ego, and Superego.'

'I know who Freud is,' I said, laughing. 'Besides, Beckie and I haven't had a late-night texting session in ages.' He had a point though. Beckie and I were renowned for looking deeply into things. Jason was undoubtedly remembering the time that she had text me to tell me that she thought her latest boyfriend was fixated at the oral stage of development due to some kind of trauma he must have experienced during his childhood.

'Website's looking good,' said Jason. 'Have you decided on a name yet?'

This was something that I had been toying with all week. I was running out of time to make a decision as it was the only thing holding the website back from going live and attracting clients for me. I wanted something catchy and memorable that let people know instantly what I was offering them.

'Everything I come up with sounds so obvious and boring,' I said, sighing.

Jason rubbed the bristles on his chin like he always did when he was pondering something.

'What about Brilliant Biographies? Everyone loves an alliteration.'

'That sounds like I'm a shop selling biographies of Z-list celebrities.'

'Um, how about Special Stories?' he ventured.

'That sounds like a bedtime story collection that teaches toddlers about good morals.'

'Ok, what about Autobiographies by Amber then?'

I mulled it over. It had an alliteration which Jason had quite rightly pointed out everyone loves. It showed that it was for autobiographies. And having my name in there made it feel personal, rather than a big company that was trying to sell to you. It was so obvious I wondered why I hadn't thought of it.

Jason sensed by my silence that he might be on to something. 'You could follow it up with a tag line. Autobiographies by Amber – Everyone's story deserves telling.'

'I love it! It's perfect.'

Jason looked smug. 'You should have asked for my input sooner. I do work in advertising, Amby.'

'Thank you,' I said leaning over to kiss him. Placing my laptop on the floor, I scooched backwards until I was nestled into him with his arm wrapped snuggly over me. I closed my tired eyes, willing my over-thinking brain to relax and allow me the luxury of eight hours of sleep before waking up to my 'Manic Monday' alarm. I was just drifting off when I remembered the promise that I had made Josh when I had tucked him into bed earlier. Letting out a big sigh, I wriggled free from Jason's arms where he was already starting to softly snore, and grabbed my dressing gown off of the hook on the door. Wandering down the stairs, I marvelled at how quiet the house was. It was an amazing contrast to the usual madness that ensued when everyone was awake. Yawning, I flicked the light on in the kitchen and picked up the needle and thread that I had left on the worktop a few hours ago. I had promised Josh that I would finish making his outfit for his dress rehearsal with his friend Daniel tomorrow. The two of them had been practising a dance that they were performing at the school talent show at the end of term. It wasn't for weeks yet, but they were so excited, I couldn't let them down. Daniel's mum had been on choreography thanks to her dance background – Josh told me she had once been a backing dancer for Beyonce, bless his little imagination – which meant that I was on costumes. After making homemade superhero outfits for Ben and Ryan when they were younger and vowing I would never do it again, I had somehow found myself agreeing to make two little outfits with MM and AM embroidered on the back, for Mr Magnificent and Amazing Man. As I started the first M,

I resigned myself to the fact that I wouldn't be seeing my bed until at least midnight. Josh's excited face when I showed him in the morning would be worth it though. I may not be a master seamstress, but Josh wouldn't notice the terrible lopsided stitching when pulling on his very own personalised superhero costume. In the eyes of my four-year-old, it would be flawless.

At 12.15am, I dragged my weary backside upstairs. I was only half way up when I heard the unmistakeable rumble of a snore leaving Jason's mouth with every breath he took. I momentarily contemplated walking straight past the door of my own bedroom and into Samuel's where I could curl up with him in his toddler bed. Jason had been at his new job for at least a month now though, and my consideration for him getting a good night's sleep had been well and truly taken advantage of. Opening my bedroom door, I decided that it was time to claim back my bed, and if that meant waking Jason with a jolt by throwing myself on the bed like a sumo wrestler taking a fall, then so be it.

Chapter 16

'Amber, I've got something amazing to tell you!'

My mum's voice came through the loudspeaker on my phone the following morning as Samuel and I were giving his play doh creation a haircut.

'Hi, Mum,' I replied, anticipating a lengthy recount of her neighbour Ethel's trip to the doctors. I picked up the play doh scissors and pretended to cut Samuel's hair with them, making him scream.

'So, yesterday, I met my friend Valerie at that lovely café that has opened up in town. Such a delightful little place you know. Valerie had the coronation chicken baguette, and I had the smashed avocado and poached egg bagel. Did you know that was even a thing, Amber? I would have called it *mashed* but the menu definitely said *smashed,* and I think it sounds kind of trendy, don't you think?'

I rolled my eyes at Samuel and thanked the heavens for the invention of speaker phone so that I could carry on playing with Samuel whilst Mum gave me far more detail than was necessary.

'Yep, totally a thing, Mum. And really, really amazing.'

'Oh, that's not the amazing thing I rang to tell you, Amber,' Mum said, completely ignoring my sarcasm.

'Ok, what was it then?' I replied absent-mindedly as I rolled another lump of play doh in my hands for Samuel to sculpt.

'Well, as Valerie was eating her baguette, I finally managed to get a word in edgeways as that coronation chicken is so messy that she had to focus on not dripping it down her chin.'

'Mum, I really don't need to know about Valerie's eating habits.'

'Yes, sorry Amber, I'm just setting the scene for you. Anyway, I told her about your new business venture, and she wants you to write her autobiography!'

Now she had my attention.

'Really?' I replied. 'That is amazing!'

'I told you it was.'

'Ok, great, so apart from struggling to eat coronation chicken baguettes, what else do you know about Valerie?'

'Well, she's pretty ordinary really. She's seventy-two years old. She's been married to the same man for nearly fifty years, and she has three children and quite a few grandchildren. I'm not too sure why she would want her autobiography written to be honest. It's not like she's led a particularly interesting life or anything.'

'That's the whole point of Autobiographies by Amber, Mum,' I reprimanded her. 'Remember the tagline, 'Everyone's story deserves telling'? It may seem boring to you, but her family will love learning more about her life. Besides, we do all have an interesting life. Sometimes, someone just needs to ask you the right questions to draw it out of the depths it's been hidden in for years.'

'Well, when you put it like that, I'm sure you'll do a wonderful job. Let me just give you her number so that you can give her a call.'

Swapping my play doh ball for some paper and a pen, I scribbled down the phone number that Mum gave me, feeling a bubble of excitement. My first real client. Sure, it had come from my mum, but it was a start. Striking whilst the iron was hot, I called Valerie straight away to explain how the process would work. I couldn't wait to tell Kayla that I had my first client.

'That's brilliant,' she exclaimed, giving me a big hug when I filled her in at school pick up. 'I knew you could do this.'

Her faith in me was comforting. It still seemed surreal that we were already so close after only meeting a few months ago.

'You have such a clever mummy, Sammy,' she said, ruffling his hair where he sat in his pushchair next to Eden.

'So, are you going to interview her in the pub so that

she can divulge her most intimate secrets like yours truly, or are you going for the more professional approach this time.'

'Definitely the more professional approach this time,' I confirmed. 'Unless, she struggles to open up. Then, I may need to feed her a little sherry to loosen her tongue.'

'Urgh, who's drinking sherry?' asked Shannon, pulling a look of disgust as she joined us.

'Amber's new client,' explained Kayla. 'That's her business strategy for stiff, cagey clients – get them drunk.'

'Seems perfectly sensible to me,' agreed Shannon. 'Where do I sign up?'

Josh appeared at my side, saving me from being swept into the conversation that was in danger of damaging my reputation before my business had even sealed the deal with its first client.

'Hey sweetie, how was your day?'

'Boring,' came the typical response he was coming to learn from his brothers.

'I'll see you guys at the slope,' I said to Kayla and Shannon. It was Kayla's son Finn's fifth birthday and he was having a party at the local donutting centre. Josh's face lit up as he remembered where we were going.

'Don't be late,' said Kayla. 'We need to be there by 3.45pm for a safety briefing.'

'I won't,' I replied. 'I'll come straight there after grabbing Ben and Ryan. Are you sure you're ok for them to join in too?'

'Of course,' Kayla said. 'Finn will love them coming

along.'

Finn loved seeing Ben and Ryan whenever he was at our house with Kayla and Eden. When I had first told them about their invitation to Finn's party, they had both looked at me like I was mad for suggesting they would go to a little kid's birthday party. They soon changed their tune when they heard that it was a donutting party though.

At 3.42pm, we raced into the party hut just in time to receive the safety briefing.

'What took you so long?' asked Kayla, looking worried.

'Sorry,' I replied. 'Ben's teacher needed a quick word. Something about finding loads of chocolate bars in his desk.'

'Why did he have so many?'

'He told me that Tommy gave them to him,' I said, shrugging my shoulders.

'Oh, ok. Look at the instructor over there. Shannon is desperately trying to get his attention, but I don't think he realises she's flirting with him.'

I looked over in the direction that Kayla had indicated and saw a very attractive man with a *just stepped out of my chalet in the French Alps* kind of vibe to him. He was fitting helmets on the children's heads whilst Shannon offered to help him make the adjustments.

'Did she actually just brush her finger against his hand whilst taking that helmet from him?' I asked.

'Yep, that's our Shannon,' Kayla replied laughing. 'She

never can resist a man who is good with kids.'

Once all twenty children were kitted out, we followed *sexy chalet man* out to the slope with the promise of getting Eden and Samuel an ice cream to console them for the fact that they were too young to take part. At about sixty-metres long, the dry ski slope wasn't nearly as daunting as I'd expected. In fact, the little jelly feeling that emerged in my legs at the mere mention of heights could almost be defined as a twinge of excitement instead.

'Josh,' I said, grabbing his hand. 'Do you want to sit on my lap for your first go?'

I had planned on asking Ben to take Josh down on his lap until he got the confidence to do it himself, but this actually looked like a lot of fun.

'No!' shouted Josh. 'I can do it myself!'

He dashed off to grab himself his own donut ring before I could stop him.

'We'll look after him, Mum,' said Ben, as he and Ryan quickly followed after him to get their rings.

Kayla smiled at me. 'You want to do it don't you?'

'Maybe just a little,' I said with a laugh.

'Go on then! I'll get Sammy an ice cream with Eden whilst you go on.'

'I'm not doing it by myself. I'll look like a right idiot in front of all these mums,' I said, indicating to the mums from Josh's class whose relationships with me hadn't progressed from the pleasantries at the school gate level.

'How about you guys go and get Sammy and Eden their ice creams and then I'll keep an eye on them whilst you both have a go,' said Francesca popping up out of nowhere. 'It will give me a good excuse not to go on!'

Francesca was definitely far too classy to let her guard down and climb aboard a donut ring with a bunch of hyperactive kids. I looked at Kayla and saw the glint in her eye that reminded me why we had clicked so well.

'Thanks so much, Francesca. Sammy, Eden, chocolate or vanilla?'

The mention of ice cream made our youngest two quickly forget that they were missing out on something incredibly fun that their older siblings were allowed to indulge in. Once they were safely nestled in their pushchairs licking their cones, Kayla and I sheepishly asked *sexy chalet man* if we could have a go, to which he winked and handed us some adult sized rings. We dragged them over to the pulley that would help us walk up the hill, just as Ben, Ryan, and Josh whizzed down the slope, holding onto each other's rings in a train before skidding to a halt.

'What are you doing, Mum?' Ben shouted over with a dubious look, wondering why all the other mums were sipping coffee in the bunker whilst his mum was encroaching on the fun.

'Kayla asked me to have a go with her,' I fibbed.

'Ah-hem, more like your mum was desperate to have a go and dragged me along too!' Kayla corrected with only a half truth.

'Come on then,' said Ryan, charging for the pulley in front of me. 'I'll race you!'

I started strong as I marched up the hill, ignoring the pulley handle next to me, determined to show the boys that I wasn't old and boring just yet. About half way up though, my legs felt the burn. Glancing back at Kayla, I saw that she had already clung onto her pulley and gladly followed suit.

'Do you want to do a train, Mum?' asked Josh excitedly as we arrived at the top of the slope.

'How about I do this one myself and then a train next?' I replied, suddenly feeling a little apprehensive as I looked down the slope which seemed far higher once you were at the top of it. I pulled my ring over to the far side and positioned it between the bars just before the tip of the slope. Kayla put her ring in the one next to me.

'How the hell do we climb in these without falling down the slope?' I asked her.

'Easy,' she replied. 'You just hold onto this bar here and plonk your bootie down inside the ring. Then you stretch your legs out either side and voila!'

She demonstrated by flopping into her ring in a very un-elegant kind of way as her ring tipped precariously over the edge. She clung onto the bar for dear life and nodded her head towards me. 'See, easy. Your turn.'

Copying Kayla's rather unorthodox technique, I managed to position myself in my ring without shooting down the hill prematurely and bumping into the poor unsuspecting child who had the misfortune of being in front of me. I unwittingly got an image in my head of lying legs akimbo in a doctor's surgery.

'I feel like I'm lying spread eagle waiting for a gynaecologist?' I told Kayla, giggling.

'Oh my God, I know what you mean,' she said laughing.

'Three, two, one, GO!' came the voice from the marshal, indicating that it was now safe to do our run.

I watched as my fearless boys didn't think twice before launching themselves off of the top of the slope. Kayla and I looked at each other for a second, and then closing my eyes, I took a deep breath and did the same. My hair whooshed backwards as I felt my stomach abandon the rest of my body a metre behind. Daring to open my eyes, I saw a bump up ahead that I hadn't noticed before. Bracing myself, I momentarily flew through the air as my body defied gravity for all of a millisecond before remembering that I was far from feather-like. My back jarred slightly upon landing to remind me that the cliché 'feel good' quotes had lied to me for years and that age actually is more than just a number. Before I knew it, I was gliding to a stop as I gently bumped into Ryan's ring.

'That was brilliant,' I said laughing, as despite myself, I had actually really enjoyed it.

'Let's do a train this time, Mum,' said Josh, grabbing my hand. Even if I hadn't wanted to do it again, my second youngest son wasn't giving me a choice!

'You go,' said Kayla, climbing out of her ring next to us. 'I'll check on Sammy and Eden and then come and join you.'

What was meant to be one or two rides, turned into

an hour of Kayla and I racing up and down the slope with twenty kids. Ben quickly got over his mortification that his mum wouldn't just sit and watch like any normal mum, and even seemed to enjoy the fact that I was joining in.

'Last go, ladies,' our new friend, Jesse, at the top of the slope told us. He was never going to be a David or a Simon, was he? With his shaggy-haired snow boarder look, he was always going to be able to pull off a *Jesse*.

'Can you spin us then?' asked Kayla. I swear she batted her eyelids at him when asking this. Jesse had been spinning the boys for the last half an hour, but I had been too scared to try it.

'What she means is, can you please spin *her*,' I said. 'I am perfectly happy with my boring, straight down approach, thank you very much.'

I climbed into my ring and waited for my last three, two, one countdown. I was just about to push myself off when I felt my ring being pushed for me. Only, it wasn't just a little nudge off the edge, it was a maximum force, spinning push! Suddenly, I was whirling my way down the slope, completely out of control.

'I hate you, Jesse!' I managed to yell just before I flew over the bump backwards. Skidding to a halt, I realised that I may have drawn a little attention to myself as all the other mums seemed to have suddenly stopped their inane chat about which kitchen design they should go for, or whether little Leonie should be doing two ballet classes a week or just one. Feeling embarrassed, I attempted to pull myself out of my ring only to fall straight back into it when Kayla's ring ploughed into the back of me. Her laughter was contagious though, and giving into it, we both lay there like hysterical old ladies with our legs in the air.

'Don't blame Jesse,' she said, in between snorts of laughter. 'I signalled for him to do it when your back was turned. I knew you'd enjoy it once you got spinning!'

'I am so getting you back for this!' I said, not feeling as angry as I pretended to look. It felt good to have a friend who knew she could get away with stuff like that. It reminded me of how Beckie and I had been at university together.

'I know what you mean about this reminding you of the gynaecologist,' Kayla said. 'That's about the only time you'll see my legs in this position these days!'

'I can't even remember the last time I went,' I replied. 'It's just one of those flashbacks that never leaves you though, isn't it? Come on, let's get out of these before we get pummelled by that massive train!'

Looking up the slope, we saw that Jesse had somehow made four trains of five children for one last finale down the slope. Any second now, they would all come hurtling towards us at top speed. We'd had our fun, and now it was time to go back to being responsible parents.

Chapter 17

'Don't you think it's time you were the bigger person, Amber?' Jason asked me the following Saturday morning, looking over the heads of our three youngest sons. They loved jumping in bed with us when they woke up at the weekends, and their little eyes were all glued to the television as they enjoyed one of the highly irritating cartoons that they insisted on watching.

'What do you mean?' I responded nonchalantly. 'I am the bigger person.'

'Well of course I know that,' Jason replied, choosing his words carefully. 'But Rob probably doesn't think that seeing as you barely ever even open the door to him when he picks Ben up.'

'I'm just always busy when he arrives,' I lied. 'If I was the one nearest to the front door, then of course I would answer it.'

'Ok, I believe you,' said Jason, looking like he totally *did not* believe me. 'Seriously though, Amby, you need to let it go for Ben's sake. It's been nearly ten years.'

He was right of course. As much as I loathed Rob, I really needed to make the effort to take our exchanges a step further than the required minimal interaction needed to arrange his time with Ben.

'I'm not talking about inviting him over for Christmas,' Jason joked. 'Maybe just start with something simple like smiling and saying hello when he knocks at the door later today.'

Instead of answering, I suddenly became very interested in the infuriating cartoon.

'Amber?' he persisted.

Reluctantly, I turned to face him. 'Ok, ok,' I relented, accepting defeat. 'When he comes to pick Ben up today, I will open the front door to him.'

'Open the door to who?' Ben asked, appearing in the doorway.

Before I could answer, Ryan filled him in. 'Rob.'

Apparently, the cartoon hadn't been so interesting that he had blocked out mine and Jason's conversation.

'You're getting taken out for pizza and to the arcade again,' Ryan continued in a sulky voice. 'It's not fair. Mum, why can't me, Josh and Sammy have two dads?'

It wasn't the first time one of the boys had shown a streak of jealousy over Ben's situation. Every time he got an extra present at Christmas or on his birthday, his brothers went green with envy. Luckily Jason never got offended. He knew that Rob was nowhere near the father he was. Any man could contribute to creating a life, but it took a real man to be a father.

'It's not that exciting,' Ben replied to his brother, and then turning to me he said, 'Do I have to go, Mum?'

'No, you don't have to go. The man is a total prick who couldn't give a toss about you when you were a baby so doesn't deserve to see you now!' is what I wanted to say. What I actually said was, 'You don't have to sweetheart, but Rob would be really upset not to see you. I'm sure you'll enjoy it once you're there.'

'Sure you will,' added Jason. 'Who doesn't love a bit of pizza!'

'I suppose so,' said Ben, reluctantly. 'Can we have pancakes for breakfast, Mum?'

'Of course, sweetheart.'

Ben's reluctance to see Rob made me want to wrap him up in cotton wool and keep him safe with me forever. If pancakes cheered him up a little, then I'd make a whole stack of them and add extra syrup! Part of me wanted Ben to have a good relationship with Rob, but the darker side of me wanted him to just vanish from our lives forever. I felt the familiar feeling of guilt arise. Guilt about making such a poor choice of husband first time round and giving Ben such a shitty dad. I knew it was irrational to think like that but I couldn't help it. Ben had a great life. He had an amazing dad in Jason, and three little brothers who adored him despite constantly annoying him. Rob was the one who had blown it. Not me. I had nothing to feel guilty about. Yet, I still did – guilt and motherhood went hand in hand like tight leggings and camel toe.

After a lazy pyjama morning, eating pancakes and playing with LEGO, it was time for Ben to go out for the afternoon with Rob. Arriving ten-minutes late, he knocked on the door and rang the bell. *He can't even knock on a door without being annoying*, I thought to myself. Taking a deep breath, I went to open the door for him, as I had promised Jason I would.

'Oh, Hi, Amber,' he said, looking taken aback. 'How are you?'

'Really good thanks,' I replied with more enthusiasm than was probably necessary as I planted a big fake smile on my face to prove it. 'Boys are great. Jason's great. Couldn't be better.'

'That's great, um, really great,' he replied awkwardly. 'Is Ben ready?'

'Yep, he's just coming,' I replied as Ryan, Josh and Samuel all appeared at the door to be nosy.

'How old are you?' asked Josh. 'You look younger than my daddy?'

'Josh!' I reprimanded, feeling embarrassed.

Before Rob could reply, Ryan followed up with another question, 'Can you buy us Christmas presents this year as well. It's not fair that Ben gets more than us.'

'Shut up, Pocket Rocket,' Ben said, affectionately using his brother's nickname as he appeared at the door, saving me from any further humiliation. 'Hi, Rob.'

'Hi, son,' Rob replied looking very thankful that he had been saved from an interrogation by my other children. 'Shall we get going?'

Ben gave me a hug and walked off down the drive. I hadn't noticed it before, but Rob appeared to have bought himself a new sports car which let out an unsociable roar as he pulled away down the road.

Cock, I thought to myself.

'Why did you just say *cock*, Mummy', asked Josh.

Apparently, I didn't just say it in my head!

'I didn't say cock,' I said feigning a confused look. 'Oh, you mean clock! I said, let's go and check the clock so we can see what time it is.'

Seeing my three youngest sons waving at the back of the car that their big brother was in until it vanished around a bend nearly sent my emotions over the edge.

Jason was waiting for us in the kitchen. 'You ok?' he asked me.

'How about we have a snuggly movie afternoon with the boys?' I suggested, moving into his arms for a hug.

'Yay,' shouted Ryan and Josh followed by a little high-pitched voice saying 'I want cop porn!' I caught Jason's eye trying not to give in to the immature trigger in my brain that wanted to acknowledge what my youngest son had just said. 'Ok sweetie, *cop porn* is coming right up! Would you like sweet or salty?'

'I want toffee!' said Ryan, fully understanding his brother's mispronunciation of their favourite movie snack.

'And chocolate buttons!' said Josh.

'And cheese balls and chipsticks!' added Ryan.

'You'll be sick if you eat all that,' Jason said laughing.

'Ben's getting pizza!' Ryan justified. 'If he gets pizza, we deserve lots of movie snacks.'

'Ok, ok, I'll see what I can rustle up,' I said reaching into the snack cupboard which was placed strategically high up so that the boys couldn't reach it. 'You guys go in the lounge with Dad and choose a movie.'

Laden with bowls full of enticing treats, I joined my family on the sofa. As I sunk into the cosy warm material, I instantly became blanketed by little feet and arms. Strategically positioning them so that Samuel, Josh, and Ryan all believed that they had prime position cuddling into Mummy and Daddy, I rested my head against Jason's shoulder and relaxed. It felt like there was a missing piece to our complex jigsaw without Ben there, but I knew he'd be back soon. Obi clambered up onto the arm of the sofa, not wanting to miss out. Ryan cuddled him thinking he was all about the dog loyalty, but I had a sneaky suspicion that he actually just had a cunning plan to catch any falling popcorn that the boys spilt.

'What are we watching then?' I asked expecting to have heard more arguments coming from the lounge over which movie to watch.

'Not sure, but Dad said it's a good one,' said Ryan.

'Yeah, he daid it got dakes in it,' said Samuel, his eyes wide with anticipation.

'And someone gets their heart pulled out of them!' added Josh looking like he was about to wet himself with excitement.

I raised my eyebrows at Jason as he cleared his throat and looked a little sheepish.

'So, you thought it would be a good idea to scare our seven-year-old, four-year-old, and two-year-old sons with a movie with snakes in it and people getting their hearts ripped out?' I enquired.

'And they eat monkey brains too!' said Josh, who at this point looked worryingly jubilant that he was going to get to watch something so gruesome.

'Ok, Josh,' said Jason. 'That's enough out of you. Why don't you eat your popcorn whilst we start the movie? Come on, Amber, it's only *Indiana Jones*. We watched it as kids and it didn't do us any harm.'

'Speak for yourself,' I said. 'The eyes of that psycho ripping the heart out haunted me for years.'

'Look, if they get scared, we'll turn it off. Let's take a vote. Hands up who wants to watch the big boy adventure movie!'

Unsurprisingly, three little hands shot up, and not for the first time in my household, I was well and truly outnumbered.

After their innocent young eyes had sat transfixed to the vivid images that would undoubtedly haunt their dreams that night, Ben arrived home and the house felt complete again.

'Did you have fun with Rob?' I asked him as he put his pyjamas on ready for bed.

'Yeah, it was ok. Did I miss out on much here?'

'No, not really,' I said, deciding not to tell him about

missing out on, in the words of Josh, 'the most awesome movie they'd ever watched'. His brothers would tell him soon enough anyway.

'Any gossip?' I asked, not wanting to pry at the same time as wanting to know every last detail of what Ben had been doing whilst he'd been away from us.

'Not really.'

'Ok, sweetheart,' I said, kissing the top of his head. 'You get a good night's sleep.'

As I went to walk out of his bedroom, he called me back.

'Mum?'

'Yeah.'

'Dad's girlfriend's pregnant.'

Not knowing how I was meant to react to this unexpected revelation, I felt blank as I tried to find the right words. An uneasy feeling crept over me that I couldn't quite put my finger on.

'Wow, I wasn't expecting to hear that,' I managed to reply. 'When's it due?'

'A few months, I think. It's another brother,' he said rolling his eyes.

That's when the penny dropped, explaining the weird feeling that I was experiencing. Ben was going to have another brother that wasn't part of me. Up until now, Rob had just been Rob - the sperm donor. Now, he was creating another family for Ben and as selfish as it was, I couldn't bear the thought of it.

Chapter 18

'When was your last smear test, Mrs Clayton?'

Since my joke on the donut slope, Kayla had been nagging me to book an appointment to get my three-yearly test. Not trusting me not to get distracted by daily life, she had literally dialled the doctor's number when I had been at her house a few weeks ago and handed me the phone when the receptionist finally answered.

'Um, probably sometime between my second and third sons,' I answered vaguely.

'Can we be a little more specific?' the nurse responded curtly, not looking away from the calendar on her computer.

'Ok, probably about five years ago,' I offered, feeling

like a child who had just been reprimanded for missing their six-monthly dental check-up and now needed a filling.

With a sharp intake of breath, she tapped away on her keyboard whilst I glanced around the room. There was a treatment couch nestled next to the window that was mottled glass to ensure our privacy. A long stretch of starchy white paper lay over it to keep it clean between patients. I shuddered as I imagined myself lying on it naked from the waist down. In an attempt to distract myself, I started reading a poster asking me if I was *At Risk of Type 2 Diabetes* on the wall next to me. It looked like it had been placed there with Blu-Tack thirty years ago and not been touched since as its edges faded to a murky yellow colour. The nurse finally looked up from her computer screen, stopping me from torturing myself any further. She looked to be about fifty years old and had a brusqueness to her voice that would have ordinarily made me avoid her, but somehow suited the situation. I didn't want to become friends with the stranger about to look up the valley in my lady garden. Curt and to the point would do me just fine in this situation, and then I could run out of here and never see her again. If being brusque meant she was efficient and good at her job then that was fine with me.

'Ok, Mrs Clayton. Go behind the curtain there and take off your trousers and knickers. There's some extra paper on the chair there that you can cover yourself up with and just let me know when you're ready.'

Walking over to the chair and drawing the blue modesty curtain around myself, I did as I'd been instructed. I cursed myself for forgetting to shave my legs, and then decided that hairy legs would just compliment the wayward bikini line that I hadn't had waxed in about five months. Again, another positive for having a fifty-year-old, unceremonious nurse to do the job. She probably had a little hirsutism going on herself underneath her crisp, clean uniform. If I hadn't felt so prone and vulnerable right then, I would have laughed aloud at the image that unwittingly flickered into my mind.

'Are you ready?'

'Ready as I'll ever be,' I replied.

The nurse appeared round the curtain holding the speculum that she was about to insert into me. I turned my head to the side, not wanting to look at the long, metal contraption that looked remarkably like a duck's bill and was about to go where no metal object should quite frankly ever be placed.

'Ok, just pop your heels together and let your legs flop to the side. If you need to tell me anything unique about your cervix, now is the time.'

Anything unique about my cervix? I thought to myself. *What a strange question.*

'Um, nothing that I know of,' I replied uncertainly.

'Ok, just relax then.'

I felt a slight discomfort as she wasted no time getting into my apparently very boring and *un-unique* cervix.

'Just a few seconds longer.'

I closed my eyes and took some deep breaths, imagining myself on a desert island to take my mind off of the reality of where I was. A flashback of a conversation I once had with Beckie popped into my head. She had told me that a nurse had once got a speculum stuck up her noony (her word, not mine!) during a routine smear test. When the nurse enlightened Beckie as to the predicament, she understandably panicked and tightened her vaginal muscles around the instrument, locking it in even more. This resulted in her being stuck, legs akimbo, for nearly an hour whilst two doctors tried to coax the thing out. Suddenly worrying that the same thing could happen to me, I started a mantra in my head to tell my vagina to relax.

'And all done,' said the nurse on my sixth repetition.

'Thank God for that!' I said, proceeding in my relief that it was all over to babble my story of Beckie's horror to her. Barely raising an eyebrow, she informed me that this was in fact incredibly rare, and suggested that maybe Beckie had exaggerated a little bit. She may have a point. Beckie did love to dramatize things when we were younger. It was probably only stuck for ten minutes as opposed to a full hour.

'I'll leave you to get dressed now and as long as the results come back normal, you'll need to have another one in three years.' And then a little more pointedly, 'Not five years, *three* years.'

'Understood,' I said, giving her a little salute with my

hand, once again feeling like a naughty child. Hurriedly dressing myself, I got out of the surgery as quickly as I could to go and report back to Kayla that I had done as she had told me to, and now she could stop nagging me.

All done, I text. I'll be there to get Sammy soon.

She replied straight away.

Almost school pick up. I'll bring Sammy and meet you there.

Looking at the time on my phone, I realised that she was right. I hadn't noticed how late it was. *Time flies when you're having fun,* I thought wryly to myself.

Before I knew it, I was back to being mum as I walked my merry troop of men home. I had planned on sneaking off to my bedroom and eating the bar of Galaxy Caramel that I had hidden in my underwear drawer to reward myself for being brave at my smear test. But as we walked, Ben asked if we could go to the pet shop to get Obi a birthday present, and I found it impossible to say no. Without even going through the front door, the five of us climbed straight into my car the second we got back. The pet shop was only a short drive away, and as long as I could get a parking space right out the front, we'd be back in no time at all.

Lady luck must have been shining on us as the small car park out the front was empty when we arrived. It was a small independent shop which had somehow survived the monopolisation by the large chain store that had recently opened in town. Pulling the handbrake on, I started to open my door when Ben asked if he could go in on his own. I hesitated slightly, and then realised that now was probably as good a time as any to allow him to feel grown up. The shop was tiny, and I could literally see him in there the whole time from the car.

'Go on then, but don't be long.'

I watched Ben wander into the shop and hesitate as the owner approached him to presumably ask if he'd like some help.

'Mummy,' came Josh's voice from the backseat a few moments later.

'Yes, sweetheart.'

'How do you tell the difference between a girl hamster and a boy hamster?'

'Erm, well one would have a willy, and one wouldn't, I expect,' thinking of the most obvious answer as I spotted Ben paying for something at the till. 'Just like boy and girl dogs.'

'That makes sense,' said Josh accepting my very basic answer. 'As Tilly the school hamster doesn't have a willy. I checked the other day and there's definitely not one there.'

'Well, there you go then,' I said, not convinced that you would find one on a boy hamster without a very strong microscopic lens.

Ben climbed into the front seat next to me holding a

very cute looking toy monkey.

'Obi's going to love that, Ben,' I told him.

'I hope so. I'll give it to him as soon as we get home.'

I smiled at my eldest son, feeling smug that he was proving my point to Jason as to how important it was for us to bring a puppy into our lives. The bond that Ben had with Obi was undeniable.

Thankfully the drive home was only short as Ben kept squeaking the monkey's tummy to make his brothers laugh. Whoever thought it would be fun to insert a squeaker into a dog toy obviously didn't like humans very much.

Obi was so excited to see us when we got home that he raced straight out of the front door to Ben. I felt guilty that he must have seen us arrive home from school and get straight in the car to go out again. I could just imagine the sad whimper he would have made as his barking efforts fell on deaf ears whilst he had watched the car drive away. Ben's present would make up for it though. He literally fell backwards as Obi jumped up and started licking him. Suddenly everything seemed to go in slow motion though as Obi spotted a cat on the other side of the street. Scrambling off of Ben, he ran towards it with absolutely no thought for what could be on the road.

Chapter 19

'The house feels so strange without Obi, Mum.'

Ben and I were lying in his bed like we used to when he was Sammy's age. As I stroked his soft hair which was still slightly damp where he had just washed the gel out, it felt nice to see a glimpse of the little boy that still hid inside of him. Ben often seemed far older than his young nine years, and I felt guilty for expecting more of him than I should, just because he was the oldest.

'I know, sweetheart. I miss him too.'

'Do you think he'll be feeling scared?'

'He's probably dreaming of running through fields and rolling in mud,' I said trying to make Ben feel better. 'And I promise you, as soon as the vet calls me in the morning, I will go straight in to get him. Ok?'

'Ok.'

'I was so proud of you today, Ben. Obi is very lucky to have you.' I kissed him on his head. 'And so am I.'

Obi was an incredibly lucky dog. After being hit by a

car, he had amazingly only suffered a broken leg. I felt a shiver run down my spine as I thought about how much worse it could have been. After initially feeling relieved that he was going to be ok, I had had a moment of panic when I'd realised that in all the stress of moving house, I had forgotten to renew his pet insurance. When Ben heard this, he didn't hesitate in telling me that he could pay for Obi's treatment. It turned out, unbeknown to me, that he had been running a secret tuck shop at school and had made nearly £500! I knew that I should have told him off for doing something that was so blatantly against the school rules, but not only had he displayed some pretty impressive entrepreneurial skills for a nine-year-old, he also hadn't thought twice about selflessly spending every last penny of it on Obi. My instinct had been to tell Ben that he didn't need to do that, and that Jason and I would find the money, but the look on Ben's face when he told me he could help was a look that I would never forget. Ben wanted to be the one to save the day. He wanted to use his money for something important, and nothing was more important to him than his best friend, Obi. We have many defining moments in our lives and this was one for Ben. I wasn't about to take that away from him.

'You need to try to get some sleep now, sweetheart. It's getting late.'

'Can you hold my hand until I fall asleep, Mum?'

Taking his right hand in mine, I softly started singing 'What A Wonderful World' by Louis Armstrong in a lullaby tone like I used to when he was a baby.

'Er, Mum.'

'Yes?'

'I said can you hold my hand, not treat me like a baby.'

'Oh, ok. Sorry.'

'I'm nearly ten, Mum. Not two. Besides, your singing is really terrible.'

I laughed softly at my son's brutal honesty. I could always rely on my boys not to sugar coat things. I'd got carried away at the idea of mothering my eldest again. The lullaby probably was a step too far. I'd just lay there quietly instead, relishing in the fact that he still wanted to hold my hand.

As Ben's rhythmic breathing signalled that he was fast asleep, I gently let go of his hand and climbed out of his bed. Walking to my bedroom, I got under my own covers and snuggled into Jason.

'So, we've got ourselves a little entrepreneur, have we?' Jason asked smiling down at me.

'It would seem so,' I replied, laughing. 'Should we tell him to stop before he gets caught?'

'What and be the ones held accountable for shattering his dreams of becoming a millionaire? Today, the school tuck shop, tomorrow, the world. Let the kid have his dreams, Amby.'

'You're right,' I agreed. 'But, if he gets caught, and we get a call from the headteacher, I'm denying all knowledge of it.'

'Sounds like a plan. Now, tell me all about your very first client, courtesy of your mother.'

'It's actually a really lovely one to start with. No dramatic family secrets being divulged. No shocking revelations. Just a straight forward, lovely recount of her life with the odd wow factor thrown in that her children didn't know about her.'

'Sounds perfect,' said Jason, kissing me on my head before yawning. 'Shall we go to sleep. I'm exhausted.'

'You're exhausted!' I exclaimed. 'Try having the day I've had.'

The drama with Obi had made me forget all about my earlier smear test, but what with that and poor Obi getting hit by a car, it truly had been a day I did not want to repeat any time soon.

Chapter 20

I was thankful for a bit of calm in my life for the next few weeks. Kayla and I came to an arrangement whereby she would look after Sammy one day a week so that I could focus on Autobiographies by Amber and I would look after Eden one day a week so that she could focus on her studies. After she had offered to let me practise my interviewing technique on her in the pub, she hadn't been able to let go of the niggling feeling that she wanted to pursue her dream of becoming a midwife. After talking it over with Luke, he was completely supportive of the idea, so Kayla wasted no time in doing her research. When her course started, she would have to do most of her studying in the evenings, so having one day a week to completely focus our time would be a huge help to one another. Luckily for Kayla, she also had family around who could help out when she needed to attend lectures. I couldn't help but admire how motivated she was when she got an idea in her head. If she hadn't pushed me to go it alone, I'd still be crying into my wine glass over my Edward Pinkerton faux-pas. Although I didn't technically need to look after Eden for Kayla until her course commenced, she insisted that we start our arrangement immediately, knowing that I would benefit from the time whilst getting my new business off the ground.

Today, was my day to focus. I just had the finishing touches to put on Valerie's autobiography before sending it to print, and then I could dedicate my time to a new client who had found me through my website that was now up and running. I was really excited about this one, as it was a slightly different brief to anything I had ever worked on. It was for a client whose mother had Alzheimer's. After seeing her grandmother go through the same thing, my client wanted to capture as much of her mother's life in a book as possible whilst she still had many lucid moments to tell her everything she could. It was actually quite a beautiful concept that I felt privileged to be a part of. After a couple of email conversations with my client, I was about to meet her on a video call with her mother to conduct the first interview.

As the connection established on my laptop, I came face to face with my client for the first time. She looked to be a similar age to me which immediately made me think of my own mum and how lucky I was to still have her around.

'Hi, I'm Amber,' I said, smiling warmly into the

camera. I felt a little nervous and hoped that she didn't pick up on it.

'Hello, I'm Jenna,' she replied mirroring my smile. 'Mum isn't having a great day, so I thought we could have a chat first, and then she'll join us in a bit if she's feeling up to it. Is that ok?'

'Yes, of course,' I said, feeling a little out of my depth with the sensitivity of the situation. I had been excited about the concept, but seeing Jenna sitting there brought home the reality of it.

'Did you have a chat with your mum about the questions I sent you last week?'

I had given Jenna a framework detailing different areas that I would usually cover and some leading questions to get her mum chatting about certain things in her life. Given that we couldn't guarantee her mum being lucid for our interview calls, it seemed like the most practical way to proceed.

Jenna nodded and placed her hands against her chest, looking down. When she glanced up, I saw that she had tears in her eyes.

'I did,' she said. 'Amber, it was amazing. The things she told me were things I never would have known if you hadn't prompted me to ask.'

I felt my own eyes welling up in response as I realised the full impact of what we were doing. Jenna was connecting with her mum in a way that she wouldn't be able to the more her condition progressed. Creating a book of her mum's life meant she would always have something to look back on and cherish when she felt like her mum was no longer there.

For the next hour, Jenna filled me in on everything her mum, Maria Denning, had told her over the past week. I was recording the conversation, partly so that I didn't miss anything important, but also so that Jenna had my full attention as she told me about her mum's life. I promised Jenna that I would do her mum justice in her autobiography, and I truly meant it. I would spend hours putting together Maria's words in a way that could be enjoyed by generations of their family for many years. I felt a lump in my throat as Jenna's mum, Maria, joined us at the end of the call, and I thought about how precious the book would be.

'Hello, dear,' she said. 'Are you one of Jenna's friends from school.'

'No, Mum, this is Amber. Do you remember I told you about her?' Jenna asked as she put her arm protectively around her mum's shoulders.

'Do you ever get a detention?' Maria asked me. 'Jenna is always getting detentions.'

Jenna looked uncomfortably into the camera as I bore witness to the reality of Alzheimer's.

'No, I haven't had a detention today,' I said not wanting to confuse her by trying to explain who I really was. 'It was lovely to meet you, Maria. I'll leave you and Jenna to it now. Bye Jenna,' I said, waving into the camera.

Jenna mouthed thank you to me as she switched off

her camera. I let out a sigh as I took in the scene that had just played out. To see your mother lose herself like that must be tougher than anyone could ever imagine, and I was going to work my hardest to give them a keepsake of the amazing woman she once was.

Chapter 21

'I can't believe he did that,' said Kayla, looking shocked. 'You must have been beside yourself with worry.'

'Oh my God, you have no idea,' I said, raising my eyebrows. 'My boys have done some pretty questionable things over the years, but this one took things to a whole new level.'

We were pushing Samuel and Eden on the swings at the park after dropping the older ones at school. After a freezing cold, few months, the warmth of Spring had arrived, allowing us the freedom to enjoy being outdoors again. The daffodils seemed to have appeared out of nowhere, growing in their vibrant clusters. The sight of their bright yellow petals never failed to trigger a feeling of happiness inside me. Most women loved expensive bouquets made of elaborately styled roses and Peruvian lilies. All I needed was a bunch of daffodils sitting in my hallway to put a smile on my face.

I was filling Kayla in on my dramatic weekend. Rob had insisted on taking Ben on a camping trip which had nearly sent me over the edge anyway. My initial reaction had been to tell him it was a terrible idea, but after chatting it through with Jason, I had realised that Rob did seem to be making more of an effort with Ben these days, and as much as I would rather that he lived in Outer Mongolia with no means of communication other than carrier pigeon, I had to accept that he may want to start seeing Ben more. Ben had been understandably hesitant given that he had only ever seen Rob for a few hours at a time up until now, but being the bigger person that Jason had encouraged me to be, I had encouraged him to go. When the weather forecast had predicted an unusually warm weekend ahead, Rob had decided that there was no time like the present and had booked a pitch at a campsite in the New Forest. As well as packing the essentials like the tent and sleeping bags, unbeknown to any of us, he also packed something extra without realising – Ryan! Feeling jealous that his big brother was going camping for the weekend, Ryan had snuck out of the house when I wasn't looking and climbed into Rob's car. He had hidden on the back seat under Rob and Ben's coats, and had amazingly kept quiet until they were almost at the campsite. When I got the phone call from Rob to say he had a stowaway, I was already a complete nervous wreck after searching the house for Ryan for the past half an hour. Initially thinking that he was playing in his bedroom, the alarm was raised when I called him down for lunch and he didn't appear. Jason had just left to go knocking on the neighbour's doors when my phone rang. Somehow, Rob had managed to convince me to let Ryan stay with them. All weekend, I had been playing out the scene in my head of Ben and Ryan arriving home. I had planned to give them the biggest telling off they had ever had. No more *Mrs Nice Mum*, making pancakes and hot chocolates! Well, that was the plan anyway. But when the boys had arrived home, they'd looked exhausted and I had decided to save the lecture for the morning. Ben had got it all figured out though. He'd told me how much fun they had had together knowing that I wanted nothing more in the world than for my sons to develop that brother bond that no-one could ever break. While Jerry Maguire had Dorothy at 'hello', Ben Collins had me at 'we truly bonded'.

'You fell for that hook, line, and sinker,' laughed Kayla.

'I know,' I admitted. 'But how could I stay angry with them after Ben's little speech about how well they got on, and how pleased he was to have his brother there?'

'But still, Amber, Ryan literally stowed away and ended up miles away from home without you knowing.'

'I know, I'm a push over,' I said, wincing at how weak I sounded.

'That's being a mum for you. They literally push you to the brink of insanity and then melt your heart with one little hug.'

'I'm still going to punish him for it,' I told Kayla, not

wanting to look like a complete sucker. 'I told him he has to clean my car after school today. Inside and out. I'll tell you what is strange though. When Ben heard the punishment, he offered to do it with Ryan! They really must have had a great weekend together.'

'Well as stressful as it was for you at the time, it sounds like it was actually worth it,' Kayla said, understanding how I felt. 'All any of us really want is for our kids to get along with each other. If Eden and Finn end up half as close as Ben and Ryan seem to be now, I'll be a happy mum.'

'Yep, totally agree. Although I'm sure it won't last. Before long, they'll be back to annoying each other. I'll tell you who has been a good influence on all of them though. Tommy! He's spent so much time at our house lately, and he loves acting like a big brother to Ryan, Josh and Sammy. I think it's making Ben appreciate them a bit more. Do you know anything about Tommy's parents? All I know from Ben is that they are insanely rich and never around.'

'Well,' said Kayla, looking like she was about to divulge some seriously juicy gossip. 'Did Ben tell you *how* they became so rich?'

Ben had told me that Tommy's parents had won the lottery. It did seem a bit far-fetched, but I didn't question it as didn't want to put any doubt in Ben's head about his new friend. We all hear of someone winning the lottery, but never does it happen to someone you actually know.

I told Kayla what Ben had told me, and she pulled a

smug face before screwing her nose up in a way that said a thousand words.

'You don't think they won the lottery?' I asked her. 'I have to admit, I did think it was a little unbelievable.'

'From what I heard,' said Kayla, glancing around to check that no-one else was in ear shot, 'Tommy thinks they won the lottery as that's what his parents told him. One day they were living a normal, frugal life just like us, then the next thing you know, they're living in a mansion. They had to tell Tommy something.'

'So where did the money actually come from then?'

'Well according to Shannon, Tommy's dad is some kind of white-collar criminal. She heard that he's been laundering money in the Cayman Islands for years.'

'Kayla, that's ridiculous,' I said, laughing. 'Stuff like that happens on Netflix, not in real life! Where on earth did Shannon hear all that?'

'I don't actually know. Shannon is just one of those people who seems to know all the gossip. You're probably right though. It does sound a bit absurd when you say it out loud like that. They probably just inherited it from some long-lost uncle or something.'

'Now that is far more conceivable,' I agreed as I pushed Samuel higher to meet his demands to touch the clouds.

'Anyway, there was something else I had to tell you,' I said, looking at Kayla. I picked Sammy up out of the swing and told him to run along to the slide with Eden. Kayla followed suit, plucking Eden up who then happily rang along after her bestie. I got my phone out of my pocket and showed Kayla the latest picture.

'Aw, so cute!' Kayla said, looking at the adorable picture of an eight-week-old cocker spaniel puppy. 'Whose is she?'

'Mine!' I said excitedly. 'I saw an advert for her last week, and I just couldn't resist.'

'You just happened to see an advert?' mocked Kayla.

'Well, I might have been thinking a bit about getting a friend for Obi so just had a little peak. I think it's fate though. The first search I did popped up this little beauty. What do you think?'

'I think Jason is going to go totally ballistic,' she answered, laughing.

She was right of course. Jason was going to be livid. I could handle him though. He hadn't wanted Obi either, and he soon fell in love with him.

Chapter 22

'What the fuck were you thinking, Amber?'

Apparently, Jason wasn't going to be the pushover I had hoped he would be.

'Obi needed a friend,' I replied, angling for a pull on the emotional heart strings tactic.

'We already have four kids and a dog. We didn't need another dog. Especially not another annoying puppy who is going to destroy everything,' Jason answered angrily.

Whereas Jason had instantly fallen in love with Obi, his relationship with our new puppy, Lola, was going to take a little more work. After a week of her howling at night, teething on everything in sight, and digging up the garden, she had, yesterday, committed the ultimate sin of chewing a hole in his new slippers. It certainly hadn't enamoured her to him, that was for sure.

Ben had already been subjected to Jason's rage whilst he hid Lola under his duvet out of reach. Now it was my turn.

'Look, she's just a little puppy,' I said. 'She'll grow out of it.'

'She'd better grow out of quickly, or she can take a one-way trip to Battersea Dogs Home.'

I knew he didn't mean it. Jason was a big softy underneath the tough act he was playing. He would come round to the idea of another dog, just like he came round to the idea of a fourth child. And until he did, I would just need to keep a very close eye on little Miss Lola... and buy Jason a new pair of slippers. Changing the subject, I checked the time, wondering out loud when Ben would be back. Rob had called him a few hours ago with the news that his girlfriend had had the baby. He had wanted Ben to go round straight away to meet his new little brother. My face must have given away the inner turmoil I was feeling as Jason suddenly softened.

'Does it feel weird?'

'A little,' I confessed. 'I know it sounds selfish, but we're Ben's family. You're his dad, and Ryan, Josh, and Sammy are his brothers. He doesn't need another family.'

'No, he doesn't need one. But whether we like it or not, he's got one, Amber.'

'I know. It just seems so unfair that Rob can be such a crap dad to the point that he didn't even bother seeing Ben when he was a baby, and then he just decides he wants to play happy families all of a sudden.'

'You're right, it is unfair. But Ben has another brother, and that little fella deserves to have someone as amazing as Ben in his life, don't you think?'

Jason always knew the right thing to say. He may be lacking in the compassion department when it came to cute puppies, but when it came to our family, you couldn't fault him. Give it a few months, and he'd see Lola as part of the family too. I took a step towards him and allowed myself to be wrapped up in his arms that were no longer waving manky chewed slippers at me.

'Maybe Rob's changed,' Jason continued when I didn't answer. 'We're all getting older, Amby, maybe Rob's finally growing up too.'

Taking a deep breath, I looked up into his eyes. 'You're right. I'll stop being selfish. This is about Ben, not me. And if there is anything Ben is good at, it's being a big brother.'

'Come on,' said Jason, 'Let's go and make a cup of tea and wait for him to get home so he can tell us all about it. But,' he added as an afterthought, 'this does not mean you're forgiven for bringing that little gremlin into our home.'

'How can you call something so cute a gremlin?' I protested. 'Just you wait, she'll be as good as gold in no time, just like Obi.'

Jason certainly didn't look convinced, and I realised that keeping quiet was probably my best tactic right then. As well as keeping Lola well out of Jason's line of vision – unless she was looking adorably angelic as she napped after rampaging round the house in her whirlwind way.

We let Ryan, Josh, and Samuel stay up a bit late with

us as we all waited for Ben to get home. We were sitting round the kitchen table playing Snap – three little boys in their pyjamas, stifling yawns for fear of being sent to bed before seeing their big brother.

'Will Ben be bringing his brother back here with him?' asked Josh.

'No, sweetheart,' I replied. 'Ben's new brother has a different mum so he will be living with her and Rob.'

'Oh, ok,' said Josh.

'But he our brudda too?' asked Samuel, looking up at me questioningly with his big blue eyes. He was too young to really understand what was going on, but his innocent acceptance of the situation wasn't lost on me.

Before I could answer him, there was a knock on the door. Everyone jumped out of their seats, scattering the cards everywhere as they raced to be the first to see Ben. Opening the door wide, Ben was leapt on by three little brothers all at once.

'Alright lads, let the poor boy in,' said Jason, attempting to scoop them off of him. I took their place, hugging Ben like he'd been away for two days, not two hours.

'So, how was it?' I asked. 'Does he look like you?'

'Not really, it's a bit cute though.'

'Did you cuddle him?'

'No,'

'Aw, why not?' I asked, taking a sip of my tea that I was still holding. 'You used to love cuddling your brothers when they were babies.'

'I didn't cuddle him, because I cuddled her,' said Ben, smiling as he emphasised the *her*.

Instead of swallowing my tea, I spat it right back out.

'You mean…'

'Yep!'

Everyone else looked perplexed, but I knew exactly what Ben meant.

'I don't have another little brother,' Ben confirmed. 'I have a little sister!'

Chapter 23

'Bloody hell, I bet you didn't see that one coming,' said Shannon as I filled her in on the surprise arrival of Ben's little sister the following Friday evening. Kayla already knew of course, and had relayed it to her, but Shannon wanted to hear all the details first hand.

'I know,' I said. 'They'd already bought lots of little blue baby grows and everything. Apparently, it was a complete shock.'

Our conversation was halted by an announcement over the microphone that we were all to take our seats. It was the night of the school talent show. Jason had finished work early so that he could come to watch. Ben had asked Rob to come along as well, but he was too busy with Cassie and the baby who they had named Jodie. That was typical Rob — come back into Ben's life pretending to want to be a dad, and then drop him at the first sign of commitment. Luckily Ben didn't seem too phased as he had his best dad there cheering him on anyway. I took my seat next to Jason feeling a pang of emotion. Just a few months ago, I had sat in the school office wondering how on earth we would get through the day as the boys all nervously entered their new school filled with terror. Now, the three of them were about to perform in front of a packed room, full of parents, teachers, and their new friends. Holding Samuel in my arms, I sat down in between Jason and Tommy.

'Sit on Dommy,' said Sammy, reaching his arms out to his surrogate big brother. When Ben had told me that Tommy's parents hadn't got tickets to the talent show, I hadn't hesitated in inviting Tommy to come with us. Gladly handing Sammy over to him, I grabbed hold of Jason's hand, thankful that I could give all our boys my full attention without worrying about entertaining our youngest. Getting Tommy all to himself for an hour was like striking gold to Samuel.

'Oh my God, look, Ryan's the first act,' I said to Jason as I saw Ryan strolling out onto the makeshift stage, looking cool as a cucumber. I felt that mixed bag of pride and nerves that every parent feels when they see their child up on stage. It doesn't matter whether it's their first wonderfully imperfect nativity play that they are performing in, or the leading role in their interpretation of Shakespeare. That feeling will get you every time.

The stage lights beamed on him as Ryan stood there confidently wearing his Arsenal football kit, holding his favourite ball under his arm. With all the signatures of last season's team, it was his pride and joy. Some music started thumping out of the speakers, and as the audience all started clapping along, Ryan gave a cheeky little wink to the crowd before starting some flawless keepy-uppys.

'I think he gets it from me,' whispered Jason in my ear.

'The football skills, or the shameless confidence?' I whispered back.

'Both.'

I felt unbelievably proud as I sat there watching my seven-year-old son showing off his skills, and heard someone behind me say, 'that kid'll play for England one day with moves like that.' My heart stopped for a moment as Ryan suddenly kicked the ball straight out towards the audience. It skimmed heads, gaining height until it dipped at the back of the hall falling straight into the basketball hoop. The crowd erupted at this point, cheering and clapping their hands. A few even climbed on top of their chairs and started whooping.

'That's my boy,' said Jason loudly, proudly taking credit for his superstar son. I laughed as I saw Ryan jump off of the stage to reclaim his ball before anyone else could touch it. I waved at him as I tried to catch his eye, but we were just a dark mass of people in amongst the bright lights beaming onto the stage. Ryan had certainly got the night off to a great start.

'He was amazing,' said Kayla, reaching over Tommy to nudge my hand.

'He was, wasn't he,' I agreed, as I noticed a man sitting next to Kayla who must have arrived after the lights went

185

down. 'Is that Luke?' It seemed amazing that in the few months that I had become so close to Kayla, I had never met her husband. The man sitting next to her in a suit and tie was exactly how Kayla had described him, only far more handsome. I guess when you had been married to someone for such a long time, you took their features for granted. The well-defined cheekbones and naturally perfect eyebrows were a winning combination that any sane woman would appreciate. You could never go wrong with a man with a good set of eyebrows, Beckie had once told me in a text message about her latest date. Unfortunately, the lack of a second date meant that Beckie never got to find out whether the eyebrows would have made him a keeper. In Luke's case, it was definitely true though. No wonder Shannon practised her flirting techniques on him.

'Hi, Luke,' I said, leaning over Tommy and Samuel. 'I'm Amber.'

'Lovely to meet you finally, Amber,' he replied with a friendly politeness. 'Kayla has told me all about you.'

'Don't believe a word of it,' I giggled and then cringed at myself for being so cliché. I was about to attempt to introduce Jason across the row of chairs when the next act came on hushing us all.

The next half an hour felt like torture as girl after girl came on stage to delight us with their sweet singing voices. I chastised myself for being so mentally scathing to them whilst respectfully clapping along with the other parents. I prided myself on being a good, kind person, but I held no responsibility for the thoughts that my brain just couldn't control. I justified it as not counting as malicious if no-one else knew my unfiltered thoughts. Oh, except for Jason. Jason and I had a rule that we could say what we liked about anyone else to each other, and it didn't count as being scathing, as long as it stayed in our little secret bubble.

I looked up to see two adorable little boys entering the stage wearing undeniably homemade costumes. Taking their positions, they turned their backs to the audience and started shaking their little backsides as the music started. It was Josh and his new best friend, Daniel, wearing the Mr Magnificent and Amazing Man costumes that I had lovingly sewn for them. I should have felt embarrassed at how appallingly made the costumes were, but it strangely added to the whole winning cuteness factor. I knew their routine by heart after watching Josh perform it over and over again as he practised it in his bedroom. To finally see him doing it in sync with Daniel was definitely a proud mummy moment.

'I think he takes after me,' I said, nudging Jason.

'No doubt there,' he agreed in a tone that could have been either complimentary or judgemental – I wasn't quite sure. Josh and I did like a good dance round the kitchen to Abba, and I planned to embrace every second of it before he grew up and started to tell me my dancing was, in the words of Ben, 'a total cringe fest'.

Josh and Daniel won the respect of every older kid in school when they ended their routine with a cocky arm fold and over the shoulder glance. They had absolutely nailed it, and I led the audience in getting to my feet and clapping louder than every parent in there.

'Just Ben to go now,' I said to Jason as Josh and Daniel left the stage. I felt my nerves kicking in as I imagined Ben standing high above the audience doing his karate act. My concerns had been belittled by Ben and Jason when Ben told me about his dare devil plans to do a karate stick kata ten-feet off the ground. I backed down, thinking that I would let the school be the ones to put a stop to Ben's plans as thought that there was no way they would allow it on health and safety grounds. Shockingly, they had given the approval for it to go ahead though, so now I had no choice but to sit there trying my utmost to contain my anxiety and control my nerves.

I didn't have long to wait, as following a budding magician and a slightly dubious contortionist, Ryan and a few of his classmates prepared the stage for Ben. He appeared moments later, wearing his Gi with his brown and white striped belt majestically wrapped around it.

'He'll be fine,' whispered Jason as I dug my nails into his hand, feeling worried. 'Ben could do this with his eyes closed.'

I wished that I had Jason's confidence, but all I could see was my little boy standing up high on some scaffolding, just inches from falling off and breaking his leg. I had to bite my lip to stop myself from shouting out, 'be careful darling.' I bore my eyes into Ben, willing him to look at me, despite knowing that we were probably just a blur of darkness to him in amongst a sea of strangers. I took ownership of any distant telepathic powers my ancestors may have handed down to me and urged Ben to be careful with the strength of my mind. I could have sworn that he looked straight at me, and then I heard a whoosh as he started twisting his stick in his fingertips. The next few minutes were a blur of kicks and punches and gasps as Ben stepped dangerously close to the edge of the platform.

'He knows what he's doing,' Jason reassured me as my nails dug in deeper with every gasp. I watched as Ben banged the stick down loudly before leaping off of the top of the scaffolding with his hand raised ready to chop the piece of wood below him in two. I momentarily relaxed, knowing that the drama was about to end. Jason had confided in me that the wood was actually two pieces of wood that had cleverly been glued together in a way that they would easily break apart when Ben's hand connected with them. He'd let me in on the secret when I had kept him up one night, stressing about how dangerous it was. My relaxation was short-lived though as the sound of Ben screaming ripped through me.

Chapter 24

I hadn't planned on spending the next few hours of my life in the accident and emergency department of the local hospital, but then again, who does ever plan for that? It turned out that some evil little witch in Ben's class had switched the fake block of wood for a real one. Thankfully Ben's hand hadn't broken and was just badly bruised. My superstitious mind kept reminding me that bad luck comes in threes. First, Obi's accident, then this. I couldn't shift the feeling that a third problem was on its way.

'Who in their right mind would do that?' I asked Jason as we lay in bed that night, unwinding after all the drama. Ben seemed to take the whole thing very well considering, and when I overheard him plotting revenge with Ryan, I didn't intervene. There is no wrath like that of a mother protecting her children, and this was a time that someone deserved a little taste of their own medicine. The suggestions I overheard were more along the lines of tying her shoelaces together or giving her a chocolate bar laced with chilli powder, so I knew they wouldn't do anything that could do her permanent harm.

'Kids can just be stupid sometimes, Amber. She probably didn't realise how dangerous it could be.'

'Maybe not, but if one of our boys ever did something so spiteful, I would ground them for a whole year.'

'You're going to have to think up better punishments than that you know. Grounding a child these days is a reward, not a punishment.'

He was right. When we were kids, being grounded was a fate worse than death. Nowadays, kids loved the thought of staying inside their cosy house full of all the electrical gadgets they could wish for.

'Hey, I've had an idea for Ben's birthday by the way,' Jason said, changing the subject. 'How about a Nerf gun party?'

Jason's eyes lit up in excitement as he said it, proving that there was truth in the statement that no man ever truly grew up.

'I think Ben would love it,' I replied. 'And I think you would love it too!' I added, raising my eyebrows at him.

'That's decided then,' Jason said smiling. 'I thought Ben might like to invite Rob along too.'

'Are you sure about that?'

I had been trying to be the bigger person lately and not regard Rob with such disdain, but having him along to Ben's party seemed like a big step... a massively big step.

191

'Why don't we ask Ben and let him decide?' I compromised.

I had to admire Jason. Not all men would be so secure as to encourage a relationship between their son and the man whose name was on the birth certificate, but Jason wanted what was best for Ben. And if he could tolerate Rob for the sake of Ben, then I at least needed to try.

With all the drama of the day and now the image of Rob playing happy families with us going through my head, no amount of melatonin was going to allow my brain the luxury of sleep any time soon. I crept out of bed and flung on my dressing gown. There was no point in tossing and turning as my mind begged for sleep for the next hour. I may as well get some work done on Maria Denning's autobiography.

Lola looked up at me from her crate with sleepy eyes and started wagging her tail as I turned the kitchen lights on. If I stood any chance of getting her to win Jason over, she had to stay firmly put in her crate at night until she had mastered the art of toilet training. For the next hour though, she could become my late-night writing buddy. She couldn't believe her luck as I opened the crate door to let her out less than an hour after she had been tucked up for the night. Stretching her front paws out and giving a yawn so cute it would melt even Jason's heart, I pulled her bed under the table and clicked my fingers for her to curl up in it. Sitting on a chair, I tucked my feet underneath her and felt immediately comforted by the warmth of her little body. Kayla had told me that if a dog sits on your feet, it means they trust you and you are 'their person'. Technically, I guess I had forced my feet to be sat on, but Lola seemed perfectly content to stay there as she gave a little sigh and drifted back to sleep.

As I opened up my laptop to continue my work, a text message came through on my phone. The only other person who ever text me at this time of night was Beckie. All the sane, mum friends that I knew would have been getting their beauty sleep whilst they could. Reaching for my phone, I anticipated either an over-sharing message about Beckie's latest date, or an explicitly detailed message describing her latest gruesome discovery at a murder scene. I really should pitch the proposal of writing an autobiography for Beckie to her. The shocking nature of her work coupled with her highly questionable track record with men would certainly make for an interesting read for future generations of her family. Thinking of Beckie made me realise that we hadn't actually text each other since the boys had started their new school, and I felt glad that she was finally getting in touch tonight.

Instead of Beckie though, it was a group WhatsApp message that had been created by Shannon, called *My Birthday!* Immediately, my Leo-Virgo dual personality rose its ugly head as I felt torn between the excitement of getting dressed up for a night out with the girls versus the temptation of snuggling up in my onesie for a night in with a bar of chocolate and reality TV. I clicked on the participants as I waited for the next message to arrive letting us know what Shannon had planned. I felt guilty as I hoped it would just say Kayla and Louisa as, as much as I tried, I just hadn't clicked as well with Francesca and Maddison yet. Even after spending the day at the spa with them, courtesy of Louisa, I still felt like my mojo only operated at half capacity with them around. I had no such luck though, as their names flashed up alongside mine, Kayla, and Louisa's. The message that followed invited us all for a meal out the following month on a Friday night. I hesitated to reply, suddenly worrying that I would agree to go only to find that Kayla couldn't make it. I really did like Shannon, and Louisa too, but Kayla was like my anchor when I didn't have the boys with me. She kept me grounded when I felt a little out of my depth in the mummy clique that I had found myself welcomed into. I then worried that Shannon would see that I was online and wonder why I hadn't replied straight away. I felt like a teenager being invited out to her first party and immediately felt like a complete idiot.

Sounds great, I messaged back as I got control of the Superego in my brain that was relaying every possible bad social outcome to me – the worst being that everyone except for me and Francesca would suddenly come down with a stomach bug just minutes before we were due to meet, and I'd be stuck politely making small talk with her about which accessories would look best on her prodigious summer door display to replace her stupendous spring door display.

Yay, came Shannon's reply. Can't wait!

No-one else joined in the conversation due to it being so late, so I messaged a thumbs up to Shannon – the ultimate emoji that translates as *it's been great chatting to you, but we're done now as I really can't be arsed any more,* – and typed out a quick message to Beckie.

Hey Beckie. Feels like I haven't heard from you in ages! How's things?

Doubting that she would reply straight away, I turned my attention to the chapters that I had written so far. Most of the information had been gained through Maria's daughter, Jenna. We had tried to schedule a few interviews with Maria herself, but with the difficulty of never knowing what state of mind she might be in, we hadn't had much luck. Seeing the distress on Jenna's face the second time that we had tried had made me decide that the best way forward would be to continue to provide Jenna with leading questions to open up a dialogue with her mum. That way, we could gather enough information to put a basic autobiography together. From there, I could then direct more specific questions to add the depth and personal touch that made a great autobiography. I had advised Jenna that it was best to reminisce with her mum in a way that she could relate to rather than directly asking the questions that I had provided her with, as this might prove too stressful for Maria if she struggled to find the answers. A much more relaxed, casual approach would hopefully trigger memories without the pressure of trying. This method meant that it took up far more time than a usual client would, but I felt so personally invested in the desire behind creating this book that I would have allowed it to take months if that's what was needed to capture Maria's life for her. A few days ago, Jenna had sent me a message barely able to contain her excitement at some information that she had to share. Most of her findings had been from conversations with her mum over a cup of tea on her lucid days. However, on this particular day, Maria had spoken to Jenna as if she were her sister from their teenage years. Whereas the inability to recognise her own daughter would have usually upset Jenna, she had responded as if she were actually Maria's teenage sister and had found out things that she would never have known to ask. Jenna was privy to experiencing a snapshot from Maria's past that most of us would love to share with our own parents. A little insight into what their life was like before they became, in your eyes, *just your mum and dad*. According to Jenna, she had been playing an old song which Maria had suddenly started singing along to, word for word. When I had accepted Maria as a client, I had done a little research into Alzheimer's so that I could empathise and adapt my questioning where needed. I had discovered a study that had shown that the musical memory part of the brain was left relatively unaffected by the disease, and as such, Alzheimer sufferers could recall and even sing along to music from their past. Jenna had seen first-hand evidence of this with her mum, and she was convinced that the sensation of happiness brought on by the song had stimulated other positive feelings from her past.

I opened my email to find Jenna's message and was pleased to see that she had replied to my previous message asking her to elaborate on certain things that she had mentioned. Now equipped with all the information, I started to weave her words together as if Maria were talking.

An hour and a half passed without me even noticing as I got lost in Maria's memories. The only interruption I had was an unexpectedly prompt reply from Beckie apologising for being so crap at keeping in touch and blaming the stresses of life. She couldn't chat now as was out on a date but would text soon. Yawning, I closed the lid to my laptop and thought to myself how I now knew Maria better than my own mother. I made a promise to myself to ask Mum round for coffee more, and have chats about what seems like nothing in the moment but means everything when you no longer have it. Beckie's text had left me a bit sad and philosophical as, reading between the lines, I could see that the distance between us was growing, and the text she had promised probably wouldn't come any time soon. Lola moaned as I wriggled my feet out from under her.

'Sorry girl, it really is time for bed now.'

I felt guilty sending her out into the cool night air as I encouraged her out the backdoor to do her business before shutting her back in her crate. The full moon lit up the night sky like it was centre stage, surrounded by shining stars. *Just like Maria*, I thought to myself. She would light up her autobiography like a moon in all its glory so that when she was shadowed into a crescent of herself and no longer seemed like Maria anymore, her family could still see her for who she once was.

Chapter 25

Unusually for my family, the month leading up to Ben's birthday was relatively drama free, allowing me to focus my full attention on Maria's autobiography every evening after the boys had gone to bed. As I sent the final draft to Jenna, I felt as emotional as if it had been about a member of my own family. Taking on such a sensitive subject for my first genuine customer, and not one pressured into it by my mother, had been ambitious to say the least. I just hoped it lived up to Jenna's expectations, and that I had done her mum justice in capturing her life story.

I needn't have worried though. The day after sending it to Jenna, she had called me full of gratitude. She had said that it had completely surpassed her expectations, and she would treasure it forever. Jenna had no idea how much her words meant to me — how much confidence they gave me in what was, unbeknown to Jenna, new territory for me. I wasn't answering to anyone anymore.

Edward *Prickerton* wasn't having to approve my writing and recommend changes to be made before handing the finished product to the client. Autobiographies by Amber was my baby, and I was sure as hell going to make it work. I was a real-life super mum taking the world by storm. I was an absolute fucking legend!

'You are literally the worst mum in the world!' Ben snapped, bringing me back down to earth with a bump. 'Why on earth would you think I would like it?'

It was Ben's tenth birthday, and we were all in the car driving to his Nerf gun party. Earlier that morning, I had packed Ben a little fondant fancy cake in his school lunch box and stuck a candle in it. Feeling smugly pleased with myself, I had imagined his little face breaking into a huge smile as he spotted his surprise. I even wrote a special birthday note with it, complete with an entire row of kisses. It would seem that I had failed in my attempt to bring a bit of birthday joy though. Instead of making my son feel spoilt and loved, I had made him feel embarrassed and mortified.

'I'm really sorry, Ben. I thought you would like it.'

'I would have liked it when I was four, but I am ten now, TEN! I am not a little kid anymore, Mum, so don't treat me like one.'

'Ok, ok, I get the message,' I relented. I was starting to see it from Ben's point of view. Maybe I had been a little over the top. I vowed to make it up to him by avoiding all embarrassing mum attributes in front of his friends at his party.

As we arrived at the party venue, the boys all piled out of the car with Tommy. As a regular fixture within our family, I had naturally assumed he would be jumping in with us. They all looked at the entrance with excited wide eyes. The gate was covered in army netting and had Nerf guns hanging all over it. Jason had certainly hit the jackpot with this idea. This was every ten-year-old boy's dream party. Thinking that it would be nice for Jason to take charge with this one, I told him to go ahead with Ben, Ryan, and Tommy whilst I took Josh and Samuel to the café. After the initial threat of a tantrum when they realised that they weren't old enough to join in with the fun, the promise of a doughnut seemed to placate them. All thoughts of his embarrassing mum appeared to evaporate as Ben raced off with his brother and his best friend. I laughed as Jason ran after them, swiftly over-taking them to beat them to the gate.

'Why does Dad get to go to the party and not us?' whined Josh.

'Because Dad is a great big kid who is about to spend an hour running around, forgetting he is a responsible adult,' I replied, hoping there would be a *responsible adult* working there who would adopt the role. 'And he's not going to be the only one,' I muttered under my breath, remembering Jason's questionable idea to invite Rob along to the party. 'Come on, you two,' I said, grabbing their little hands in mine. 'Let's go and get some extra jammy doughnuts.'

We headed into the café and took a seat next to the

window where we could catch a glimpse of the obstacle area that the boys would be using as cover when playing their first Nerf gun game. Jason had read all about it on the website when he had booked the party and had relayed it to me in scrupulous detail. As Josh and Samuel dripped jam down their chins, I took a sip of the Mocha I had treated myself to and saw a familiar figure running past the window. 'Bloody typical,' I said, shaking my head.

'Bloody typical,' mimicked Samuel, as Josh giggled. An old lady at the table next to us tutted loudly as she poured herself a cup of tea so diluted that it looked like the café was trying to save costs by re-using tea-bags between customers. The Nerf gun venue was at the back of a garden centre, and as such, the café was typical of a regular haunt of the over-seventies. Ignoring the judgemental onlooker, I hypocritically told Sammy that *bloody* was not a nice word to use unless he was describing a cut on his knee, and watched as Rob ran breathlessly into the tent where Ben was waiting with all his friends. He couldn't even make it to his son's birthday on time.

After stretching the hour out by getting Josh and Samuel milkshakes to follow their doughnuts, and looking at the pet corner in the garden centre, I told my youngest two that we could head over to the party just before it was due to finish. In their excitement, they ran ahead of me and through the gate before I could catch them. My cries to wait for me fell on deaf ears as they charged off, eager to see the fun that their big brothers were having. Knowing that they couldn't escape once through the gate, I decided to be kind to my pelvic floor and speed walk after them rather than give chase in a full-blown panicked run. The scene that I found upon entering the enclosure, however, made me think that I may have been a little naïve to the impact of the damage that two mischievous little boys could do when unsupervised for five minutes. Somehow managing to acquire a Nerf gun each, they ran off into the distance and proceeded to shoot Ben on his backside! Their squeals of delight at their unexpected success, quickly turned to squeals of terror as Ben raised his own Nerf gun to shoot them back. As if in slow motion, I saw Jason suddenly dive out of the bushes like Rambo to protect his youngest sons. I winced as I saw the bullet that Ben had intended for them hit Jason square on the nose. I felt like I had fallen into a badly made slapstick comedy as Jason then started chasing Rob who had appeared on the scene out of nowhere. I had no idea what Rob had said to Jason to cause that reaction, but deciding it was best to let the two of them fight it out with their Nerf guns, I picked up my pace to gather up Ben and his friends, along with my other sons, two of whom were practically rolling around the floor in hysterics. In the space of five minutes, they had caused complete chaos in what I assumed had otherwise been a great party.

'I think we have what we call a bit of male ego going on here, boys,' I announced. 'Let's leave the pair of them to it and cook some sausages on the camp fire.' If Jason's enthusiasm about this party hadn't already sold the idea to me, then the fact that the party food consisted of the rare opportunity for the kids to cook their own sausage over a fire certainly would have done. This was the easiest kids party we had ever done.

After about ten minutes, Jason and Rob, both joined us, panting away like they had run a marathon. Rob's left ear now looked as sore as Jason's nose where he had obviously taken the full impact of a close-range Nerf bullet.

'You complete and utter dickheads!' I said to them both in a hushed tone before adding the child friendly version for all to hear, 'You two should be ashamed of yourselves. What must Ben's friends think of you?'

The two of them, looking suitably chastised, offered each other a half-hearted apology. Luckily everyone seemed to find the whole thing hilarious, and I overheard someone saying that this was the best party ever. I dreaded to think what they would be telling their parents when they picked them up though. Not only did Ben have an embarrassing mum who put a mini cake complete with birthday candle and cringey note in his lunch box, he also had a complete bell-end for a father. And to make matters worse, Jason had uncharacteristically chosen to act like a bell-end for the day. We were certainly more *The Simpsons* than *The Waltons*, that was for sure.

Chapter 26

Two weeks later, I got my number three that I had warned Jason would be coming. Superstitions existed for a reason. Breaking a mirror, opening an umbrella indoors, sleeping with your head pointing north – they all brought bad luck and I must have done all three of them given the luck that I was having at the moment. My smear test had been long forgotten with all of the drama since, so when the unmistakeable envelope of a medical nature arrived through the front door, I tore it open without giving it a second thought. Expecting it to say everything was normal, I scanned my eyes over it and was shocked to see words such as *abnormal, HPV,* and *cancer* jumping out at me. It didn't matter that it said the word *not* before the word *cancer*, all I saw at that point was *cancer*. I was to go to the hospital the following week for a colposcopy.

I walked in a daze to the kitchen and saw Ryan, Josh, and Samuel playing outside on the trampoline. Knowing that Ben was upstairs with Tommy, I picked my phone up and text Kayla.

Hi, got my smear test results back.

All good?

Not exactly. Need colposcopy as got abnormal cells.

Shit Amber, thank God you got it done! You ok?

Not really.

I'll be right over.

No more than ten minutes had passed when Kayla knocked on the front door with Eden and Finn in tow.

'The boys are playing out on the trampoline,' I told them, as Kayla gave me a hug. 'Go and join in, but tell them I said no more wrestling!'

I heard Samuel squeal with delight as he saw Eden running out to join him. 'Cuppa?' I asked Kayla.

'Yes please. Chocolate biscuit?' she trumped me, taking a packet of M&S luxury chocolate chip cookies from underneath her coat. 'I've been hiding these from the kids all week. I've got a whole stash of them to get me through the school holidays!'

We were just a few weeks into the summer holidays, and I could completely relate, only my secret stash came in the form of prawn cocktail Pringles and wine… lots of wine.

I put the kettle on and showed Kayla the letter I had received just fifteen minutes earlier.

'You know, this is a good thing,' said Kayla, after reading it properly rather than skimming to the scary bits like I had. 'It's much more common than you think. Chances are they've caught it before things get really nasty.'

'You mean before it turns to cancer,' I said sombrely.

'Amber, it's not going to be cancer,' Kayla replied resting her hand on my arm.

'We don't know that.'

'No, we don't, but the chances are they've caught it early enough and it hasn't turned into cancer yet.'

I looked into Kayla's eyes, feeling a lump forming in my throat. 'Thank God, you pushed me into going for that smear test, Kayla.'

'You are very welcome,' she replied giving me another hug. 'You're not the first woman to have received a shock like this through the post, Amber. Why do you think I was being so pushy with you about booking an appointment?'

Kayla looked at me with her determined hazel eyes which told me what she was thinking without her saying a word as the penny dropped.

'You've had abnormal cells before too?'

'Yep, when I was twenty-two. Seems like a life time away now. But I remember feeling exactly like you. In fact, I was worse. I called my sister straight away in complete hysterics. Within minutes, she had arrived on my doorstep holding a tub of cookie dough ice cream which she said she kept in the freezer for emergencies.'

I let out a little laugh which was more of a puff of breath through my nose with a noise resembling a lamb's bleat. I pointed at the packet of chocolate chip cookies on the breakfast bar. 'She taught you well.'

'She certainly did.'

'How bad was it?'

'I'm not going to lie to you, Amber. It wasn't great. I had third degree abnormal changes which meant that they had to remove quite a bit of the tissue inside my cervix. But they did it. They got to me in time, and now I'm a healthy mum with two kids. The tragedy would have been if I had ignored my reminder to go for my smear test. If I had done that, things would have been so much worse.'

'Thank God, you went,' I said thinking how unimaginable it would have been to have never met Kayla if she had died from a cancer that she could have prevented.

'And thank God, you went too,' Kayla said, putting her hand on top of mine. 'They'll remove whatever nasty cells you have in there and that will be the end of it. Right?'

'Right,' I agreed, trying to sound as strong as my friend.

We were interrupted by a knock at the door. I

answered it to find one of my neighbours standing there with her daughter. I'd met her the week we moved in but hadn't really seen her again, and judging by the look on her face, she wasn't coming around to invite me to her house for a neighbourly cup of tea.

'Hi,' I said tentatively as I opened the door.

Evidently not wanting to exchange pleasantries, she roughly spun her daughter round to show me the back of her head. 'Look what your son has done to my daughter's hair!' she snapped at me.

'My son?' I asked feeling perplexed. 'How has my son done that?' And then as an after-thought, 'Which son?'

Without taking a breath, she launched into a tirade about how Ben had been charging kids in the street for haircuts. Apparently, his attempt at little Alice's locks hadn't gone too well as I now witnessed the considerable difference in length between the back and the front.

'Oh my goodness, I'm so sorry,' I blurted out. I had over-heard Ben and Tommy talking about setting up a hairdressing business earlier, but had just thought they were discussing future career possibilities. I had no idea they were actually doing it. It did mean that there was absolutely zero doubt in my mind that my neighbour and her daughter were telling me the truth though. I shouted up the stairs for Ben to come down and face the music. I had needed a distraction from my current situation, but this was taking things one step too far.

Chapter 27

'Seriously, Ben, what were you thinking?'

He looked at me with sheepish eyes as I sat on the edge of his bed after a bedtime reading marathon with Ryan, Josh, and Samuel. Obi and Lola had positioned themselves between us and as I stroked Lola, Ben did the same with Obi. Fur therapy was a tactic I had learnt long ago and came in very useful not only when the boys were upset, but also when I needed them to sit still for an interrogation.

'I didn't mean to cut it so short.'

'Well, you did, and now that poor girl is going to have to have it all chopped to that length to even it out. That is about four years' worth of growth, Ben.'

He shrugged his shoulders at me, obviously not fully comprehending the magnitude of how that could feel to a little girl given that his hair had never grown beyond a grade three.

'How embarrassed do you think I felt when her mum

knocked at the door?'

'How annoyed do you think I felt when you made me give them all of the money that Tommy and I had made?'

'Very annoyed I'm sure, so I hope you remember that feeling next time you think about doing something so stupid.'

Rather than arguing back this time, Ben slid further down the bed so that his head rested on Obi. Feeling myself soften, I remembered how he had spent the money that he'd made from his last money-making scheme.

'Look Ben, I know you want to come up with ideas to make money, and it was great how you used it for Obi's operation before, but you need to sometimes think a bit more about what you're doing, ok? A secret school tuck shop is pretty harmless in the scheme of things, but cutting kids' hair is another thing entirely. Surely you can see that?'

'Yeah, I guess,' Ben admitted. 'I thought it would be easier than it was.'

'Let's just say, I won't be employing your skills as a hairdresser any time soon. And also, count yourself lucky, I'm in a forgiving mood.'

I had far too much on my mind to be thinking up punishments for Ben. Besides, making him hand over all of the money he had earnt today so that his victim could pay a proper hairdresser to fix his disaster was exactly the punishment that he would regard as most severe. I couldn't help but admire his business prowess and had

211

no doubt that he would follow his dreams of becoming an entrepreneur. I needed to discipline him to a level that was acceptably necessary without dampening his desire to succeed.

'Now, are there any other business plans that you and Tommy have been concocting that I should know about?' I asked.

'Nope.'

'You sure about that?'

'Yep.'

My mother's instinct warned me that Ben wasn't being entirely truthful with me, but I decided to leave the lecture for now. If truth be told, I was emotionally exhausted and just wanted to have an early night.

'Ok, well you get some sleep now. It's getting late.'

I tucked Ben's duvet around him and kissed the top of his head.

'Night, Mum,'

'Night, Ben, love you lots.'

As I was leaving his bedroom, Ben called out to me.

'Mum, do you think time travel is possible?'

Jesus Christ, it was going to be one of those nights.

'Yes, I do sweetheart. Night night.'

'Ok, time's strange though isn't it, coz one minute we're here, and then before we know it it's the next day, and it's just all a bit weird.'

Ben and I had had many a night like this. There were days when he would barely speak to me all day long, and then when his brothers were all fast asleep and he had no distractions like his Xbox or Tommy, he would decide that it was the perfect time for an in-depth chat. Sometimes it would be about the meaning of life, sometimes about something that was bothering him, and sometimes just about things in general. I never ducked out of the late-night chats though, no matter how tired I was, as knew how precious they were. When the teenage years hit, I'd be lucky if he muttered two words to me every day, and one of those would probably be incoherent to the parental ear.

Reversing back into the room, I reclaimed my position on the end of his bed and grabbed a cushion to get comfy, knowing that I would be there for a while. The conversation of the concept of time was no stranger to us, ever since I had allowed him to watch *Back to the Future* with me one day last year when he had a nasty cold and couldn't go to school.

'Maybe you could use that entrepreneurial brain of yours to invent a time machine,' I suggested. 'That would make you a millionaire for sure.'

'Don't be silly, Mum, I'm not the little five-year-old that you used to trick into thinking that planes that flew up high were really space rockets travelling to the moon. I know you can't make a time machine.'

'Hey, don't you give the game away on that one,' I said. 'Josh and Samuel still believe the space rocket fib.'

'Yeah, well those two bozos also think Father Christmas and the Tooth Fairy are real.'

I felt a pang of sadness as Ben said this. He was only

ten, yet he seemed so much older.

'Don't grow up too quickly, Ben. There's plenty of time for you to run businesses and make money. Just enjoy being a kid for a bit longer yet.'

Instead of acknowledging this, Ben yawned and asked if I could give him a head massage. Knowing that this never failed to relax his mind that was as over active as mine, I gently ran my fingers through his hair. Lying down next to him, the stress of the day forced my eyelids to close and sleep consumed us both.

Chapter 28

'Are you sure this is ok?' I asked Shannon as I stood on her doorstep with Kayla and our six children.

'Of course,' she replied, smiling. 'We're going to have so much fun. Maisie found all her old toys for the little ones to play with. She's been looking forward to them all coming.'

'Thanks, Shannon,' said Kayla, giving her friend a hug. 'We'll come and get them in a few hours.'

'No rush, just come whenever you're ready.'

I said a quick goodbye to each of the boys who thought Kayla and I were going shopping for the morning. Stepping aside, Shannon let them run into her house to create chaos. I'd been inside Shannon's house a few times before and remembered it having a lovely, girly feel to it where she and Maisie didn't have to compromise with any males in the house. I was in awe of the Champagne pink sparkly wallpaper that covered a feature wall in her hallway which she had told me was created using real glitter particles when she had caught me feeling the texture with my fingertips. Francesca probably would have balked at the possibility of me leaving smudges on it, but Shannon had been flattered by my interest, and had told me it was her favourite feature in her and Maisie's little home.

'Are you ok?' Kayla asked as I fastened my seatbelt in her car.

'Not really,' I replied honestly. 'Thanks for coming with me though. I really appreciate it.'

It was the day of my colposcopy at the local hospital, and Kayla had arranged for Shannon to look after all the kids so that she could come with me for moral support.

All too quickly, I was lying with my legs held up in stirrups whilst Kayla sat in the waiting room. A kind nurse held my hand as two doctors stood looking at a part of me that really should be left to the imagination.

Why the fuck does it need two of them? I thought to myself, knowing full well from their introductions that one of them was a trainee doctor and needed the experience.

I felt violated as they shone a light into my most intimate parts, and looked through their binocular lens that I knew as a colposcope thanks to my trainee doctor showing off his knowledge.

'See there,' I heard the doctor in charge say. 'We're able to tackle that right away with a loop excision.'

What the fuck?

'We just give a little injection to numb the area, and

then cut the cells out with the electric current before burning it to cauterise it.'

Seriously, what the fuck?

Kayla hadn't said anything about electrical currents and burning. I thought they were just going to take a tiny little biopsy. I must have tightened my hold on the nurse's hand as she bent down so that her face was on my level. Her mouth was covered by her mask, but her eyes were caring as she explained.

'Sorry, Amber, doctors forget that they're dealing with actual real people with feelings sometimes.'

She looked pointedly at the doctors who were preparing their instruments for the procedure.

'The doctors think they're able to treat you right now to get rid of those nasty cells.'

'Yes, Amber,' said the doctor who up until now seemed to think he was working on a mannequin. 'You have quite an extensive area of abnormal cells, but I'm confident we can cut them all out today. Is that ok?'

I nodded, unable to get any words out as I lay there feeling uncomfortable in both mind and body. I flinched as I felt the burn of the needle numbing me, and a warm, silent tear trickled down my cheek as my hand started to shake. I closed my eyes and tried to take my mind to the beach like I had in my smear test, but the intensity of the situation was too much to distract myself. I heard a sound like a small vacuum cleaner followed by pressure inside me.

'I can smell burning,' I said to the nurse as I opened

217

my eyes in a panic. 'Why can I smell burning?'

'That's perfectly normal, Amber, try not to worry. We've got you. Have you ever tried the five-senses-technique to calm yourself when you're feeling anxious?'

I shook my head at her feeling vulnerable and helpless.

'Ok, let's do it together,' she said. 'Firstly, we're going to look for five things that we can see in this room. You look around and tell me what you see.'

Moving my head to take in the minimal view that I was graced with as I lay flat on my back, I saw a big bright light extending from an arm attached to the ceiling. I obediently reported this to the nurse, and told her that I could also see her which seemed obvious but five things seemed a lot to find in a relatively sparse operating theatre. Behind her, I could also see a table covered in blue paper and a tray of surgical instruments on it which technically counted as two things.

'And one more thing,' the nurse said, kindly listening to my rambling answers as she continued to hold my quivering hand.

'And I see a surgical cap with a picture of a pug on it,' I sniffed as I braved a tilt of my chin to look toward the end of the bed.

'Yes, you do,' chuckled the nurse. 'We try to tell him it's not a good look but he doesn't listen. He's obsessed with pugs.'

'Don't you mock my pug,' came a voice from between my legs. 'I'll have you know, it's my lucky cap.'

Are they seriously bantering whilst holding an electrical

instrument up my fanny?

'Now, four things you can touch, Amber.'

I tried to ignore the physical pressure that I felt and brought my finger up to the top of my surgical gown, feeling the texture of the flimsy material. I then pressed the tip of my thumb into the tip of my index finger next to it until the skin around the nails turned white. With little else to touch given my current immobility, I ran a finger over one of my eyebrows and then my bottom lip.

'You're doing great, Amber. Let's focus on three things you can hear now.'

The constant vacuum cleaner like noise that filled the room invaded my ears as I tried hard to listen for two other things that I might be able to hear.

'Can your voice count?' I asked the nurse.

'Yep, that can definitely count,' she replied. 'And one other.'

The doctor started humming a very tuneless version of Ed Sheeran's 'Shape Of You'. Thinking that I'd rather my cervix had his full concentration but feeling in no position to make demands that he stop, I simply added it to the list.

My cheek felt tight where the salty tears had been falling whilst the doctor removed the cells that had had the audacity to invade my body. I realised that although I was still uncontrollably shaking, I had stopped crying.

'Just two things that you can smell now, Amber. You're nearly there.'

Up until then, my nurse's clever strategy had helped

somewhat in distracting me, but focusing on things that I could smell made me even more aware of the smell of burning coming from my body. The nurse must have realised this as she bore witness to my widening eyes and quickly moved on.

'Maybe that one doesn't work so well in this situation,' she said, looking apologetic. 'Let's move on to something you can taste.'

I could still taste the mint on my tongue left over from the chewing gum that Kayla had given me on the drive to the hospital so told the nurse this.

She gave my hand a little squeeze. 'Great job, Amber. You just hang in there a little longer and this will all be over.'

I mustered up a small smile to show my appreciation to her for her efforts to calm me down. I wasn't ready to lay back and think of England, but she had undoubtedly averted the panic attack that I had felt overwhelming me ten minutes before.

'All done,' announced the doctor with the pug fetish.

I let out a puff of breath and released my grip on the nurse's hand, feeling guilty as I suddenly became aware of how tightly I'd been holding her.

'Thank you,' I said, which felt weird to say to the man who had been inflicting such torment on me for the past fifteen minutes.

'I think we got it all, Amber. We'll send some off to check for cancer and let you know.'

The matter-of-fact way that he said it was startling.

This was something that could have a catastrophic impact on my life, yet he spoke like he was sending his dog's DNA off for genetic testing. The bedside manner module of a medical degree needed some serious reconfiguration.

Feeling drained, I got myself dressed and returned to the waiting room to find Kayla. Despite my inner turmoil, I smiled as I saw her talking to a heavily pregnant girl who looked to be about seventeen. She would make an amazing midwife. As she spotted me, Kayla said goodbye to the girl and came straight over.

'You ok?'

'Yeah, I'm exhausted though.'

'I'm not surprised. It's overwhelming going through something like this. Let's get home.'

Kayla linked her arm through mine, and we headed to the exit. Neither of us spoke as we navigated our way through the strangers who had all found themselves in the hospital at the same time as us. Normally, I would have imagined scenarios in my head as to why they were there, but the only thought in my head right then was the worry about what the biopsy result would show.

Chapter 29

Four weeks of worry. Four weeks of imagining the worst. Four weeks of feeling guilty that I might not be there for my boys as they grew up. Four fucking weeks! Four weeks during which I wanted to curl up under my duvet and binge watch Friends whilst eating share size bars of Galaxy chocolate. But I couldn't do that as I was a mum. Waiting for results that would tell me whether or not I had cancer, I had to put a smile on my face and survive the daily school run that hit with a vengeance as the summer holidays came to an end.

I read the letter three times to make sure there was no mistake on the morning that it arrived through my door. I then repeated the most important words to myself out loud to make it real. '…showed no signs of cancer.' The relief that washed over me was immense. I took my phone out of my pocket and text Kayla before even calling Jason.

Got my biopsy results. No Cancer!

Kayla replied instantly.

Best news EVER! I knew you'd be fine!

Thanks. Calling Jason now.

Ok hun. Just waiting for a call from Louisa. Will come to see you after. X

Louisa had left for Australia a few weeks ago. I had been so caught up in my own worries that I would have forgotten she was going had Ben not reminded me. My suspicions about him liking Lottie had been confirmed when he came home devastated after finding out that she was moving to the other side of the world with her family. Louisa had told Lottie a few days before they left after sticking to her plan to wait so that she didn't spend weeks upset about leaving her friends. According to Ben, she needn't have worried though, as Lottie was thrilled at the news and couldn't wait to start her new adventure.

After calling Jason to tell him that our scare was over, I went outside to join the boys on the trampoline, literally feeling like a weight had been removed from my head. Samuel and Josh squealed with delight as they realised that I was going to join in with the chaos instead of telling them to calm down. As I bounced holding their little hands, I breathed in the fresh air and felt the warmth of the sun on my face. Calling for Ben and Ryan to join us, we lay down on the trampoline and looked up at the wispy white clouds that dotted the blue sky.

'Look at that one there,' I said, encouraging them to join in with one of my favourite things to do with them. 'It's a pirate ship with a wave crashing over it.'

Josh pointed to the cloud next to it. 'And that one's a dragon breathing fire.'

'Wow! That is one enormous dragon, Josh. What do you see, Sammy?'

'I dee a dog,' he said pointing.

'I can totally see that,' I agreed, looking at the cloud that had a tail trailing at the end of it.

Before we could express our imaginations any more, the three of us catapulted into the air as Ben and Ryan leapt onto the trampoline, destroying the moment of tranquillity. Laughing, I relished in the whirlwind that was my family.

With Obi and Lola barking away in the garden as they sensed the vibe of happiness, I didn't hear the doorbell go when Kayla arrived.

'Hope you don't mind us just letting ourselves in!' she called out as Eden and Finn charged over to join in the fun.

'Of course not,' I replied, pleased in the knowledge that she felt she could just reach over to unlock the back gate and make herself at home. Giving me a big hug, she produced a bottle of Prosecco from her handbag.

'Not quite a Bollinger, but the bubbles can let us pretend it's Champagne,' she said.

We left the kids to their own devices as we went to the kitchen to find some glasses.

'I remember my sister coming round to me with some Cava the day that I got my biopsy results. We made all these plans about what we would do with the rest of our twenties.

'Did you do it all?'

'To be honest, the only thing that I remember, given the fact that we moved onto a bottle of Vodka when the Cava had run out, was that amongst all the crazy stuff that we had planned, I just wanted to be a mum.'

'Well let's cheers to that one,' I said, clinking my glass against Kayla's. 'Eden and Finn have fulfilled that one for you.'

'Yep, they certainly have. Did I tell you I had to have a stitch in my cervix to make sure they stayed in there? I was so worried they would come out early after having my loop excision.'

'Is that really a thing?'

'Yep. Trust me, Amber. You're lucky you had yours done after you had kids.'

I certainly hadn't felt lucky four weeks ago as I lay feeling violated on the hospital bed, but Kayla was right. I was lucky. Lucky that I had a friend who had relentlessly badgered me to have the smear test that saved my life. Lucky that I had been blessed with four children when other women who didn't get treated in time may never even get to have one.

'You know what we should do?' I said to Kayla.

225

'What?'

'Make our own list of plans. Like you and your sister did.'

'That's a great idea. Grab a pen, I've got one for you to get us started.'

'Ok, what is it?'

'Go camping with the kids!'

I looked at Kayla hesitantly. 'Camping? Are you sure?'

'They'd love it!' she exclaimed seeming tipsy already with our day time celebratory drink.

'Oh, and here's one for us too. A girl's weekend in Marbella!'

'Now you're talking,' I said as my Leo personality imagined cocktails in sarongs and ignored my Virgo alter ego trying to shout it down with visions of my plane crashing as I left my boys to go frolicking in another country.

An hour later, Kayla and I had an empty bottle of Prosecco, a list of goals to achieve over the next five years, and six hungry children.

'Who wants to order pizza?' I yelled into the garden, feeling jubilant.

I looked back at Kayla, shrugging as the deafening sound of children who couldn't believe their luck filled the garden. 'What else am I meant to feed them all? I've got no chicken nuggets left in the freezer!'

We both started laughing uncontrollably, realising that it wasn't even that funny but unable to stop ourselves as the effect of the Prosecco took hold.

'Are you two drunk?'

I looked behind me to see Jason had arrived home from work early, carrying a bottle of Taittinger.

'I see you beat me to it,' he said indicating to the empty bottle of Prosecco on the worktop.

'We only had the one,' I said, indignantly. 'We're still highly capable of adulting.'

'We're just not used to having a drink in the day,' justified Kayla. 'It makes us a bit giggly.'

'I can see that,' said Jason, walking over to give me a kiss.

'I knew you'd be ok, Amby.'

Grabbing an extra glass out of the cupboard, he sliced his car key across the foil on the neck of the Champagne bottle and aimed the cork towards the ceiling. Our obligatory shrieks filled the room as the distinctive pop resonated around us. There was nothing more disappointing than a mild whump from a dud cork. Jason's expertise didn't let us down with this bottle of Taittinger. Or it could have been pure luck given that expensive Champagne was not a regular on our weekly shopping list. As bubbles filled our glasses, Jason raised his up in a toast.

'To Amber, for surviving a month of worry. And to Kayla, for being the amazing friend who gave her a much-needed kick up the backside.'

Chapter 30

'I would like to propose a toast,' said Kayla, raising her glass. 'A toast to one of the best friends a girl could have. Happy Birthday, Shannon!'

'Happy Birthday,' we all joined in as we clinked our Prosecco filled glasses. The five of us were seated around a table in Shannon's favourite pub, looking at the dessert menu. There was something about a cosy pub restaurant that I enjoyed far more than eating at other restaurants. This one, whilst traditional on the outside, had décor that had been modernised over the years to give it a nice welcoming, bistro feel. After telling the staff that it was Shannon's birthday, they had seated us in prime position in the conservatory overlooking the River Wey. The terrace outside was lit up with lanterns which flickered in the drizzle that had started to fall, making us feel all the more cosy at our candlelit table.

'I couldn't possibly eat another thing,' said Kayla, patting her stomach.

'Me neither,' agreed Francesca. 'I am well and truly stuffed.'

I prayed that the others wouldn't follow suit. I had spotted the millionaire's cheesecake on the menu, and it was just crying out to me to be ordered. I couldn't be the only one to have dessert though.

'Sod that,' said Shannon. 'It's my birthday, so I am having the sticky toffee pudding with extra cream.'

I guess that cheesecake was coming my way after all!

'Ooh, that sounds good,' agreed Maddison. 'Shall we share?'

'No way, get your own,' laughed Shannon. 'I want mine all to myself.'

I knew I'd always liked Shannon for a reason.

'Well, if you're having one, I might try the cheesecake,' I said, like I was mulling over the possibility when really, I could already taste the caramel dripping over my tongue.

'And I'll have an Irish coffee,' said Kayla.

We gave our orders to the waitress, with Francesca deciding at the last minute that she would join Kayla with the Irish coffees. I was already feeling a bit tipsy from the three glasses of Prosecco I had had with dinner, and judging from the no-filter conversations that we'd been having for the past few hours, the others were all feeling a little merry too.

'I miss Louisa already,' said Shannon. 'I know she's

only been gone for a few weeks, but it feels like forever.'

'I miss her too,' said Maddison, slurring a little on her words. 'Let's make a toast to Louisa. May she love every second of her new life surrounded by sun and beaches.'

'Urgh, I'm so jealous,' said Shannon. 'She has a frigging swimming pool for crying out loud.' She gently banged her head down on the table in mock despair.

'Yes, but she doesn't have her best friends ten minutes down the road anymore,' said Kayla. 'Good friends are way more important than all that material crap.'

'She's right,' I agreed. 'I was never good at the mum-clique thing until I met you guys, but my life is so much better with friends like you in it.'

'Aw, Amber,' said Kayla, reaching out her arms to give me a hug. 'I do love you, you know.'

'I love you too,' said Shannon, reaching over the table to join in our hug. 'And I love you,' she said, pointing at Kayla. 'And you, and you,' she added pointing at Francesca and Maddison in turn. 'Let's make a pact to always stay mum-friends, even when our kids are all grown up and no longer need us.'

'Absolutely,' we all agreed.

'A good friend is like a four-leaf clover,' Francesca said wisely. 'Hard to find and lucky to have.'

'Well, I certainly got more than my fair share of luck ending up with you lot in my life,' said Shannon.

I took a sip of my drink, feeling relaxed. I even felt comfortable in the presence of Francesca and Maddison for the first time since I'd met them. I would never be as close to them as I was to Kayla and Shannon, but it felt good that I no longer felt like an outsider when they joined us. If I was being honest with myself, they had probably intimidated me slightly when I had first met them, with their expensive looking haircuts and immaculate houses. But when you stripped all that away and got them out for a drink with the girls, they weren't all that different to the rest of us. Our auras would never gel in the way that the universe dictates when it draws us to certain people over others, but our mutual friends had forced us into a relationship, and there were certainly far worse people that I could have in my close circle. If Shannon and Kayla considered them good friends, then that was reassurance enough for me.

'I want to hear more about this new man,' said Francesca, narrowing her eyes at Shannon. 'Please tell me you didn't meet this one on Tinder!'

'No, actually, I didn't,' replied Shannon looking smug as she chose not to elaborate any further.

'Why are you being so coy about this one?' asked Kayla, looking suspicious. 'Usually, you can't wait to give us all the juicy details. I still can't get the image out of my head from when you described your date with that guy you met in Tesco's.'

'Yeah, I could have done without knowing that as well,' laughed Maddison.

'Now I'm intrigued,' I said, wanting to catch up on the juicy gossip they had all shared before I became part of their friendship group.

'Just because you lot are all married,' said Shannon, feigning annoyance. 'Us single girls are allowed to have a more eventful sex life, thank you very much.' Giggling like a little girl, she returned to the initial question that had been directed her way. 'Ok, I'll tell you, but you have to promise not to tell anyone else, ok?'

'Oh my God, I know who it is,' said Kayla as a lightbulb suddenly went off in her head.

'Who?' the rest of us asked in unison, intrigued as to how Kayla had suddenly guessed who this mystery man was that Shannon had been out on a date with last week.

'It's Mr Sturridge, isn't it?' Kayla asked with a tone of confidence that suggested there was little doubt in her mind.

The table fell silent as we all stared at Shannon waiting for her to confirm it. The glint in her eye said it all.

'You mean, *stubbled jaw line of Matt Bomer, hair of Patrick Dempsey,* Mr Sturridge? I asked, remembering the day that Shannon had described the Year Five teacher to me.

'The one and only,' confirmed Shannon, unable to contain her secret any longer.

'But he's only been split up from his wife for five minutes,' blurted out Maddison.

'Actually, it's been more like five months,' retorted Shannon, sounding hurt. 'Besides, it's nothing serious. We just had one date, that's all.'

'And?' asked Kayla, nudging her friend.

'And, what?' replied Shannon, suddenly finding her drink very interesting.

Kayla rolled her eyes at her friend. 'Did you have fun? Did you plan a second date? Did you kiss him? Can I be your midwife when you have your first baby together?'

'Did you shag him?' blurted out Francesca, in a very *un-Francesca* like way.

'No!' squawked Shannon so loudly that the people at the next table turned to look at us. 'I mean, *Yes*, to did we have fun, *Yes,* to we plan to have a second date, *Yes,* to I kissed him, but *NO,* to the shagging part. Definitely no! And so, *No,* to the midwife part too. You will make an amazing midwife Kayla, but I am not planning on having a baby with Mr Sturridge! Imagine seeing him at school after dropping off Maisie. And what if Maisie ends up in his class, and I have to look him in the eye knowing that he's seen all my wobbly bits?'

'That would be awkward,' I agreed.

'So, you don't think he's the one then?' asked Kayla.

'Of course, he's the one!' replied Shannon, looking dreamy eyed. 'You heard Amber. He has the stubbled jaw line of Matt Bomer, the hair of Patrick Dempsey, and he is great with kids. He is literally the perfect man.'

'So, what's the problem then?' asked Kayla.

'I'm not the perfect woman,' replied Shannon matter-of-factly. 'I seriously lack a filter at times, I will always be that little bit chubby, and I found a white eyebrow hair last night, which means that if I look really hard there is bound to be a white pubic hair hiding somewhere underneath my knickers right now. A woman like me doesn't get to keep the perfect man.'

'Shannon, you are amazing,' said Kayla grabbing her friend's hand. 'You are one of the strongest women I know. Plus, you are beautiful inside and out. Any man would be lucky to have you, white, wiry pubes and all.'

Shannon got a tear in her eye as she listened to her best friend's words. Coming from someone else they might have sounded cliché and like a motivational Facebook post, but coming from Kayla, they couldn't have been more sincere.

We were all saved from drunken tears of emotion breaking out by the arrival of our dessert. My mouth watered at the sight of the millionaire's cheesecake that was set before me. The gold flecks on top of the chocolate layer glittered in the candle light. I paused for a moment, considering that it was almost too much of a work of art to eat. That feeling didn't last long though as I sunk my fork into the gooey top layer feeling it crunch onto the biscuity surface below. This was literally heaven in a bowl.

Once we had all finished eating, drinking, and divulging far too much information about ourselves than was necessary, we decided we should probably get home to bed. An indulgent, carefree evening was great, but the reality was, we would all be back to being mums as soon our kids woke up, and that was never fun with a hangover. If I hadn't already felt part of this little mum-clique, I certainly did after tonight. Despite thinking that I knew Kayla inside and out after practising my interviewing skills on her, I now also knew that she had a secret crush on Shakin' Stevens when she was fifteen and had Googled him just the other day to see if he still '*had it*'. Confident, sassy, Shannon had let slip her insecurities that she would never find the perfect man to spend the rest of her life with and was destined to have sporadic relationships with men who would always leave her in the end. And Maddison, with the help of a little Prosecco, had confessed that she had once been arrested for mistaking a beach in Spain for a nudist beach when she was on a girls' holiday in her teens. But the complete shocker of the evening was when Francesca divulged her motto for maintaining a balanced equilibrium in her mental state. *Masturbate to recalibrate!* Apparently, after visiting a yoga retreat several years ago, she was gifted the knowledge that an orgasm had the power to take away physical pain and mental stress. The power to balance you from within... to recalibrate! We had all sat there fixated on Francesca as she unashamedly chanted her motto like a mantra after sharing this unexpected revelation with us. I realised that there was definitely a great deal about my new friends that I had yet to learn. My disclosure about my first failed marriage seemed somewhat undramatic in comparison. I vowed to match my new friends' level of secret-sharing next time we had a night out.

Kayla linked arms with me as we walked out of the pub restaurant. The rain that had been kept tightly in the clouds as we arrived earlier that evening had now powerfully broken through.

235

'I'm so glad you moved here,' she said, wiping a rain drop off the end of her nose. 'I honestly don't know what I'd do without you.'

'Aw, I know,' I replied. 'You're like the sister I always wanted. Only better, cos you don't steal my clothes.'

It was amazing how Kayla and I had only known each other for a short while, but I was closer to her than friends I had known for twenty years. I had always loved the saying that people were in your life for a reason, a season, or a lifetime. Kayla had undoubtedly come into my life for a reason, and our first season had seen our friendship click in a way I never imagined would happen to me.

'Wait up, guys,' shouted Shannon, laughing. 'Francesca's got her heel stuck. Can one of you come and hold her whilst I yank it out? Maddison's still in the toilet.'

'I'll go,' I said to Kayla.

'Ok,' she said. 'I'll go and grab that taxi over there.'

Kayla carried on walking towards the road where a taxi was parked up just a little way down from the pedestrian crossing. Suddenly feeling chilly, I wrapped my coat tightly across myself as I headed back to help the others. The curls that I had framed around my face at the beginning of the night were now a mess of frizziness where the drops of rain hung heavily on them.

I had almost reached Francesca and Shannon when I heard a car screeching as it skidded on the wet road. Turning around, almost in slow motion, I heard the bang before I saw it. A soft thump, followed by the clang of metal against metal. A sound that would stay with me forever. A red glow from the traffic lights glazed over the scene. A traffic light that was now bent over precariously with a car bonnet buried into it. I saw a man climbing out of the car with his head in his hands. He walked over to something in the road and knelt down. Hearing a voice screaming, I realised it was my own. Running back towards the road, I felt numb. I looked at the taxi, hoping, praying that I'd see Kayla at the window talking to the driver. Making him laugh with the tale of how four friends would join her in a minute once they had extracted one of their heels out of a crack in the path. There was no sign of Kayla there though. Running faster now, I crossed in front of the cars that were stopping in the road amidst the commotion. It was then that I saw her. My friend… my friend for a reason… my friend for a season… my friend for a lifetime. I knelt by her side and held her hand in mine.

'It's going to be ok, Kayla. I've got you. You're going to be ok.'

Her body lay twisted at a strange angle, and a trickle of blood ran from her left nostril. I stayed beside her, unaware of the wetness of the road seeping through my clothes. Keeping hold of her hand in mine, I wrapped my other hand over the top of it, just like I did when I got into bed with Sammy when he woke up crying. Her eyes were wide with terror, looking deep into mine.

'Oh my God, what happened,' wailed Shannon, kneeling down on the other side of Kayla. I couldn't speak as I looked up and met Shannon's scared eyes with my own. We knelt there with her until we heard the sirens, at first a distant, faint whine, but then getting closer and closer until the loud yelping made no mistake that they were travelling at speed towards us. It can't have been more than a few minutes, but it felt like time had stopped. Everything around me was a blur as I saw two paramedics approaching Kayla. Francesca and Maddison pulled me and Shannon to our feet and wrapped their arms around us.

'She's going to be ok,' Maddison said shakily taking charge. 'Let the paramedics take care of her in the ambulance. We'll follow them in the taxi.'

I didn't feel in control of my body as I watched them load Kayla into the ambulance as the unfamiliar smell hit my nostrils. It smelt of hospitals. Disinfectant... latex... death – souls of the bodies that they had been unable to save. I looked down at Kayla who now lay in there on the stretcher as one of the paramedics set to work on her. I heard the shudder of the engine start and they were off, racing away in the dark night, racing to save Kayla's life.

Chapter 31

Nine days it had been. Or was it ten? I wasn't even sure anymore. Every day just seemed to merge into one as I replayed the events of the night over and over again in my head. One minute we were five mums laughing and over-sharing, and the next, everything changed.

If only we had left the restaurant five minutes earlier. If only we had both turned around to help dislodge Francesca's shoe. If only Francesca hadn't got her heel stuck in the first place. If only the driver hadn't skidded in the wet at the crossing. If only we hadn't gone out at all that night. If only, if only, if only.

I stood in the bathroom, gazing at my reflection in the mirror. No matter how much Touche-Eclat I pasted on, my puffy dark circles just wouldn't fade. I looked down at my dress. *You can't go wrong with a little black dress*, they say. But this felt wrong. Everything about this felt wrong.

'Amber, are you ready?' Jason shouted up the stairs. 'Luke will be here any minute now.'

'I'll just be a sec,' I replied, leaving the bathroom to go to my bedroom. Opening the wardrobe door, I reached in to find the bright yellow silk scarf that I had bought on a whim one summer and never worn. I smiled as I draped it around my neck, feeling the luxurious softness of it against my skin. It brought back memories of seeing the daffodils in the park with Kayla when spring started to appear. Taking a deep breath, I composed myself and headed down to Jason.

'How are you doing?' he asked.

Unable to answer for fear that I would break, I just reached out a hand to him. He took it and squeezed it reassuringly. 'The others are in the kitchen, waiting for you.'

Sitting at our breakfast bar, sipping cups of tea were Shannon, Francesca, and Maddison.

'Mummy, can Eden wear my other Piderman costume,' Sammy's little voice shouted from the lounge. 'We want to be batching!'

'Of course, she can sweetie. You've got to be quick though. Run up to your bedroom and grab it. We're leaving in five minutes.'

Eden followed Samuel out of the lounge. Seeing the two of them together made everything seem momentarily ok. The pain of the last week almost as if it had never happened. And then I spotted Finn sitting quietly on the sofa, looking at his iPad, and the tears threatened to overflow again.

Sensing me looking at him, Finn looked up. 'Will

Daddy be back with Mummy soon?' he asked.

'Yes, sweetie,' I replied walking over to sit down next to him. I put my arm around him and hugged him in tightly.

'Daddy will be back any minute.'

'He's here,' announced Jason from the hall. 'Eden, Sammy, time to go.'

'Right, Finn, how about you jump in with us so you can sit with Eden and Sammy,' I said. 'Do one of you guys want to come with us too,' I asked, looking at my three friends.

'I'll jump in with Luke,' said Shannon.

'Yeah, I'll go with Luke too,' said Francesca.

'Do you want me to come with you and Jason?' asked Maddison, 'help you with the kids?'

'Yeah, sure,' I said.

'Can I go with Dad?' asked Finn.

'Sure you can, buddy,' said Jason. 'Come on, I'll take you out to him.'

With Sammy and Eden ready in an uncharacteristically fast time, we all left the house together. Jason put his hand on my knee as I sat in the passenger seat next to him. We drove the short drive up to Newlands Corner. I had always loved walking the dogs there, and one day when Kayla and Eden had joined us, she had taken us on a trail through the woods that I hadn't known was there. She had shown us her favourite spot to sit under a Rowan tree where we could see for miles over the rolling hills. It was where Luke had proposed to her. And today, Luke would be scattering her ashes there.

Kayla had died in the ambulance on the way to the hospital. I remembered vividly the words being said to us as we ran into the emergency department, desperate for news after following the ambulance on that fateful night. *'We are so sorry. We did everything we could, but your friend's injuries were too severe. She died on route to the hospital.'* She died, *she died, she died.* Those two words just repeated over and over again in my head. How was this possible? One minute she was there and alive, and the next she was gone. Just like that. It didn't seem real.

Shannon and Francesca had taken a taxi round to Luke's house to break the devastating news and to look after Eden and Finn whilst Maddison and I waited for him at the hospital. Francesca was meant to drive him back to us, but the second he had heard, he'd grabbed his keys and charged out the front door to his car before they could stop him. I would never forget the look on his face when he'd arrived. You could see a part of him that still held hope. Hope that it was all a huge mistake. Hope that couldn't diminish until he saw Kayla for himself and could see that she was gone. He had driven us all home from the hospital in a daze of disbelief. Shannon had promised that she would stay there with him as Maisie was spending the night at her grandmother's house. Feeling helpless, the rest of us had taken a taxi home to our own houses. None of us had said a word. There was nothing to say as we had all sat lost in our own thoughts, immediately sobered by the events of the previous few hours. It was only when I'd climbed into bed with Jason that the tears came. Tears like I had never experienced before. My whole body racked with sobs that I just couldn't control as I had realised that I'd lost my best friend.

That was over a week ago. The crying had been replaced by an ache that I knew would get better with time, but right now felt like I was constantly suffocating underneath a weight that I couldn't see. We had held the funeral this morning which was a beautiful celebration of Kayla's life. She had been loved by so many people. Friends, family, even mums from school that barely knew her but had experienced the warm smile that she greeted everyone with every day, making them feel like they mattered, like someone was seeing them when others just walked by. Kayla was one of those people that everyone automatically warmed to. She would have made the most amazing midwife. Whereas the funeral had been open to everyone, Luke had asked that just close family and friends attend the scattering of the ashes.

As we walked from the car to the spot that Luke had chosen, we saw a small gathering up ahead, underneath the unmistakeable Rowan tree that grew elegantly above the shrubs below. You could see some red berries starting to form to replace the white flowers that had appeared in the spring. A tree steeped in mythology, and thought by many to bring protection, it was the perfect place to scatter Kayla's ashes.

'We should put a bench here for her,' I said to Jason

as Eden and Samuel spotted Finn and ran ahead to him. 'Put a plaque on it to remember her.'

'That's a lovely idea, Amby.'

Jason put his arm protectively around my shoulders, hugging me into him as we walked with Maddison to catch up with Shannon and Francesca. The only other people there were Kayla's parents, her in-laws and her sister. Finn wandered over and clung tightly to Luke's hand. Luke hugged the urn containing Kayla's ashes into him with his other arm. Despite the air being quite warm, a shiver went through me as I pictured the contents inside. Being five, Finn understood much more than Eden did. Eden had moments of sadness, but then would play with Samuel like she didn't have a care in the world before asking again if Mummy was coming home soon. She had spent a lot of time at our house the past week to allow Luke the space he needed to make arrangements and process his own grief. It broke my heart every time I explained to Eden, as patiently as the first time she had asked, that Mummy had gone to heaven. I hugged her tight every time and noticed that Samuel would keep hugging her too, even though he didn't really understand why. The simple acceptance of his gesture always brought a tear to my eye. Finn, on the other hand, understood that Kayla wouldn't be coming back. Whilst spending time at our house since the accident, we had written a little book together of all Kayla's favourite things, from her unusual love of the bounty chocolate that everyone else left in the box of Celebrations, to her favourite song to sing them at bedtime. Finn then drew a picture of his mum on the front with a big heart around it. He kept the little book made of just a few pieces of paper and staples with him wherever he went, so that he could add to it whenever he thought of something else. I could see it right then, in fact, poking out of the top of his trouser pocket where he had folded it inside.

Kayla's mother-in-law called Samuel and Eden over with the promise of 'a sweetie' each as Luke cleared his throat. Jason scooped Samuel up into his arms as she did the same with Eden.

'Firstly,' said Luke, his voice breaking a little. 'I want to thank you all for being here with me, Finn and Eden. Every person stood here right now meant the world to Kayla.'

He cleared his throat again, pausing to regain his composure as a sob escaped. 'If it's ok with everyone, I thought it would be nice if we all said something about Kayla. Whether it is what she meant to you, or a special memory you had of her, or even something funny that she once said.' And then looking at Kayla's mum, 'Would you like to go first, Annabelle?'

As the rays of the sun created shadows under the Rowan tree, we all cried and laughed as we shared our memories of Kayla. We all knew her in different ways, but there was an unmistakeable essence of warmth and love that everyone had felt. She was sunshine in a human form. She was a soul that touched people and left her mark forever. She was someone who made all of us a better person. She was the wife, daughter, mother and friend who had made the world a better place.

Chapter 32

As the next few months passed, we all fell into a routine of helping Luke with Eden and Finn. Kayla's family lived nearby so helped out whenever they could, and between us all, we made it work. When Luke went back to work, Shannon, Maddison, Francesca, and I all took it in turns to have Finn and Eden after school. When Shannon found Luke a lovely mum from school to use as a childminder for Eden during the day, I had insisted that I have her for two days a week. This way, she still had the familiar routine of playing with Samuel like she used to when Kayla and I would meet up for a cup of tea and a chat that would consist of all the random nonsense that true friends shared.

There were times where I felt the loss so acutely that it was like I couldn't breathe. I had never understood the feeling of emptiness before. When Rob left me, I had felt relieved, but that didn't stop me feeling pain too. This was a different pain like no other though. There were days where I would sit watching Eden and Samuel play, and I would feel pressure building up in my temples as my cruel mind replayed the night over and over again. There was truth in the cliché saying that time heals though. As the days passed, things did get easier. When you have children, you have no choice but to continue. Life went on. The boys went to school. They made me laugh with their questionable antics. They made me mad with their incessant bickering. But they all continued with normal family life, and I had no choice but to be swept along with it. Jason was amazing, as he always was in a crisis. He regularly popped in to check up on Luke, initially under special request from me, but before long, because the two of them formed a genuine friendship that men seem to find so hard once they enter the maturity of fatherhood. As mums, we embrace the shared experiences of motherhood, many of us forming friendships closer than any of us have ever experienced before. I was never blind to the fact, however, of how much harder it was for Jason to bond with new friends at this stage of his life, friends he didn't have shared memories of boyish escapades with. So, to see his growing friendship developing with Luke in the same way that mine had with Kayla made me happy.

As the evenings started to draw in, the festivities of December began to approach. There was nothing like the excitement of children embracing all that the build up to Christmas had to offer to lift spirits.

'How was Luke when you saw him today?' I asked

Jason as we lay in bed.

'He actually seemed pretty good.'

'Really?' I asked, surprised. 'I was getting worried that all the Christmas things going on would make things hit him hard again.'

Understandably, there had been moments since Kayla's death where Luke had hit rock bottom in his grief. But he had Eden and Finn to think of, and with help from the rest of us, he had pulled through. Approaching Christmas on his own could not be easy though. The firsts of everything would be tough. The first birthdays without Kayla, the first wedding anniversary, and coming up all too quickly, the first Christmas.

'Maybe we should invite him over with the kids for Christmas,' I suggested.

'If you like,' Jason replied, 'But I think he said he was spending it with his parents.'

'Ok, no worries. It was just a thought. Maybe mention it to him, just in case. You know, so that he knows he's welcome, any time.'

'You know someone you could invite for Christmas don't you, Amby?'

'Who?'

'Rob, Cassie, and Jodie.'

I rolled over to stare at Jason in shock. 'Why on earth would you want to invite my ex-husband and his new girlfriend over for Christmas? Have you gone mad?'

'He's not just your ex-husband, Amber. He's Ben's dad. And Jodie is Ben's baby sister. When you were talking to Ben the other night about him splitting his time between here and Rob's over Christmas, you could see he felt a bit weird about it all. As much as he moans about his brothers, I can tell he'd rather be here with them. But Jodie is his sister now too, and we could solve everyone's problems by just having them all here instead.'

'Jason, I love that you would even suggest this,' I said, shaking my head in amazement at how unselfish Jason could be. 'And it just goes to show what a fantastic dad you are, but absolutely no way! That man does not deserve to spend Christmas here with us. I don't have a problem with Cassie. She seems very nice. Probably completely and utterly stupid if she's in love with Rob Collins. But nice, nevertheless. And Jodie is undoubtedly adorable. But Rob is still a complete and utter twat, and I am not spending Christmas with him. Capiche?'

Jason held up his hands in defeat. 'Ok, ok, just an idea. No problem. I was just thinking of Ben, you know.'

'And that is why I love you,' I said, kissing him. 'You always put our boys first. Have you forgotten how you shot him at Ben's party though? He probably wouldn't want to come in case you had a Nerf gun hidden in your Christmas cracker.'

We both laughed at the image conjured up in our heads at the memory.

'Oh yeah, I'd forgotten about that, ok, not the best idea I've ever had.'

'I'll tell you what you could do to be the best dad in the world though,' I said, reaching into my bedside drawer for my bright pink nail varnish.

'I already told you no, Amber,' Jason said in a tone that told me he wasn't going to budge. Earlier that evening, I had told him about my latest idea for the naughty elf we had bought for the boys. Ben and Ryan were suspicious that he wasn't real, so I really had to up my game with the devilish behaviour. Pretending the elf had painted Jason's toenails was genius. The only problem was, he hadn't agreed to it as readily as I'd hoped.

Jason leant over to kiss me before turning off his bedside lamp. 'Now stop bugging me and let me go to sleep.'

'Night.'

As the all too familiar rumble began, I was reminded that he may be the perfect dad, but the perfect husband would most definitely not snore. I waited ten more minutes and then, satisfied that he was fast asleep, I climbed out of bed, pulled the duvet off his feet, and took the lid off of the nail varnish. Jason would just need to take one for the team!

Chapter 33

'What the hell has happened to my toes?'

The boys and I ran down the stairs to the sound of Jason discovering what I had done whilst he slept. We all collapsed onto the sofa in hysterics as we heard Jason's footsteps above us. He appeared at the door looking dishevelled where our laughter had woken him up with a start.

'Amber! What the hell?'

'Mummy didn't do it,' interrupted Josh. 'The naughty elf stole her nail varnish whilst you were sleeping and put it on your toenails!'

I gave Jason a look above the boys' heads to implore him to play along and keep up the pretence. I mouthed *sorry* to him before the boys' laughter became contagious again. Jason really did look funny standing there with bright pink toenails. He seemed to relax a little, and even smiled slightly as he started to see the funny side.

'That naughty elf,' he played along. 'I guess it could be

worse. A little bit of Mummy's nail varnish remover will sort this out.'

Oh shit! I'd run out of nail varnish remover a few months ago and hadn't got round to buying anymore.

'Yeah, about that,' I said, biting my bottom lip. 'I'm not sure I have any.'

Jason looked at me as if he was about to explode again, but try as I might to look serious and apologise, hearing the boys' laughter grow even more uncontrollable as they realised that their dad was going to have to go to work with bright pink toenails hiding underneath his socks, I just couldn't. I laughed until there were tears rolling down my cheeks. I laughed like I hadn't laughed since before the night of Kayla's death, and this fact wasn't lost on Jason. His threat of spontaneous combustion eased away as he joined in our hysterics and came over to give me a hug.

'It's good to see you laugh again. Even if it is at my expense.'

'It's good to laugh,' I said, and I meant it.

'Now, you lot,' he said grabbing at the boys. 'I think we need to get Elvis to paint some nail varnish on your toes. How do you like the sound of that?'

A unanimous, 'NO' resonated around the lounge as the boys all charged off out of Jason's reach. As funny as they found their dad falling victim to Elvis' antics, they did not want to be next on his list.

When all the excitement had died down, I miraculously got Ben, Ryan, and Josh to school on time and took Samuel home for some *Sammy and Mummy time* as he had started calling it. I marvelled at his little innocent face, stirring the spoon as we made some cookies. To look at, you would think that butter wouldn't melt, but under those big, angelic blue eyes was a mind full of mischief. Just two days into December, he had opened up all of the doors on Ryan's advent calendar and eaten every last chocolate. We had found him under the kitchen table with his face smeared in chocolate and even then, he had had the audacity to try to tell us it must have been Lola. I couldn't stay angry with him though. If Kayla's sudden death had taught me anything, it was that life is precious and every day with my boys was a gift. I wasn't going to waste it being angry with them. Jason had warned me not to become a soft touch though.

'Four boys will walk all over you if you let them, Amber,' he had said to me one night. 'They know you love them, and they need to know boundaries, so make sure they don't take advantage of your kind nature, ok?'

He was right, of course. I wouldn't do them any favours going all soft on them. I would just make sure that I got those extra cuddles in whenever I could, and keep being that mum who baked cookies and knew when to make the hot chocolate and marshmallows.

Since Kayla had died, I hadn't been able to focus on building my business, but just last week, I had received an email from a potential client. Laughing with the boys this morning had been exactly the therapy that I needed to give me a kick up the backside. Kayla had loved the idea of Autobiographies by Amber, and I could just imagine her here now telling me to sort my act out. Whilst the cookies were baking in the oven, I gave Samuel some toy cars to make a traffic jam with, and turned on my laptop. Pulling up the email, I read it properly after only skimming it when it came through last week. It was from a gentleman who was a friend of Michael Lamb. He had got in touch with the agency after reading Michael's autobiography, and rather than directing him to another writer, Magda had given him my details. *Thank you, Magda.* Edward Pinkerton would have flipped his lid if he had found out, but Magda's loyalty to me was fierce. She knew that it was the writers that made his firm the success that it was whilst he just sat about getting rich off of our words. My words had inspired Michael's friend to follow suit, and Magda had made sure that he found his way to me. I made a mental note to send her a box of chocolates to show my appreciation.

I started typing out a reply to my new client. It felt good to be moving forward with it again. For the past few months, I had been working on a special, personal project whilst the boys had been sleeping at night, and it was almost complete. It was definitely time to take on some more paid work doing what I loved.

Following an afternoon of realising my lack of sculpting talent whilst making clay animals with Samuel, I felt a new surge of energy as I picked the boys up from school. I saw Shannon at the gate and gave her a hug.

'How's your day been?'

'Not bad. Luke told me he was working from home so I popped by to check up on him and give him a lasagne.'

Shannon had been amazing at helping Luke out. We all took our turns supporting him with the kids, but she had taken it to another level, often making extra portions of dinner for him and the kids when she cooked for her and Maisie. He had even mastered the art of plaiting Eden's hair thanks to Shannon after Eden had told her one day that he had put her hair into a pony tail by sucking it up into the hoover nozzle. Luke was doing his best at looking after the kids without Kayla, but there were some things that he just couldn't replace her with.

'That's really sweet of you,' I said, waving at Josh as I spotted him coming out of the classroom door. 'Are you still ok to have Finn and Eden tomorrow too?'

'Yep, no worries. And you've got them the day after, right?'

Our routine worked really well, and Maddison and Francesca did their bit too. I had grown closer to the two of them since our night out, and I reprimanded myself for how quickly I had judged them when I first met them. Once you broke through their school gate mum personas, they were actually both quite nice, and their attachment to Kayla made me want them in my life still. Shortly after Kayla's death, Shannon had changed the title of our WhatsApp group to *Kayla's girls*. She had typed an emotional message to us straight afterwards, saying how much she loved us all, and how we should make sure we looked out for each other, just like Kayla always had for all of us. Not a day had gone past where we didn't chat on it at some point, usually late at night when our emotions always seemed heightened, sometimes just through tiredness, but often thanks to enjoying a glass or two of wine after dinner. I found myself messaging Beckie less and less, and felt bad for replacing her with my new mum clique. She was busy in her own life though, and often didn't reply for weeks when I did message her. I had always thought that we wouldn't drift apart, but maybe we were heading into the 'friend for a season' territory and our season was coming to an end.

Chapter 34

'Hey, check this guy out on the local news,' Jason called from the lounge.

We were having an afternoon at home after a disastrous visit to see Father Christmas. Any other kids would gaze in awe as they told the kind soul who had taken the time to pretend to be this wondrous man what they would like for Christmas. My sons, however, interrogated the poor man to within an inch of his life, and then tugged his fake beard off whilst proclaiming that he was an imposter who had tricked them. I was sure that we'd laugh about it in years to come, but there were times when I wished that my spirited boys could just toe the line a little more like other kids.

Walking into the lounge, I saw a man dressed as Father Christmas flash onto the TV screen. I felt a glow of warmth rush through me as I listened to how he had been spotted around town performing random acts of kindness.

'That really is lovely,' I said, walking over to sit down next to Jason. I felt tears pricking my eyes as I watched the mystery man handing out cosy socks and hot chocolate to some homeless people.

'Why are you crying, Mummy?' asked Josh, as he climbed onto my lap and hugged me. 'Are you sad again?'

Sniffing, I squeezed him tightly. My boys had seen far too many tears falling from my eyes these past few months.

'No, sweetheart. These are happy tears. I'm feeling emotional because someone's doing something so lovely.'

Satisfied that I was ok, Josh got up and went to find his brothers, no doubt for a bout of *Wrestle Mania*.

'I mentioned to Luke about coming over for Christmas,' Jason said. 'He said to tell you thanks, but he's going to take the kids to his parents.'

'Ok, no worries.'

'He did say that he wanted us all to go round for New Year's Eve though.'

'That'll be nice. Francesca, Maddison, and Shannon too?'

'Yep. He said that Kayla always loved New Year's Eve, and having you lot round is what she would have wanted.'

'Then that's what we'll do,' I said feeling the tears brimming my eyelids again. 'For fuck's sake, I just can't stop these bloody tears, today.'

'Mum! You said fuck! Ben, Mum said fuck!' yelled Ryan.

Oh shit, I'd thought they were out of earshot!

'No, no I didn't,' I said quickly. 'I said, duck.'

'Very original,' muttered Jason, smirking next to me.

'Sounded like fuck to me,' replied Josh, narrowing his eyes suspiciously.

'Fuck, fuck, fuck, fuck,' chanted Samuel.

Great, now he chooses to pronounce his words properly!

'Who wants to play some football, you Mother Fuckers!' shouted Ben, joining in on the new found acceptance of expletives.

'Ben!' Jason and I shouted in unison.

'What, I thought it was fair game now Mum was saying it.'

'Mum is not saying it,' I answered, putting on my best look of disapproval. 'Mum just had a little blip, and accidentally said a word that you boys are not allowed to repeat. Understood?'

'For fuck's sake, you didn't tell Ryan, Josh, and Samuel off, but the second I say it, you're all like *BEENNNNN!* Just because I'm the oldest.'

'Enough!' shouted Jason, coming to my rescue. 'Let's all shout it together after three to get it out of our systems, and then I don't want to hear another person in this house use the F word ever again, ok?'

I looked at Jason like he'd gone crazy, and hoped the neighbours were well out of ear shot as, after a count of three, we all yelled 'Fuck' as loudly as we possibly could.

It felt strangely therapeutic.

'Everyone good now?' asked Jason as the boys all started laughing in disbelief at what they'd just been allowed to do. 'Now the next time you utter that word, you need to be at least eighteen and have a damn good reason. Capiche?'

'Like we've dropped a bottle on our toe?' asked Ryan.

'Exactly like that,' confirmed Jason. 'But not before you're eighteen, remember?'

The boys all nodded and followed Jason out the back door for a game of football in the garden.

As I watched them go, I smiled to myself. I'm not sure getting your kids to shout *Fuck* as loudly as possible to get it out of their system would win us any parenting awards, but Jason was definitely up there with the best of the best. I found myself thinking how if I died, Jason would do an amazing job with our boys, and then chastised myself for thinking morbid thoughts yet again. I made a mental note to mention it to *Kayla's girls* in our next WhatsApp chat. I was sure I couldn't be the only one having intrusive thoughts like that.

Chapter 35

OMG Yes! came Francesca's reply on *Kayla's girls* when I broached the subject of thoughts of dying flashing into my head, later that night. Jason and the boys were all fast asleep in bed, and my plans to work on my latest autobiography client had been interrupted when the familiar ping sounded from my phone to let me know that I had a message. I sipped my glass of gin and tonic, and felt a satisfied tingle down my spine. Pink grapefruit gin had been Kayla's favourite, and when we had all had a glass to toast her after scattering her ashes, I decided that it would now become my favourite too in her honour. I was still partial to a glass of full-bodied red wine, but feeling the sharp taste of the gin on my taste buds made me feel close to Kayla in a way that I couldn't explain.

Maddison - Yep, totally get that.

Shannon - Me too.

I breathed a sigh of relief as I realised that my irrational thoughts maybe weren't so irrational after all, and were all part of the process of dealing with the trauma we had experienced.

Francesca – My therapist says it's totally normal.

Shannon – I didn't know you were seeing a therapist.

Francesca – Well more of a reflexologist but I seem to pour my feelings out to her when she presses certain parts of my feet and she gives really great advice.

Maddison – I couldn't bear someone touching my feet! Urgh!

Me – My friend once dated a guy with a foot fetish!

I thought to myself how six months ago I would have cringed at my lack of a filter, blurting out a statement like this to Francesca, Maddison and Shannon. Now, it just felt normal. Good friendships were all about bizarre conversations that would have outsiders committing you to a mental institute. I felt comfortable with these ladies in a way that I had never thought would be possible.

Shannon – I once dated a guy with a teeth fetish!

Maddison – What even is that!?

Shannon – He started licking my teeth when he kissed me!

Francesca – Ew, yuk!

Maddison – I think I'm about to throw up!

Me – That is possibly the grossest thing I've ever heard!

Shannon – Haha, I didn't go out with him again after that!

Francesca – Have you met any eligible men lately Shannon?

Shannon – Did you see that guy dressed as Father Christmas on the news?

Francesca – Don't change the subject Shannon!

Me – Yes! How lovely is he doing all those acts of kindness!

Maddison – I wonder who it is?

Me – I don't know but whoever it is must be such a great guy.

Francesca – Maybe you should try to meet him Shannon?

Shannon – Why are you so obsessed with my love life
all of a sudden?

Francesca – Because I have been having boring married sex for years and have nothing interesting to bring to the table!

Maddison – that's not what you told us on our night out!

It was the first time any of us had referred to *that* night in a way that wasn't filled with sadness. The text conversation fell silent for a few minutes as we all sat lost in our own thoughts.

Maddison – sorry, I didn't mean to bring it up.

Francesca – don't worry! I had actually forgotten all about my over sharing that night! Can you please forget that I did?

We all went to our friend's aid, knowing that she was probably cringing in her soberness.

Me – Forget what? No idea what you're talking about.

Maddison – Consider it forgotten!

Shannon – Not a clue what you mean! And, for the record, I won't be seeking out our lovely secret Santa. He is obvs far 2 much of a saint for the likes
of me!

I felt a surge of protectiveness for Shannon. She was such a lovely person and an amazing mum ,but she always seemed to pick the wrong men. She really needed to believe she deserved better.

Me – You deserve a good man Shannon!

Maddison – Totally. Any man would be lucky to have you.

Shannon – Aw, you guys. I'm the lucky one having all of you in my life. Did you hear the gossip about that mum from Year Six?

I couldn't help but notice that Shannon was keen to swerve the chat away from her single life that she had found herself back in after her fling with Mr Sturridge. The word gossip distracted everyone nicely. After spending the next ten minutes debating whether there was any truth in the rumour that a mum from school was leaving her husband for another woman, I tapped out what I intended as my last message of the night to say I had to get back to work on the autobiography. This led to another debate on how I could call it an autobiography when I was writing it for someone else, which in turn led to another discussion on ghost writing. So, another eleven messages and thirteen sips of gin and tonic later, I returned to my intended reason for another late night – my latest client.

He may have been a friend of Michael Lamb's, but his story was completely different. That was part of the gift of what I did. To see the two friends sharing a beer together in their local pub, you would imagine they came from similar backgrounds. Maybe father and son given their considerable age gap. Or perhaps distant cousins, or friends from work. This is usually just a small piece of the intricate puzzle that makes up human relationships though. To really get to know someone and understand them was a privilege, and the honour of people trusting me with their life story would always be at the forefront of my mind. I pressed play on the recording of the interview that I had conducted with Lee Meadows a few days ago. Too busy to meet in person due to the nature of his work and the physical distance between us, we had spoken via a video call. As a doctor working at the Great North Children's Hospital in Newcastle, Lee wanted to share his experience of his medical career. Whereas most people just wanted me to ghost write their autobiography as a keep-sake for their family to cherish, Lee hoped to publish his to inspire others to follow in his footsteps.

I wondered to myself if it would be unprofessional to attempt a little matchmake between Lee and Shannon. I was only five minutes into the interview recap and already I was remembering how perfect he was. A doctor who saves children's lives and wants to inspire others to do the same — that was definitely the type of man Shannon should be dating. Not Pete, the mechanic from Tinder, whose profile picture was lacking some serious clothing in the chest area. I grabbed my phone to send Shannon a quick text.

Me - Shannon, found the perfect man for you!

She replied instantly.

Shannon - I didn't want to say in the group chat but there is someone I think I might have a connection with already.

I stared at my phone and read the message twice to make sure I hadn't made a mistake. Shannon always told us about the men she was seeing, usually before she'd even learnt their middle name!

Me – That's great. Why didn't you say?

Shannon – Just kind of wanted to keep it quiet for a bit.

I could understand that. We'd all become really close since Kayla had died, but she had been the main person that Shannon had always confided in. It probably felt strange to her to tell us when she couldn't tell Kayla.

Me – Totally get it.

Shannon – Thanks hun. Gotta go. Need some sleep.

Turning my phone off to avoid any further distractions, I turned back to my laptop so that I could give Dr Lee my full attention. After a short while, I pressed pause on the recording and started typing.

My earliest childhood memory is of lying in a hospital bed. It's not the actual room that I remember though, it's the smell. The heavy, abrupt smell of disinfectant that never seemed to fade. Doctors would come and go. Speaking over the top of me to my parents. Barely able to make eye contact with me. One day, after being prodded on my stomach by a doctor with hands so cold that I questioned whether he was actually alive himself, I made the decision. The decision that if I was granted the gift of living, I would grow up to become a paediatric doctor. A doctor who warmed my hands up before examining a child. A doctor who actually talked to children rather than above their head. A doctor who understood that this wasn't just another statistic passing through their ward, but a child with fears and dreams and hopes. I decided that I would be that doctor they would trust. I would be that doctor who would save them. And if I couldn't save them, then I would damn near kill myself trying.

Taking a deep breath, I took my hands off the keypad and re-read my introduction. Forget setting Dr Lee up with Shannon. After writing his introduction, I wanted to marry him and have his babies myself!

Chapter 36

There was an air of anticipation as we arrived at school for the yearly Christmas play. The boys were unusually guarded about it as had been sworn to secrecy by their teachers. I allowed myself a moment of gratitude as I saw them piling out of the car. Ben crouched at the door so that Samuel could climb onto his back before charging off down the street with him as he squealed with the thrill of it. Ryan attempted to do the same with Josh, but the pair of them soon collapsed to the ground in a giggling heap. Jason scooped them up so they could catch up with Ben and Samuel. It was only 5.30pm, but the sky was already as dark as midnight. If it had been a monotonous January day, it would have felt gloomy, but the month of December held an entirely different vibe. The blackness was lit up by hundreds of twinkling lights that glowed on the outside of houses in the build up to Christmas Day. Jason preferred a simple string of warm white bulbs lining the tip of a roof or a garage door. I, on the other hand, saw the blend of vibrant colours interspersed between driveways as a show of comradery, defying the darkness and extending hope as we ended the year and entered a new one.

Catching up with the boys at the school gates, I extracted Samuel from Ben's back before my three eldest sons charged off together to find their respective classrooms where they would get changed into their costumes in amongst the hubbub of excited children.

'Hi, Amber.'

A whirlwind of emotions shot through me as I turned around and saw Rob hesitantly looking at me with his daughter, Jodie, in his arms. My first instinct was that of hatred and contempt as the memories of how he had treated me came to the forefront. But then my maternal instincts kicked in as my gaze was drawn to the baby who smiled and reached out her little mittened hand. This was Ben's little sister. A sister who hadn't come from me and wasn't a sister to my other sons. She was an extra part of Ben's life that was separate from the rest of us, and meeting her for the first time felt surreal.

'Hi,' I replied, drawing my eyes away from Jodie. 'She's a cutie.'

'Hi, Rob, how's it going?' Jason said, extending his hand out to Rob. It was the first time they had seen each other since the Nerf gun incident, so I felt thankful that

Jason was being the bigger man.

'Not bad, mate, not bad,' Rob replied accepting the handshake.

A woman appeared at his side, slightly out of breath, looking flustered. 'Sorry, I couldn't find a space for the car. I'm so glad I didn't miss the start.'

She looked to be about five years younger than me, although it was hard to tell as she was bundled up in a scarf and hat against the cold evening. Taking Jodie from Rob's arms, she turned her attention to Jason and me, giving us a warm smile. I really, really didn't want to like her. I wasn't meant to like her. She was my ex-husband's girlfriend. I was meant to loathe her. The script for a scorned wife dictated that I mock her with my friends over a glass of wine whilst they applauded my speech about how I *had a lucky escape from the wanker*. But something about the way her smile reached her eyes so naturally made me feel at ease. She was the mother of Ben's sister.

'Do you guys want to sit with us?' I heard myself saying before I even realised the words had left my mouth.

Rob raised his eyebrows in surprise. 'Ok, great,' he said. 'Cassie, meet Amber and Jason. Ben's mum and...' He paused for a minute trying to find the right word for Jason. '...And Ben's other dad.'

The acceptance of the words used wasn't lost on any of us. Jason deserved the title of *Dad* without a shadow of doubt. He had been more of a dad to Ben that Rob ever had, but there weren't many men out there who would willingly allow another man the title.

'It's so lovely to meet you both finally,' Cassie said, breaking what was going to very quickly become an uncomfortable silence as we all overcame our emotions in this significant moment. 'Ben's such a lovely boy. Jodie is lucky to have him as a big brother.'

'Well, he's certainly had a lot of practise in the big brother department!' I said laughing. 'We'd better get inside before we really are late.'

I picked Samuel up, and grabbing Jason's hand I led our unlikely group towards the school hall. I felt the comfort of Jason's hand squeezing mine, acknowledging what a big step this was for me. Meeting Rob's girlfriend and his baby sister, talking in a civil manner to the man I had harboured abhorrence towards for so long, and inviting them to sit with us, all in the space of five minutes — it was a lot for anyone to take in.

We walked into the school hall to the loud rumble of voices chatting away in enthusiastic anticipation of seeing their little ones up on stage. I spotted Shannon, Francesca, and Maddison sitting together, and was relieved to see Luke alongside Francesca's husband with Eden perched on his knee. There were three seats spare next to them which would have been perfect, but given that I had just invited my ignoramus ex and his seemingly delightful girlfriend and undeniably adorable daughter to sit with us, I headed towards the next available row. As we filtered into the seats, I unintentionally found myself in between Rob and Cassie. I considered asking Cassie if she'd like to swap places, but quickly noted how closely compacted all the seats were, and realised that rearranging would inevitably render my backside brushing up against either Rob, Cassie, or the poor unsuspecting grandad in the seat in front. My decision to stay put was further reinforced when Jodie reached her podgy little arms out to me, indicating that I was to be blessed with a cuddle.

'How old is she now?' I asked Cassie, as I put Ben's little sister on my lap like it was the most natural thing in the world.

'Coming up six months.'

'Such a lovely age.'

'I don't know how you did it with four. Just one is hard enough!'

'Oh, it's not too difficult,' I said, stretching the truth liberally. 'I'm lucky to have them.'

I'd got so used to my stock lines defending my entourage over the years that they just came out automatically now. Any further conversation was halted, as the headmaster of the school came on stage to welcome us and give the *'in case of a fire'* spiel.

The next hour was the most entertaining I had ever seen at a school Christmas play. Given the boys' excitement, I had known that there must be more to it than the massively repetitive story of Mary and Joseph that we usually had to endure year after year, but this really went beyond expectations. I travelled an emotional rollercoaster as tears fell down my cheeks when Finn appeared on stage and delivered his line. I allowed myself the pretence that Kayla was sitting somewhere in the dark, holding Luke's hand and cuddling Eden on her lap whilst waving at Finn hoping he could spot her in the crowd. My tears turned to laughter though, when Josh came onto the stage larger than life, dressed as a 'cool wise man' complete with sunglasses and a cap on back to front. Forgetting his lines, he started to freestyle Vanilla Ice's, 'Ice Ice Baby' lyrics that he had played relentlessly on a singing Christmas penguin toy that I had bought at the beginning of the month. I looked on in wonder at his confidence, as the audience clapped and cheered him. Somehow, Ryan had managed to get a football trick act in by doing it dressed as an innkeeper and asking the audience if they liked *the innKEEPers KEEPY UPPY's*? Thankfully everyone laughed in the right place at his cringey joke. I couldn't help but feel sorry for Ben, as he walked on stage dressed as a donkey whilst carrying a girl called Emily on his back – she was none other than the little witch who had sabotaged his talent show act. I sent him silent, telepathic messages, begging him not to buck her off. Given their history of rivalry, I wouldn't have blamed him if he had, but I didn't think the other parents would see it quite the same way. The shocker of the night came when the teachers appeared on stage, singing a very respectable 'Oh Come All Ye Faithful' before whipping off their black cloaks half way through to reveal sparkly jumpsuits, and proceeding to belt out 'Merry Christmas Everybody' by Slade! It was a far cry from days gone by where the music teacher destroyed Little Donkey on the piano.

All too quickly, the show was over, and the audience stood to gather their coats and wait outside their children's classrooms to take them home.

'Shall I go to get Ben and Ryan, and you get Josh?' I asked Jason.

'I can get Ben if you like?' interrupted Rob. 'You know, if it helps. Three adults, three boys. Kinda makes sense.'

'Perfect,' said Jason. 'I'll get Ryan, you get Josh, Amber, and Rob can get Ben. '

'Ok,' I agreed, feeling a little put out that Rob would be the first to congratulate Ben on his performance, but acknowledging that it made sense.

'Great,' said Rob, looking pleased. 'Shall we all meet out the front when we've got them?'

'Sounds like a plan,' I said.

Wow, are we actually getting on ok after all these years? I thought to myself. The image of Jason suggesting we invite Rob, Cassie, and Jodie over for Christmas flicked into my head. Maybe he was right. Saying goodbye to Cassie, I gave Jodie another little hug. *It would be nice to have a baby in the house on Christmas Day…*

Shaking my head, I brought myself to my senses. Sitting with Rob in the dark, not having to talk to him for an hour was one thing. Sitting round the dinner table making pleasant conversation with him was quite another.

I spotted Luke waiting outside Josh and Finn's classroom. Shannon, Francesca, and Maddison were circled around him, protecting him from sympathetic stares of other parents. Walking over, I reached out to give him a hug, as Samuel tugged on Eden's hair to get her attention.

'How're you doing?' I asked him. I felt the familiar lump in my throat but, refused to let it give rise to tears. I needed to be strong for Luke. This was the first school event he had attended since Kayla had died and it was probably taking every ounce of strength that he had to hold it together.

'Oh, you know,' he said with a deep intake of breath.

'Yeah, I know,' I replied. We held each other's eyes for a moment, sharing the pain we both felt without Kayla. Luckily Shannon interrupted the moment before we both caved under our emotions.

'Oh my God, Amber, Josh was hilarious!'

'I have no idea where he gets it from!' I said as we all laughed. 'He's such a little show off!'

'He was brilliant!' exclaimed Francesca, and everyone nodded their agreement. Just then, the classroom door opened, and a swarm of excited children rushed towards us to lap up the praise of their waiting parents. My heart melted as I spotted Josh with his hat still on backwards. Picking up Samuel, I waved in his direction so that he could see me. He pointed me out to his teacher, and then ran over to us, beaming from ear to ear. Feeling on a high, he didn't stop talking the whole way to the car park to meet the others. I didn't stand a chance of getting the boys to bed anywhere near their usual bedtime tonight.

'How about we celebrate with some late-night hot chocolate and marshmallows when we get home?' I suggested to my two youngest sons.

'Yay! Thanks, Mum,' approved Josh.

'I love hot locolate!' Samuel concurred with his cute mispronunciation. I remembered how not so long ago, Josh would get his words mixed up too and contemplated the great paradox of parenting – whilst the days passed in slow motion, the time itself went so fast.

Chapter 37

'Ben, I can't just drop everything to take you and Tommy into town. I've got your brothers to look after.'

It was the Saturday after the Christmas play, and whereas I had planned on having a family day at home, it would seem that my eldest son had other plans.

'Let's all go,' said Jason, walking into the room. 'We can get our secret Santa presents whilst we're there.'

A couple of years ago, we had adopted the secret Santa tradition so that the boys could learn the gift of giving at Christmas rather than just receiving. Last year, Ben had gone slightly over our £5 budget, buying me a huge jar of toffee bonbons, secure in the belief that I would share it with him. The secret part of who bought which gift never stayed a secret for long once the presents were given.

'Yeah, let's go,' joined in Ryan as he overheard the conversation. 'We can see if there's any chocolates left on the Christmas tree in the town centre.'

He was referring to another good deed by the mystery man, dressed up as Father Christmas who locals had named Saint Christmas. Last week, he had decorated the huge town centre tree with Christmas chocolates just like we always did on our one at home.

'You never know,' said Jason, 'Maybe Saint Christmas will be doing something in the town centre again today. We might catch him in the act.'

Ben and Tommy exchanged a sneaky glance which I interpreted as a feeling of smugness that they had got their way.

'Ok,' I relented. 'Shoes on everyone.'

After fifteen tortuous minutes of trying to perform what should have been a simple task, but instead was hampered by a son who insisted on wearing a lost batman cape that we eventually found on our very tolerant dog, we all piled into the car.

'So why are you so keen to go into town this afternoon, Ben?' I asked turning around to look at my son suspiciously.

'Like Dad said, I need to get my secret Santa present.'

My mum radar told me that Ben wasn't being totally honest with me. There was definitely more to this than he was letting on. Before I could interrogate him and Tommy, Ben started winding Samuel up which only ever headed in one direction within the confined space of the car. Just as I was about to intervene, Jason turned the radio up.

'Shh,' he snapped. 'Listen!'

A hush fell over the car as we all registered the excited tone of the radio DJ where we caught his conversation half way through.

'…he'll only come down when the crowd has donated at least £10,000 to little five-year-old Darcey Edwards, who needs to go to America for some ground breaking treatment to save her life.'

Everyone in the area knew about Darcey. She had a rare disease that her parents couldn't afford the treatment for. They'd been doing all kinds of fundraising events, but still didn't have enough.

'Come on, folks. Get yourself down to Guildford Cathedral now to see the man in action. Forget the Father Christmas from Lapland. We have our very own Father Christmas in Guildford who is an absolute saint,' the DJ continued.

Ben immediately demanded that Jason take a right at the next roundabout instead of turning left to the town centre. His sudden change of direction made me think that maybe I was wrong to be suspicious of his reasons, and perhaps he and Tommy were genuinely just a bit bored and wanted to go into town for something to do. The opportunity to see Saint Christmas in real life was instantly far more appealing to them than shopping, and the feeling in the car was unanimous.

'Do you think he's climbed up the big tree next to the cathedral?' asked Josh.

'I bet he's climbed up the flag pole,' joined in Ryan.

282

'We'll soon find out,' I said, as Jason pulled the car into the cathedral car park. There had obviously been a lot of other people tuned into the radio at the same time as us, as we witnessed a massive crowd walking in the same direction.

Gathering everyone out of the car, we joined the masses in wonder of what we were about to see. As we got closer to the cathedral, we followed the upward gaze of the other onlookers around us. Saint Christmas wasn't up a tree. He wasn't even up the flag pole. There, 160-feet off the ground, sitting next to the angel statue, was the unmistakeable silhouette of a bearded man dressed as Father Christmas. I squinted against the sunlight that shone low in the December sky behind him as it began its descent. Wispy clouds glowed coral pink in places and fiery orange in others as the light fragments passed through them with intensity, smattering the blue sky that would soon darken. I hugged my coat into myself, glad of the hat that I had found in my handbag. Sometimes it felt like a winter sun just showed itself every now and then to blind you, offering no warmth or calm as you squinted behind the wheel of your car. Bearing witness to a sunset such as this was a true privilege though, and something that I would never take for granted in this complex world. Francesca had shared her reflexologist's words of wisdom that it was important to notice a part of nature every day, and that was one bit of well-meaning advice that I had gladly taken on board.

'Look at those beautiful clouds,' I said to everyone but

no-one in particular.

'Forget the clouds, Mum!' Ben said, looking anxious.

I followed his gaze to the man on the roof, pulling my poetic thoughts back to earth. 'Look,' I said, 'he's got a rope tied around his waist. He must be planning on abseiling down when he's raised enough money for Darcey.'

Ben looked reassured as he acknowledged the rope, but I couldn't help but notice that he seemed a little on edge.

'Ho, Ho, Ho,' came a crackly voice through the crowds.

I grinned at all my boys who were surveying the scene with wide open mouths, in awe of hearing the mystery man speak. A cheer erupted around us as everyone showed their support for Saint Christmas.

'If you raise £10,000 for little Darcey, I will abseil down this cathedral,' he boomed. 'However, if you manage to raise £20,000, I will also reveal my true identity when I get to the bottom.'

I felt myself getting wrapped up in the furore and started speculating as to who might be behind the disguise.

'I bet it's Darcey's dad,' I whispered to Jason, not wanting to spoil the anticipation for the boys as they waited for the big reveal.

'Guaranteed,' Jason agreed, nodding.

'Yep, I'd put money on it, definitely Darcey's dad,' I continued. 'Such a great idea to raise the money they need.'

'How about we donate our secret Santa money to this good cause?' Jason suggested to all of us. 'If we all put £5 in, that's £30 we can put towards helping little Darcey.'

The boys didn't hesitate in agreeing with Jason, and I had a moment of reassurance that we must be doing something right in the parenting department.

'How do we go about giving money to this crazy dare devil?' asked Jason, looking around. 'Is there a bucket going round or something?'

Right on cue, we heard the crackling of the megaphone again, as the man we were all looking at in admiration told us how to donate online. A sea of mobile phones appeared in hands where people logged on to donate. There must have been hundreds of people who had turned up to see the unexpected drama unfold, and many more were still swarming up the path towards the cathedral which was glowing majestically in the sunset.

Astonishingly, after a mere fifteen minutes, Saint Christmas announced that the target of £20,000 had already been hit. I felt a warm rush of adrenaline, knowing that our little contribution as a family had helped. A countdown started amongst the crowd, as he prepared to make his descent down the cathedral wall.

'I hope his rope's tight enough,' I said. I couldn't bear heights, and just watching this stranger lean backwards was enough to make my legs feel like jelly.

'Imagine if he ended up going splat!' Josh said.

'Dat would be funny,' giggled Samuel, who had been

mastering his F sound nicely lately.

Before I had a chance to reprimand them for their insensitive morbidity, Ben tackled them for me.

'Oi, shut up, you two. This isn't one of the stupid TV shows you watch. This is real life. He's a real person you know!'

I might not have appreciated his 'shut up' approach, but I was certainly proud of his sentiment, and his little brothers seemed to be pulled into line straight away.

Within minutes, Saint Christmas had made it half way down the cathedral wall. As he manoeuvred his way around to complete the final part, I was distracted by Ben suddenly shouting, 'come on' as he grabbed Josh and Ryan's hands and pushed his way through the crowds.

'Ben, where are you going?' I shouted after him.

Jason was still gazing up at the cathedral, oblivious to the fact that his sons had suddenly bolted away. Grabbing his hand in much the same way as Ben had done with his younger brothers, I gave pursuit, mumbling *excuse me* and *sorry* as I barged between people, not taking my eyes off of the four unmistakeable heads bobbing up and down through the crowd next to Tommy's big head of curls.

We caught up with them round the side of the cathedral just as Saint Christmas was navigating the last few metres of his stunt.

'Ben, you shouldn't have charged off with your little brothers like that,' I reprimanded him. I would have said a lot more too, but that was just about all I could manage in between puffs after the exertion of my power walk. I paused for a second to catch my breath, hoping I'd then be able to speak again. Before I could utter another word though, Ben dashed over to Saint Christmas and flung his arms around him.

I stared at him, feeling confused. This was not typically characteristic behaviour at all from Ben. He wasn't the type of child to run up and hug random strangers. Even if they had just done something incredibly heroic and admirable.

I looked up at Jason with questioning eyes and saw that he looked as baffled as me. Saint Christmas removed his sunglasses that had been part of his disguise throughout his mysterious acts of kindness and looked at Ben. Then he addressed the crowd who all instantly fell silent in anticipation of the big reveal.

'Ladies and gentleman, boys and girls. Thank you so much for your amazingly generous donations for little Darcey. Thanks to all of you, we now have double what she needed for her treatment, which means that we can donate the rest to other sick kids too.'

'It's definitely Darcey's dad,' I whispered to Jason again, feeling smug that I had guessed his identity.

'Without doubt,' Jason nodded.

'He literally must be the best dad in the world to do this for her,' I said in hushed tones, before quickly adding, 'except you of course,' in case Jason got offended.

'Now, as promised,' Saint Christmas continued, 'I will reveal my true identity.

Ben looked over at me, grinning as the mystery man

whipped off his hat and fake beard to a massive round of applause.

My mouth literally dropped open as my brain registered what it was seeing. The images of everyone else around me blurred together as my gaze homed in on the one person that everyone was looking at, but who I was really seeing for the first time in a very long time.

'I knew I recognised that voice,' I muttered in disbelief.

Chapter 38

I still felt in shock when I climbed into bed with Jason that night after an enlightening chat in Ben's bedroom. He had filled me in on how his suspicions about the true identity of Saint Christmas had arisen when he had seen a social media video that someone had captured of him dancing. As Ben had laughed at the embarrassing dance moves, he had detected the unmistakeable atrocious singing alongside it. Sharing his supposition with Tommy, they had calculated that there was a high chance that he would be performing more acts of kindness in town like he had every other Saturday throughout December, and that's where I had come into their plan to give them a lift into town. Ben couldn't believe his luck when the radio had divulged Saint Christmas' exact location.

'Who would have thought?' I said to Jason as I

snuggled into the cosy duvet.

'Your face was a picture!' Jason said, laughing at me.

'I was so convinced it was Darcey's dad. I should have known as soon as I heard him shouting through that megaphone. And the way that Ben seemed anxious about him falling. It all makes perfect sense now.'

'Rob Collins,' Jason said shaking his head in wonder. 'Never in a million years would I have guessed it.'

Ben's biological dad. The man I had referred to as 'the sperm doner', 'the dickhead', 'the plonker' for so many years, was the same man that I had been using words such as 'admirable' and 'heroic' for, just a matter of hours ago. He was the Saint Christmas that everyone had been talking about as he had performed random acts of kindness which culminated in nothing short of a valiant, Herculean act of selflessness.

'Maybe he really has changed,' I said. 'He was still an immature prick when I married him, but I guess that was ten years ago. Look how far we've come in ten years. Four children, two dogs, you a successful advertising exec, me running my own business after my defamation of my boss. A new house, a new school. If this much can change for us, maybe life has changed him too.'

'The Rob you knew wouldn't have done all this, Amber. I've done some pretty stupid things in my past that I wouldn't dream of doing now. Maybe Rob just grew up a little later than he should have done.'

'Maybe.'

'I think this needs to be a turning point, Amby. You

can go on hating Rob forever more for how he treated you and Ben, or you can be the bigger person and accept that it's time to move forward. For Ben's sake. Remember my suggestion to invite them over on Christmas Day?'

I let out a big puff of breath as I contemplated what Jason was saying. It was hard to alter my perception of someone that I had harboured such resentment towards for so long. He would always be the man who left me and his baby son for another woman. But maybe it was time to let go of that resentment.

'Bitterness is for those who have been left without, Amby. That's not you. You often say that Rob did you a favour leaving. I'm certainly glad he did,' he said chuckling, 'or I'd never had had a chance to charm you into bed with me.'

I swatted him playfully on the arm for the implication that his affections had been little more than an act of *charming me*.

'When did you get so wise?' I asked pulling a sulky face as I knew he was right. The childish part of me wanted to hold a grudge forever, but learning this newfound information about Rob, and seeing Ben's reaction to him when he had proudly discovered his identity was reason enough to let it go. Like Jason said, for Ben's sake. It wasn't just him and Rob now. It was Cassie and Jodie too. They were a family. Ben was lucky enough to have two loving families, and if I was any kind of a mother, I needed to embrace that for him.

291

'I guess I'd better buy some extra crackers for Christmas dinner then,' I said to Jason.

Jason leant over and kissed me.

'They may already have plans,' he said, 'but just the gesture of you inviting them speaks volumes.' He reached over me and grabbed my phone from the bedside table, handing it to me. 'No time like the present.'

Knowing full well that I may think up a convenient excuse to change my mind in the morning, Jason was forcing me to strike whilst the iron was hot. Rolling my eyes at him, I dropped the phone on the bed. 'It's too late to text. They've got a baby remember?'

Not being defeated, Jason said. 'Then he'll see it when he switches his phone on in the morning.' He picked up my phone, and started searching for Rob's number himself. 'Surely you have his number on here, Amber,' he said when he couldn't find it under R.

I looked sheepishly at him. 'Try looking under P.'

'Why P?'

'P for Plonker.'

Jason laughed. I'd told him about the alarm clock that Rob used to have that screeched out, 'Get Up You Plonker'. It had seemed a fitting tribute to him, and also quite a tame form of contempt in case one of the boys flicked through my phone and saw it!

Accepting defeat, I took my phone back from Jason and typed a short, brief message to 'Plonker'.

Ben was really proud of you today. What do you think about having Christmas Day with us here?

'There,' I said to Jason. 'Done. Why are you pushing this so much anyway, out of interest?'

'Because I know what it's like to have two different families that you split things like Christmas between, Amber, and trust me, if those families can get along with each other, it makes it so much easier for the kids.'

Jason's parents had split up when he was ten – the age that Ben was now. He understood what Ben was going through far more than I ever could. The fact that he would rather invite Ben's other family into our home on our special day than make Ben miss out on being with one of us just went to show the kind of man he was.

'Thank you,' I said, giving him a kiss. 'For making me see sense. And for being the best dad Ben could ever wish for. We're so lucky to have you.'

'Speaking of good dads. Luke seemed to be doing…'

His sentence was left hanging as an unexpected ping sounded to alert me that I had a text message. Jason and I looked at each other startled. Neither of us had expected Rob to still be up.

'It's probably just *Kayla's girls*,' I said, reaching for my phone.

'Or Beckie,' he said

I hoped it was Beckie. I hadn't heard from her in ages.

Flicking the screen on, I was faced with the reality of the olive branch that I had just offered as the name

Plonker flashed up with a little envelope next to it.

'Well, it's not Beckie or *Kayla's girls*,' I said to Jason, raising my eyebrows.

'Rob?'

I nodded, still not opening the message.

Jason grabbed the phone off of me, sensing my obvious reluctance. After a brief pause, he took my hand in his, and broke it to me that the overture wheels had been set in motion.

'I think you'll be needing those three extra crackers after all, Amby.'

Chapter 39

Luckily, with Christmas Day approaching so rapidly, I didn't have time to work myself up about being in the presence of Rob. In the moments of self-doubt, I repeated the mantra, *'Ben is worth it, Ben is worth it, Ben is worth it,'* in my head. Unfortunately, Francesca's mantra of *'masturbate to recalibrate'* tended to invade my brain straight after my more family-oriented words. Damn Francesca for teaching us such a catchy mantra. What if I unknowingly started chanting it in my sleep? I had been known to ramble incoherently as my over active brain refused to rest. Or even worse, what if I blurted it out at the Christmas dinner table in a moment of awkwardness where my brain loses all filters!

Ben had been so proud of his discovery that Rob was Saint Christmas that he had even written an article about it for a newspaper competition and was chuffed to bits when he won! There was no doubt in my mind that having Rob, Cassie, and Jodie with us all for Christmas Day was what was best for Ben. We had decided to keep it a secret and surprise him with it when he came down for Christmas dinner.

Before I knew it, the momentous day arrived. The boys were so excited about Father Christmas coming that we finally let them get up at 5.30am after sending Samuel and Josh back to bed twice already. The last thing we wanted was cranky kids all day where they were overtired. Their excitement was contagious though as they noisily ran to wake up Ben and Ryan. Ben knew the truth behind the presents that mysteriously appeared overnight, but he had vowed to keep the dream alive for his younger brothers which I was thankful for. He'd have to keep the pretence up even longer now that he had a little sister to play along with too!

As the boys played with their new toys, Jason and I spent the morning preparing the Christmas dinner. At midday, Jason ushered them all upstairs to get dressed so that I could sneak three extra place settings, including a high chair, around the table. My head was a whir of mixed feelings. I felt anxious about having Rob in my home, but excited about seeing Ben's reaction when he walked in and saw both of his families together. The contradiction of my emotions was enough to give me a headache. I decided that the only way forward was to pour myself a cheeky gin and tonic that I could pretend was a lemonade. Tasting the sharp yet comforting texture on my tongue immediately made me think of Kayla and how proud she would have been of me for taking this step. Another conflicting emotion that I was experiencing was the desire to cuddle little Jodie again. I remembered my initial reaction to Ben having a baby sister. I was ashamed to admit that it was one of jealousy. I was jealous that Ben had another sibling that hadn't come from me. And moreover, a little sister. I wouldn't change my four boys for the world, but to have had the four of them and a little girl would have been the icing on the cake. Now that I had actually met Jodie though, and experienced the familiar baby smell that she had, I felt nothing but maternal towards her, and the thought of seeing her again made me feel happy and content. It literally was as simple as that. No extravagant word was needed to describe it. Not propitious, or felicitous, or auspicious like I may swerve towards when writing someone's autobiography. Simply happy and content, like the innocent world of a baby itself. Taking a sip of my drink, I acknowledged that if I allowed it, the emotions of excitement and happiness could overcome the feeling of anxiety that bubbled away underneath. *Ben is worth it, Ben is worth it, Ben is worth it, masturbate to recalib...' Oh shut the fuck up brain.*

'Ben's in his room trying to connect his new speaker,' announced Jason, coming into the kitchen with our other three sons in tow.

'Is it true what Dad said, Mum,' asked Ryan. 'Is Rob really coming to lunch with Cassie and Jodie?'

A knock at the door confirmed it for him as he

squealed with excitement. He'd been asking to join Ben and Rob on one of their arcade and pizza trips ever since he had connived his way onto their camping trip. I had thought that the appeal was the adrenaline rush of the arcade, but maybe he actually just wanted to see Rob again.

I had text Rob that morning to say that I wanted to surprise Ben, so he wasn't at all baffled when I opened the door to him without a word and put my finger to my lips to indicate to him to be quiet. I ushered him into the kitchen with Cassie and Jodie where I then proceeded to cover up any unease that I felt by picking Samuel up in my arms and directing my attention to Jodie. Cassie had dressed her in a gorgeous red Christmassy dress with pictures of white reindeer on it. She was the definition of cuteness.

'Thank you so much for inviting us over, Amber,' Cassie gushed. 'I hope you haven't gone to too much trouble.'

'No, none at all,' I lied, as an image of hunting high and low for Samuel's old high chair flashed into my head.

'Yeah, thanks, Amber,' Rob said coming over and taking Jodie from Cassie. 'It'll be nice seeing Ben on Christmas Day.'

'You're welcome,' I said as Jason came and put a supportive arm around my shoulder, feeling the tense formality of my politeness. 'Can I get you both a drink?'

I busied myself getting Cassie a glass of white wine and Rob a beer whilst Ryan, Josh, and Samuel stood staring at them.

'Y'alright boys?' Rob said, sounding a little uncertain.

'What did you get Ben for Christmas?' asked Ryan, getting straight to the point.

'Ryan,' Jason said giving an uncomfortable chuckle. 'You'll find out when Ben opens it, speaking of which, I think it's time to let Ben in on this surprise.'

'I'll pretend I need his help in the kitchen!' I said. 'Come with me to the hall you lot but not a word! Rob, why don't you and Cassie sit at the table with Jodie so that Ben finds you there?'

'Perfect,' agreed Rob.

'This is so exciting,' Cassie enthused in a way that a few months ago I would have wanted to find irritating, but actually quite warmed to in my heightened mode of acceptance.

Ryan, Samuel, and Josh ran to the hall giggling. After an unsuccessful attempt to get Ben down with my requests up the stairs to help me in the kitchen, I realised that my tactics were way off the mark. Ben never hurried down to help out in the kitchen.

'Ben, what's taking you so long,' shouted Jason.

'Alright, alright. What's the hurry? It's Christmas Day. We're meant to have a lazy day!' came his distant reply.

'Come on, Ben!' joined in Ryan.

When Ben still didn't appear, Josh and Samuel couldn't contain themselves any longer and rushed upstairs to his bedroom. Bursting in, they grabbed a hand each, and literally pulled him down the stairs. Ben looked bewildered as the five of us stood there, grinning at him like complete lunatics.

'What?' he asked hesitantly, pulling a confused face.

'Nothing,' I replied, keeping my act up. 'It's just time for Christmas dinner.'

'Yeah, and we didn't want you to miss out on pulling the crackers,' added Ryan, looking pleased with himself.

'You lot are so strange sometimes,' Ben said as he walked towards the kitchen. 'Come on then, I'm starv…!'

He didn't finish his sentence as he bore witness to the most delicious looking Christmas feast, circled by not just six chairs but eight chairs and a high chair. Rob and Cassie got up from their seats as Ben stood there speechless.

'We thought that this Christmas, we could all be one big happy family,' I said as my eyelids brimmed with tears at the emotion etched on Ben's face. 'You, me, Dad, Ryan, Josh, Samuel, Rob, Cassie, and Jodie.'

'Happy Christmas, son,' Rob said, looking a little teary himself.

'Happy Christmas,' Ben replied with a shy, soppy grin on his face.

Rob and I then both went to hug Ben at the same time which was narrowly saved from becoming a moment of awkwardness by Cassie suddenly joining in the hug too. As wrong as it should have felt, it bizarrely made it feel less inappropriate. Before I knew it, Jason had also joined the group hug along with six other little arms where Ryan, Josh, and Samuel didn't want to be left out. The moment was both cringey and precious all at the same time.

'Now, let's eat before all this food goes cold,' I said, keen to end the moment before the notion of *precious* faded completely into the shadow of *cringe*.

With Ben strategically seated between Jason and Rob, we were all about to pull our crackers when Ryan piped up, 'Does this mean that we all get a present from Rob this Christmas too?' Hence revealing the real reason that he was so excited when he heard that Rob would be joining us today.

Amidst the laughter, Rob surprised us all by saying that he had in fact bought presents for everyone. I wondered if Ben might feel a bit put out by that. One of the highlights of him having two dads had always been the extra Christmas and birthday presents that he got. He didn't look the slightest bit perturbed, however, as he expertly pulled two crackers at the same time, one with Rob and one with Jason.

And that is how you do Christmas, blended family style, I thought to myself smugly. We were only half an hour into it, but I had a good feeling that I could actually pull this off.

'Can I help you clear up, Amber,' Cassie asked as we all sat satiated after eating far too much. I could tell that she felt the need to be useful so welcomed her into the kitchen with me whilst Jason and Rob took the kids to see what Christmas movies they could find to watch whilst Jodie had a nap.

Any lingering notions that I had held about not liking her had vanished during lunch. She genuinely was a pleasure to have around and certainly someone I'd be happy for Ben to have in his life – just as long as she knew the boundaries on her mum duties! I still needed to be the one that Ben came to with his first heart break, let's just make that clear.

'So, how did you and Rob meet each other?' I asked. I had been wondering about this, and it felt like a good time to be nosy.

'Well, it's actually quite a funny story,' Cassie said. 'I was standing up on the bus on my way home from work, and Rob asked if I wanted to sit on his lap.'

'Oh my God,' I said. 'That's so typical of him! I hope you told him where to go.'

'I didn't have time to say anything, as an old lady who got on after me overheard and said *'don't mind if I do young man!'* The next thing I knew, she'd barged her way past me with her shopping bags and sat straight down on Rob's lap. His face was a picture.'

Cassie laughed at the memory as I got a vision in my head of Rob sitting frozen to the spot as a lady in her eighties with a curly blue rinse wiggled her bony backside on him.

'Oh, karma is a wonderful thing,' I said, laughing.

'Isn't it just!'

'So how did you go from that to dating, moving in together and having a baby?'

'I saw him on the same bus the next day and instead

of asking me to sit on his lap, he stood up and offered me his seat. We laughed about the incident together, and he admitted that he had been a total idiot attempting to flirt with me in that creepy way. We got off at the next stop, had a drink together, and the rest is history as they say.'

'Well, you have certainly changed him for the better,' I said. 'Credit where credit's due, Cassie, the Rob I've seen since you had Jodie is a different man to the one who I delivered Ben into the world with.'

'I'm sorry he was so awful to you, Amber.'

I was taken aback by the direct way she said it. I don't know why, but I had assumed that she would be in the dark about the man that Rob was ten years ago, seeing him only through the rose-tinted glasses she wore.

'He told you about that?' I asked. 'What did he say?'

'I think his exact words the first time I asked were something along the lines of an analogy to a footballer scoring a goal, and then getting pissed to celebrate rather than practising his skills for future matches.'

'How eloquent,' I said sarcastically.

'He's elaborated on it since though,' she continued. 'He knows he was a complete dickhead, Amber. Having Jodie has woken him up to how hard it must have been for you and Ben. He knows he can't make up for what he did, but he's a good man now, I promise you, and he wants Ben in his life more than anything. He wants to make up for being a lousy dad all these years.'

'I can see that,' I admitted. 'I just want what's best for Ben, you know. He was so proud of Rob when he found out that he was Saint Christmas, and I know that he adores little Jodie. And as much as I didn't want to like *you*, I actually really do.'

'Well thank you,' said Cassie blushing where her cheeks were already a little tinged from the wine. 'I'd really like us to be friends.'

Surprising myself, I added, 'I'd like that too.'

Hanging up the tea-towel, I realised that we had finished clearing up and excused myself to go to the toilet. I sat down on the seat and sent a text to Beckie.

You'll never guess who's spending Christmas with us?

I didn't expect her to reply straight away. After all, she hadn't replied to the last three texts that I'd sent. I hoped with it being Christmas though, she'd want to get in touch. I'd read an article recently about someone ghosting an old friend as their lives naturally followed different directions. I had never thought that it would happen to Beckie and me, but there was little other explanation for her lack of effort over the past year. Our friendship was evidently just fading away as so many did when old friend's lives went in different directions. Leaving the bathroom, I went downstairs to the sound of Jason dealing out the cards for a game of Happy Families, laughing to myself at the irony of it.

Chapter 40

After the abyss of a week where no day warranted its own name as they all merged into one big time blip — which I declared to Jason should be officially named as 'Eat Cheese Week' — it was New Year's Eve, and time to go to Luke's for the party. It felt wrong to use the word *party*, as how could it be a party in Kayla's house without Kayla there?

'Can we just call it a get together?' I asked Jason as he asked if I was ready.

We had decided to get all dressed up in honour of Kayla. I realised that I'd never had the privilege to spend a New Year's Eve with her as had met her in January, just as all the festivities ended and the days of gloom set in. I was reliably informed by Luke, Shannon, Francesca, and Maddison that she had always loved it though and never failed to get glammed up for the occasion, so *glam it up* we would! I was wearing a long black dress with beige lace interwoven across the chest. It dipped down towards my navel, and from a distance you could be forgiven for thinking it was my nude skin peeping through. I had wrapped my hair up on top of my head and allowed a few tendrils to escape to frame my face. I looked at myself in the full-length mirror in my bedroom, feeling like an imposter. It was a far cry from my jeggings and long jumpers that I seemed to live in these days.

'Twit twoo,' said Jason, appearing in the mirror next to me. He rested his hands on my hips and ducked his head down to kiss my neck. 'Looking good, Mrs Clayton,' he murmured.

'You don't scrub up too badly yourself,' I responded swivelling round so that I was facing him. Jason's stubble was the perfect length to guarantee him the *'attractive older man'* look that he still possessed. The men had decided not to go quite as over the top as us ladies, but he had still made an effort with a crisply ironed shirt and a dash of expensive smelling after shave. It reminded me to put my perfume on, so wriggling out of Jason's grasp, I picked up my bottle of Coco Chanel that he had bought me for my birthday last year. I gave it a little sniff hoping that it hadn't turned musty as I barely had occasion to wear it now. Satisfied that it had stood the test of time, I squirted it onto my wrists and my neck as Josh ran into the room.

'Mummy, you smell!'

'What you meant to say is, *'Mummy, you smell lovely'*,' I corrected.

'No, you don't, you stink,' confirmed Ryan, joining his

brother in his lack of charm.

'I really need to teach you boys the art of complimenting a lady,' I said, taking no offence at all. I had learnt long ago that my boys preferred me perfume-less, make-up-less and in my jeans. Au naturel was the way to win their hearts.

'Are you ready to go?' asked Jason.

'Can you get the boys out the front door? I just need to grab something from downstairs.'

As the boys stepped out excitedly into the dark night with their pillows, sleeping bags, and teddies, I opened up the cupboard where I kept my Autobiographies by Amber paraphernalia. Finding the item that I was looking for, I pulled it out and held it to my chest for a minute, lost in my thoughts. The abrupt sound of shouts to hurry up alerted me to the fact that I was taking too long, so putting it in my bag, I said a quick goodbye to Obi and Lola, and ventured out into the cold December air.

My glamourous look had been finished off with a nice pair of cosy Ugg boots. I had contemplated putting a pair of heels in my bag to change into after the short walk, but knew full well I'd take them off within the first hour of socialising and give in to the bohemian barefoot look. Anticipating this, I had painted my toenails a deep red for the occasion and clasped a delicate gold chain around my ankle.

Seeing Kayla's front door up ahead made me feel awash with emotion. Nearly four months on, it still felt surreal not to see her smiling face opening the door.

Instead, we were greeted by Francesca, who looked like she was about to step onto the red carpet, with her hair swept up into an elaborate style that she had undoubtedly paid over the odds for at the hairdresser earlier today. She looked amazing in a white flowing dress that wouldn't have looked out of place on the front cover of a bridal magazine.

'Come in, come in,' she said, air kissing both me and Jason as we ushered the boys through the front door. 'Everyone else is here already.'

'Thank goodness you're here!' Luke exclaimed, walking into the hall with Eden wrapped around his leg. 'See, Eden,' he said, attempting to extract her, 'I told you Sammy would be here any minute.'

Seeing her bestie had arrived, Eden let go of Luke's leg without a second thought and raced over to grab Samuel's hand. The excitement of having him there after bedtime was just beyond belief. As the two of them charged off together, bumping the walls with his sleeping bag and pillow, Luke turned to my three eldest.

'You boys, come into the lounge with the other kids. There's enough lemonade and sweets in there to keep you awake all night.'

Ben, Ryan, and Josh didn't need telling twice. Without looking back, they rushed off to join the other children in the lounge where Luke had set up treats, movies, and even table football to keep them entertained. Winking at us, he said, 'One night of being spoilt won't hurt them.'

'Oh, it's absolutely fine by us,' Jason replied. 'Gives us

the perfect space for some adult time.'

'Exactly what I thought,' said Luke.

I was pleased to see how upbeat Luke was. Jason had said that he was coping well, but I'd been concerned that he may just be appearing so on the surface whilst struggling deep inside. We walked into the kitchen to the sound of music and voices. Maddison and Shannon were seated at the breakfast bar whilst Maddison's husband, Isaac, stood chatting to Francesca's husband, Darryl, about the best places to play golf on the Costa del Sol. Jason went to join them whilst I fell in naturally with the girls, giving them all a hug before claiming my own bar stool.

'What are we drinking?' I asked.

'Kayla's favourite,' replied Shannon, chinking her glass against Maddison's and Francesca's. 'Pink grapefruit gin and tonic.'

'And here's one for you,' Luke said appearing by my side with a glass in hand. Thanking him, I took the drink and sipped through the ice cubes, my tongue tingling as the now familiar taste hit it.

'It reminds me a bit of Drumstick lollies,' said Maddison.

'Oh my God, it totally does,' agreed Shannon. 'I knew it reminded me of something.'

Shannon and Maddison were looking equally as stunning as Francesca, albeit a little less over-the-top. Maddison was wearing an emerald green, strapless, long satin dress which accentuated her slim figure. Shannon was looking bodaciously, bootilicious in a classic black dress with a plunging neckline where her chest sparkled in the fairy lights Luke had decorated the room with.

'Have you got glitter on your boobs?' I asked her.

'Maybe a little sprinkling,' she said, giggling. 'I thought Kayla would approve.'

Kayla would have most definitely approved.

'I felt a bit strange about doing this tonight,' I confessed. 'You know, having a party here without Kayla. It felt wrong when I was thinking about it, but now I'm here, it really does feel like what she would have wanted. Do you know what I mean?'

My friends all nodded. They understood in the same way that had connected all of us throughout this tragedy. Maddison glanced over at the men to check they weren't listening in, and then said to us in a hushed tone, 'I know it's stupid, but I've been worrying all day, as had this completely unfounded thought pop into my head that Luke might have met someone. I know it's ridiculous and I've got no reason to think it, but I just couldn't shake the idea and half expected to turn up tonight to find a strange woman here.'

'The thought of him meeting someone else had crossed my mind too,' I admitted. 'But my brain is always coming up with extreme scenarios so pay absolutely no attention to me.'

'Can you imagine?' said Francesca. 'That would have been way too soon. I don't think I could have coped with that.'

Shannon sniffed, looking teary.

'Oh God, sorry to get all serious and make everyone cry so early in the night,' said Maddison. 'We should have had at least five drinks each before the emotional stuff set in. Just ignore me. I'm talking absolute rubbish anyway.'

Reaching for a tissue, I dabbed my own eyes, wishing that I hadn't been so enthusiastic with my mascara. I should have known that tonight would come with its fair share of tears.

'Let's ground our emotions by having a good old gossip,' said Francesca. 'I have something very top secret for you.'

'Ooh, do tell,' said Shannon, pulling herself together.

'Ok, she did swear me to secrecy, but I think it's only a matter of time before she tells you too, so I'll just save her the trouble.'

As comfortable as I was with Francesca now, she was definitely not someone I'd share my deepest, darkest, private thoughts with. One of her favourite pass times was divulging the latest gossip she'd heard. She paused for dramatic effect, making sure that she had our full attention.

'Louisa was right about her husband!'

'What do you mean?' Maddison asked.

'She was right to call him a 'cockwomble'. In fact, she should have called him far worse. He had been lying to her. She may have got her emojis confused, but her built-in wife radar had been right all along.'

311

'No way,' I said. 'How did she find out?'

'I don't actually know yet. She literally messaged me on my way over here. I replied straight away, but she said she'd call me tomorrow to tell me everything.'

'Wow, poor Louisa,' said Shannon.

'Do you think she'll come back to England?' I asked.

'I'd be surprised,' said Francesca. 'She loves it out there, and Lottie has just got settled in at her new school. I've got a horrible feeling she'll forgive him.'

'Why do men seem incapable of seeing when they're on to a good thing and keeping it in their pants,' exclaimed Shannon.

'Oi,' said Luke, overhearing. 'We're not all that bad!'

'Sorry,' blushed Shannon. 'Present company excepted, of course.'

Any further discussion was halted by Josh running into the kitchen with my bag. 'Mummy, what's this?' he said, pulling something out of it.

'Josh, what are you doing in my bag?' I said, taking it from him.

'I was looking for my LEGO figures I put in there to show Finn. What's that?' he persisted, pointing at the item I had safely tucked against my chest.

Ignoring him, I rummaged in my bag and sure enough found five LEGO figures that I had no idea Josh had put in there. 'Here you go,' I said handing them to him. Upon seeing his LEGO, he immediately forgot his interest in what I was holding and ran off to show Finn his pride and joy. Everyone else looked at me suspiciously.

'What have you got there that's so secret?' Jason asked playfully.

I had been waiting for the perfect time to get it out, but it seemed that Josh had now made that decision for me.

'It's a gift for Luke,' I said, taking a deep breath as I told myself to hold it together. I pulled it away from my chest so that everyone could see it. It was a book with Autobiographies by Amber printed on the bottom of the spine. A book that had been my project for the past few months. A project that I didn't even tell Jason about as I worked on it in secret. It was a book with a picture of a beautiful young woman on the cover, with a smile that would light up the darkest of days. It was a picture of Kayla.

There was silence in the room as all eyes went from the book that I was holding to Luke. He had been so composed and together moments before, but now you could see the heartbreak in his eyes, and I instantly wondered if I should have chosen a different time to give it to him. A time when it was just the two of us.

'Is that what I think it is, Amber?' he asked softly.

I nodded, holding his eyes with mine. 'Remember the night that Kayla came out for a drink with me so that I could practice my interviewing technique on her?'

'How could I forget?' he asked, chuckling. 'You got her so drunk that she woke me up to show me pictures on her phone of Morten Harket.'

'Who?' Jason asked looking blank.

'From Aha,' explained Maddison.

'From *Awho*?' Jason retorted.

'Never mind,' I interrupted. 'I'll educate you later.'

'Well, that night, Kayla told me a whole lot more than just about her crush on Morten Harket,' I explained. 'She told me three hours of things about her life. Three hours of pure, unadulterated, unfiltered gems that I feel honoured to have learnt about her. So, I wrote them into an autobiography for her... for you... to keep forever. You, Finn, and Eden.'

Luke was silent for a moment, and then tears flooded his eyes.

'Amber, I don't know what to say,' he stuttered. 'Thank you, thank you so much for doing this.'

He walked over and hugged me as I sat on the stool. I hugged him back, relieved that I could finally share it with him, and that he liked it. Releasing me from his hold, he took a step back, and I handed the book to him. He flicked through the pages with his thumb and shook his head in disbelief.

'This is honestly the most precious thing you could have ever given me. Being able to show this to Finn and Eden, and to let them look at it as they grow up and remember their mum in a way that they might otherwise have forgotten — it's just amazing, Amber.'

I felt Shannon's hand close over mine and saw that she had tears in her eyes too. In fact, I don't think there was a dry eye in the room at that moment.

'I think this is the perfect time for a toast,' said

Francesca. 'To our friend, who we will never, ever forget, Kayla.'

'To Kayla,' we all joined in, raising our glasses in the air.

The next few hours consisted of much drinking and laughing. After the emotions triggered by the surprise gift, we all promised each other that we would not shed another tear of sadness. We were all there together because of our love for Kayla, and she would want us to laugh. She would want us to smile… to sing… to dance. So, turning the music up, that's exactly what we did. Worried that they were missing out on all the fun, the kids all suddenly piled in together. High on the sugar rush of the sweets they had consumed, they too joined in the crazy dancing. Taking charge of the controls for a moment, I searched for the song that would, after that night, become *Kayla's girls* anthem.

'This,' I said, grabbing Jason round the waist, 'is your education.'

The unmistakeable sound of the synthesizer reverberated around the room as Shannon, Maddison, and Francesca squealed in recognition, and started playing invisible keyboards whilst chanting a very out of key *de-ne-ne-ne-ne-de-ne-de-ne-ne-ne-nah*. The kids all looked at us like we were lunatics as we mumbled various inaccurate lyrics between us until the chorus hit and we belted out Aha's 'Take On Me', loud and proud. When the song finished, we all sank onto the bar stools feeling exhausted.

'That one was for you, Kayla!' I shouted, and we all grabbed our near empty glasses and chinked them together.

Francesca picked up her phone and after tapping away for a minute she turned it round to show us a picture of modern-day Morten, announcing 'I still would!'

'You'd still what, Mum?' asked Francesca's daughter, Melody, who was in Ben's year.

We all smirked into our glasses at Francesca's faux pas as she forgot that little ears were listening.

'I still *would*... enjoy dancing to that song,' recovered Francesca. 'Come on, Melody, dance with me.'

That was the cue for all the kids to flee the room back to the safety of their sweets and movies before we could involve them in any more embarrassing mum dancing.

'I think that one's just about finished me off actually,' puffed Francesca. 'Shall we take a break?'

'Good idea,' agreed Shannon.

'We can't be far off midnight now,' said Luke.

'It's 10.57pm exactly,' declared Jason, slurring slightly where he'd had a few too many beers.

'Let me get everyone another drink,' said Luke. 'Then, I've got something to tell you all.'

As Luke wandered off to refuel his guests, I got a niggling feeling that there may be some substance to Maddison's premonition. I looked at him as he busied himself in the kitchen. Trying to read his body language, I deduced that he definitely looked more on edge than he had moments before when we were all dancing. Whilst Luke prepared the drinks, Maddison and I went to check on the kids who seemed surprisingly quiet all of a sudden.

'Maybe they've all gone to sleep,' said Maddison.

'Not a chance with my lot after all that lemonade and sweets.'

We were met with a tangle of arms and legs sprawled under duvets as they lay gazing at the TV screen like zombies.

'I think they've surpassed their high and have now entered their sugar slump,' Maddison said laughing.

'Are you all ok?' I asked.

'My tummy hurts,' said Eden.

I sat down on the floor next to her, and she immediately climbed onto my lap where I snuggled her in.

'I'm not surprised after all those sweets,' I said, stroking her hair. Samuel crawled across us to cuddle into me on the other side. Giving a big yawn, he lay his head down next to Eden's and pulled my other hand over to stroke his hair too. I glanced over at Finn, hoping that he was ok. Eden didn't think twice about letting all of us mother her in the absence of Kayla, but Finn tended to keep himself more distant. I'd asked Ben to make a special effort with him tonight. Finn could do with a surrogate big brother around to take him under his wing. I smiled to myself as I saw Finn on the sofa between Ben and Josh. His weary eyes looked like they could lose their fight to stay open any minute, but every time they started

317

to drop, I saw him blink them back open again in his determination to see in the stroke of midnight with the older children. Eden and Sammy, however, had succumbed to the relaxation of the little head massage I was giving them as I stroked their hair. Maddison arranged some pillows and duvets in the corner of the room, and between the two of us, we successfully manoeuvred them over there without waking them. Satisfied that everyone was either about to doze off or content watching the movie, we headed back to the kitchen to hear Luke's announcement.

'What do you think Luke's going to tell us?' whispered Maddison, pausing in the hallway.

'I'm not sure, but I can't help but think I'm not going to want to hear it,' I whispered back. 'What if your instincts were right and he's already met someone else?'

'No way,' Maddison rebuked, shaking her head. 'That was just me being stupid. It's far too soon. No-one could replace Kayla just four months after she died. No-one.'

'She would have to be pretty damn perfect to fill Kayla's shoes, that's for sure,' I agreed. 'Besides, Luke wouldn't even look at another woman yet. You can see how much he misses Kayla.'

'Hurry up, you two,' Francesca yelled from the kitchen. 'Luke won't tell us what's going on until you're here too.'

Maddison and I walked into the kitchen without a hint that we'd been lingering just outside the door, gossiping. Francesca and Shannon were still seated at the breakfast bar, as the men leant against it. Everyone had their drinks replenished, and there was an air of anticipation about what Luke was about to tell us. I suddenly became acutely aware of my senses, as I felt my anxiety heighten. If Louisa returned to England tomorrow and walked in here, she wouldn't believe us that Kayla had gone. The canvas on the wall of Finn and Eden's tiny hands grasping her fingers as her hand lay on a bed of lush green grass smattered with daisies. The top of the cupboards that she had transformed into a bookshelf, creating her own book ends out of glass jars filled with aqua coloured stones and LED lights that glowed a warm white accentuating their tones. The sign on the wall that said, *'Please excuse the mess, we're busy making memories'* that just summed up her approach to life. It all carried the essence of Kayla within it, and if I closed my eyes for just a minute and shut everything else out, I could pretend that Kayla was still there too. If Luke told us that he had met someone else, that was almost like the final acceptance that Kayla was gone, and selfishly, I didn't think I was ready for that.

'Firstly,' began Luke. 'I just want to say thank you. To all of you. Losing Kayla was the hardest, hardest thing to ever happen to me.'

Pausing, he took a deep breath to compose himself before his emotions engulfed him. I pursed my lips together and folded my fingers in, digging the nails into the palms of my hands in my own attempt to contain my anguish.

'But you have all helped us more than you will ever know,' he continued. 'The way you have supported me and been there for Finn and Eden is something I will never forget.'

'Oh, Luke,' Francesca said going over to hug him. 'How could we not? We loved Kayla. She was like a sister to us. All of us. You were part of Kayla so now you're part of us.'

'Whether you like it or not,' added Francesca's husband with a chuckle, trying to lighten the mood a little.

We all smiled and did that little *puff of breath accompanied by a low squeak* laugh that really needed its own name. A snort would come closest but didn't quite nail it. Maybe a *lanort,* or a *puffaugh,* or a *braugh.* That was a good one actually, a *braugh.* I marvelled at how my brain could be so random at a moment of such emotion. Whilst Francesca was saying words of comfort to Luke, I was inventing a new word for a long neglected bodily action. Kayla would have understood. The random conversations we would have over a cup of tea whilst Samuel and Eden played had never failed to disappoint, and were the privilege of a true friendship.

I glanced at Shannon who hadn't said a word yet. She had always been so accepting of my time spent with Kayla, despite me worrying that she would think I was stepping on the toes of their long-established friendship. Not once had she displayed any kind of jealousy though. In fact, she had been the complete opposite, embracing me as a new member of their clique. After nine years of feeling on the peripheral of the *school gate mum club,* I had become a fully-fledged member of my own lovely clique, courtesy of Kayla. She had welcomed me in a way that only Kayla could, and if Kayla embraced me, then it seemed to be an unwritten rule that Shannon embraced me too. Shannon was looking at Luke with worried eyes. I walked over to her side, knowing that she too was feeling anxious about what Luke was about to tell us.

Luke took a sip of his drink as if delaying his next words. Maybe he had changed his mind. Or maybe Maddison and I were being completely paranoid and had let our imaginations run away with us, and he actually had just wanted to thank us all for our support.

'There is something I need to tell all of you though,'

I guess not!

'There is someone who I have become unexpectedly close to during this time.'

I felt like someone had just punched me in the stomach. How could he meet someone else just four months after Kayla had died? It felt like he was confessing to cheating on her which I knew was irrational, but, as her friend, my immediate response was to jump to the defence of a betrayed wife.

'But Kayla's only just died,' I blurted out. 'How could you have met someone already?'

An uncomfortable silence followed which Maddison's husband felt the need to fill with an inane comment that would only come out the mouth of a man, 'Did you meet her on Tinder?'

He instantly regretted his mistimed attempt at humour when four pairs of female eyes bore on him like lasers.

'I don't understand,' said Francesca, looking confused. 'How have you even had the time to start dating when you've been grieving Kayla?'

Luke looked at Shannon with pleading eyes, as if hoping for some understanding.

'He's not been dating anyone,' she said, coming to his rescue. 'And he didn't mean for this to happen so soon after Kayla…' She couldn't finish her sentence as her eyes filled with tears.

'You knew?' Francesca said turning to Shannon, accusingly. 'You knew, and you didn't tell us?'

Luke walked over and stood next to Shannon putting a protective arm around her. 'I asked her not to say anything,' he said. 'Not until we were sure about things.'

'Oh, bloody hell, Luke,' said Francesca. 'It's your therapist, isn't it? The grief counsellor we convinced you to go and see. Of course, it is. I knew I should have found you a man instead of a woman!'

'No, Francesca,' said Luke with a chuckle of disbelief. 'It's not my therapist. And it's not someone from Tinder,' he added, looking sceptically at Maddison's husband.

'So, who is it then?' demanded Francesca.

I didn't need to wait for the answer though. Looking at Luke right there and then, I knew.

'Shannon?' I softly questioned, before I even realised that I had voiced my thoughts out loud.

'I'm sure Luke can tell us himself now, Amber,' said Francesca, missing my meaning, obviously feeling incensed that Luke had told Shannon and not her.

Shannon looked me in the eye, and I needed no further confirmation. I looked from her to Luke and back to her again. Of course, it was so obvious now. I put my hands together and brought them to my mouth knowing what this meant. I walked over to Luke and Shannon whilst everyone else in the room stood there, their minds hanging about thirty seconds behind ours. My show of support gave Luke the confidence he needed to finally make his announcement.

'It's Shannon,' he said, as everyone's jaws looked like they were about to drop to the ground. 'The person I have a connection with is Shannon.'

Chapter 41

Everyone stood there in shock, as they filtered this new found information into their brains.

'Ok,' said Maddison, being the first one to gather herself. 'This feels so weird right now, and it's probably none of my business, but I really need to know. How the hell did this happen with none of us noticing?'

Luke looked at Shannon, and the affection between the two of them was undeniable. I couldn't comprehend how I'd missed it before.

'We didn't mean to hide it from you,' Shannon said. 'I was going to tell you in our group chat that day when you were trying to set me up, but it felt more like something we needed to tell you face to face… together.'

'Oh my God,' blurted out Francesca. 'Please tell me you two weren't having an affair when Kayla was alive. You were, weren't you? You were having an affair behind her back!'

Luke and Shannon both shouted, 'No,' in unison.

'I loved Kayla,' defended Luke. 'I still do love her. The thought of being with Shannon never crossed my mind when Kayla was here.'

Francesca and Maddison didn't look convinced.

'It crossed Shannon's though, didn't it, Shannon?' Maddison said in a tone that I don't think she would have used had she not had that last drink Luke had poured her. 'You've never made a secret of thinking that Luke was perfect husband material.'

Shannon's cheeks went red, and she looked like she was about to burst into tears. Feeling protective, I went to her aid.

'Do you really think Shannon and Luke would have had an affair behind Kayla's back?' I asked incredulously to the two woman who were supposed to be some of her closest friends. 'They didn't plan this! Shannon and Kayla had a bond closer than any of us. How could you even think that Shannon and Luke would betray the trust of Kayla. She thought the world of both of them.'

I glanced back at Luke and Shannon just to check that my faith in the pair of them wasn't about to make me look like a complete gullible tit. 'You didn't have an affair, did you?' I muttered under my breath.

'No,' they both assured me, looking offended.

'So, how did this happen then?' repeated Maddison in a calmer tone this time.

Luke and Shannon proceeded to fill us in on the part of their friendship that none of us knew had been growing over the past few months. We had all done our bit helping Luke, but none of us were naïve to the fact that Shannon had been there for him the most. In the early days after Kayla's death, she had taken him meals several nights a week, she'd often helped get Finn and Eden to bed, and we knew that she had stayed over a few times as well when Finn went through a stage of waking up with nightmares and it had all seemed too much for Luke.

When they had told us everything, Shannon looked at all of us with tears flowing. 'We only kissed for the first time, last week,' she said, looking worried that we would judge her. 'We both felt the connection we had, but neither of us acted on it before then, knowing it would be wrong. But when we kissed, it didn't feel wrong. This was Luke, my best friend's husband, and it shouldn't have felt right, but it did. And I don't know how to explain it. And I didn't know how to tell you guys because I knew that you would hate me for it.'

'Why would we hate you for it?' I interrupted, taking Shannon's hand. I was a far cry from the person who had felt anxious about Luke declaring a new love for an unknown person as I'd whispered in the hallway with Maddison. That would have been too hard to take. The thought that Kayla had meant so little to him that he had just switched his feelings off and moved on to the next thing he could find. But this wasn't like that. This was him finding love with someone that Kayla also loved. I knew that it was time to show them a page from the autobiography I had written for Kayla. Words that I'd

326

been repeating in my mind since the revelation presented itself.

'I need to show you all something,' I said. I picked up the book that Luke had placed at the end of the breakfast bar so that he could succumb to it in a moment of quiet where he could breathe in the words that Kayla spoke to me those short few months ago. I absent-mindedly wiped my hands on my dress to protect the precious cover from any smudges my fingertips may unwittingly leave there. Trying to remember the exact page that I needed, I thumbed through until I found what I was looking for. Without speaking, I took it over to Luke and Shannon so that they could absorb the words before everyone else became privy to them.

The room was silent, as everyone looked on with curiosity. Laying the book down with the page open in front of them, I touched Luke and Shannon on their shoulders and stepped around to where Jason stood. He looked at me questioningly, as he put his arm around my shoulders. I saw a tear escape from Shannon's eye, as she brought a hand up to her mouth. Time seemed to stand still around us, as I allowed the poignance of what they were reading to sink in, as our other friends stood staring, wondering. When Luke finally looked up, I could see that he was crying too.

'Thank you,' he said quietly, looking deep into my eyes. His eyes said so much more than his words, and the impact of what he was feeling hit me like a tidal wave. Kayla had given me the power to give Luke and Shannon so much more than her blessing. She had told them something that they would never in their wildest dreams have expected to hear.

'Are you going to let us in on it?' Francesca asked tentatively. Hopefully feeling sheepish after her assumption that Luke and Shannon had been having an affair for years, her voice was much softer than its usual commanding tone.

'I don't think I could read it without my voice breaking,' said Shannon.

'Can you read it, Amber?' Luke asked, passing me the book. 'They're your wise words.'

'Kayla's wise words,' I corrected him. 'I was just the vessel through which she channelled them.'

Taking a sip of my drink, my mind took me back to the night that Kayla and I had sat in the pub, laughing and sharing far more than we'd ever realised we would. Probably far more than anyone should.

'Ok, so the night that I practised my interviewing skills on Kayla,' I explained, 'we spoke about a whole tonne of things as I already told you. And some of those things were rather random to say the least. One being a revelation as to who she would choose as a husband if Luke left her for Gal Gadot.'

Luke blushed as I revealed his secret celebrity crush.

'And,' I continued, 'who she would choose as a wife for Luke if the roles were reversed. So, this is what Kayla said to me, pretty much word for word.'

As I started reading, it was my voice that the rest of

the room listened to, but to me, it was Kayla's voice that I heard, softly and clearly in my head. I felt like she was there with us, willing me to bring us all back together from the moment of distance created when Maddison and Francesca wrongly assumed that Luke and Shannon had done the unthinkable and betrayed the person closest to them.

'…but if Luke didn't choose to leave me for Gal Gadot and I suddenly vanished in an alien abduction or a plane crash which left me stranded in the Amazon jungle with no choice but to wed the tribal chief to stop them from eating me…'

'How much had you two had to drink that night, Amber?' interrupted Jason.

'Erm, just a little bit,' I replied.

'It sounds like the two of you were having a drunken game of *Would You Rather,*' smirked Maddison. 'Would you rather die in a plane crash or spend the rest of your life tending to the animalistic needs of a tribal chief?'

'Shush, you lot', Francesca said impatiently, 'I want to hear the rest.'

'…there is only one person I would want him to replace me with,' I continued. 'Someone who is beautiful inside and out, and deserves a man like Luke as much as he would deserve a woman like her if I couldn't be that woman to him.' I paused as everyone looked intently at me, waiting to hear me say what surely, by now, they must have all realised was coming.

'Shannon Rose Mitchell.'

Epilogue –
Six months later

'I'm just going to nip to the loo quickly,' I said to Jason, getting up from the table.

'You only went ten minutes ago, Amber,' he replied, rolling his eyes.

'I know, but I'm nervous, and this wine is going right through me. I'll just be a sec.'

Failing in my attempt to walk elegantly with poise, I stepped out of the six-inch heels that had seemed like such a good idea when the advert for them had flashed up on my phone after a conversation with Shannon. The spy technology that invaded our lives did have its perks. I wasn't so keen, however, on the random appearance of adverts about things that I was sure had only ever been apparent in the confines of my over active imagination and never voiced out loud. That intrusive conundrum had left me uncomfortably baffled on more than one occasion.

Picking my shoes up in my hand, I admired the beauty in the topaz blue trim detail that looked so pleasing to the eye whilst bearing untold pain on the feet. It reminded me of a blue ringed octopus, alluring yet deadly. I was wearing the same dress that I had worn on New Year's Eve as couldn't justify the expense of a new one that I wouldn't wear again any time soon. I had felt much more glamourous wearing it with my new shoes rather than the Ugg boots I'd chosen last time, but after two hours of ignoring the pain, I couldn't bear it any longer.

Shannon appeared at the door as I was washing my hands with the luxury liquid soap that hinted at the expense of the night.

'Come on, Amber! Jason sent me to get you. It's nearly time.'

Taking one last look in the mirror, I patted down a tendril that had escaped its hair grip and smiled at Shannon. Linking her arm with mine, we walked back to the table where Jason was seated with Luke, Francesca, and Maddison, and their husbands. All around us were tables of other people dressed up to the nines, drinking Champagne and laughing. You could have thought we'd accidentally walked into a wedding reception that we hadn't been invited to had it not been for the banners around the room emblazoned with *New Business of The Year* on them.

A year ago, the thought that I would be seated here

tonight, would have never crossed my mind. But thanks to my passion for creating an autobiography for Maria Denning so that her family could remember the person she once was as her Alzheimer's took hold, Autobiographies by Amber had gone from strength to strength. Maria's daughter, Jenna, had been so happy with the finished product that she had shared it with an Alzheimer's support group she was part of online which inspired other families to follow suit. In less than a year of setting the business up, I had created nearly twenty autobiographies, and had enough commissioned to keep me going for the foreseeable future. I couldn't have hoped for a better start. There was no doubt in my mind that Kayla was shining down on me every step of the way.

Knowing that I was too humble to put myself forward for an award, Shannon, Francesca, and Maddison had secretly submitted an application on my behalf, two months earlier. Four weeks ago, they had surprised me with the news that I had been shortlisted for an award that I hadn't even known I'd entered.

The noise in the room faded as the room darkened and lights shone onto the stage. A man I didn't recognise, but Jason assured me was well regarded in the local business community, addressed the tables of guests, informing us that the main award of the night was about to be announced.

'Put your shoes back on, Amber,' Shannon hissed at me from her seat. 'You can't go up on the stage barefoot!'

'I won't need to,' I whispered back. 'I won't win.

There's so many great businesses here.'

I was thankful to have been shortlisted, and grateful to my friends for having such belief in me and showing their support for Autobiographies by Amber, but felt ninety-eight percent certain that I wouldn't win. Obviously, there was that tiny two percent of my brain that allowed me the indulgence of thinking *maybe, just maybe.* But two percent certainly wasn't enough to make me put my shoes back on for the miniscule chance that I would have to make my way up onto the stage in front of all of these people. *But what if I did have to, and everyone was looking at me struggling to squeeze my feet in?* Feet that had suddenly expanded to a width never destined to comply with the unnaturally narrow shoes they had obediently succumbed to a few hours before. Changing my mind, I allowed myself the two percent indulgence as I hurriedly navigated my toes in, wincing as I squished them on top of each other to make room.

I nervously picked up my glass of wine, acknowledging that my state of tension maybe indicated that a more realistic ten percent of my brain was hoping for my name to be called. Jason took hold of my other hand, and leant over to kiss me on the cheek.

'Good luck, Amby,'

I pulled an anxious face at him, allowing my eyes to reveal the hope that I was feeling increase by the second as the moment of truth drew near. I don't think I'd allowed myself to ponder on the reality of winning before. It had felt safer to tell myself that I didn't stand a

chance, and give the cliché line that *having my friends nominate me made me feel like a winner already.* I had focused on the excitement of an actual night out with grown-ups, getting glammed up and enjoying the fine food and wine. Now there was a part of me that did actually want to win, although the rational part of my brain kept
reminding me that that wasn't likely to happen.

'And the winner of New Business in the Southern Region this year goes to....'

I closed my eyes. There was silence around me, except for the drum roll of someone's hands on a table nearby. This established entrepreneur that everyone in the room seemed to know except for me certainly knew how to create tension with a dramatic pause. I imagined myself on camera at The Oscars and quickly snapped my eyes open ready to show my gracious loser face as all eyes watched me, hoping that I'd betray myself by getting caught swearing in disappointment, thinking no-one could see me. Even now, at such a momentous point in my life, my imagination was running wild. These awards, whilst poignant to me, were hardly television worthy.

'A business that has been born from passion,' continued Mr Entrepreneur himself. 'A business routed in *com*passion. A business that will thrive under the ethos of its leader.'

Bollocks, it's not me. I'm not a leader. It's just little old me in my business.

'A business that is so distinctive in its approach that is today, the entirety of just one person, but will undoubtedly grow under their direction.'

Oh, could be me still. Back in the running!

'A business that…'

Oh for fuck's sake. Just get to the bloody point, Mr I Love The Sound Of My Own Voice!

'I take great pleasure in presenting this award to Autobiographies by Amber!'

The room erupted into applause as I sat dumbfounded, wondering if I had actually heard him right or whether my mind was playing tricks on me. There was no doubt in my friends' minds though as Shannon, Maddison, and Francesca all squealed at once, and leapt up to rush around the table to hug me in celebration. Allowing us our moment, Jason held back and then ushered me to my feet, as I realised that I needed to go and collect my award and give a speech.

I suddenly wished that my ego had allowed me enough confidence to factor winning into my game plan so that I could have at least prepared something. Practising a speech had been pushed firmly to the back of my mind, as had seemed far too arrogant and a waste of time as my self-doubt kept telling me that I was just here for a night out with friends.

Thankful that I had put my heels back on just in time, I ignored the pain and made my way to the stage, feeling the burn of everyone's eyes on me. I walked in a slow and measured way, as I put all my effort into not tripping over. I was just going to have to wing the speech when I got up there.

I walked up the makeshift steps which wobbled a little under my weight and accepted the outstretched hand of the presenter. At about fifty-years-old, with a nice full head of grey hair, he looked and smelt expensive.

'Don't look so scared,' he whispered to me away from the microphone. 'You have a business to be proud of.'

I looked him in the eye and felt guilty for calling him *Mr I Love The Sound Of My Own Voice* in my head. He had a kind face, and I wondered if he had been part of the judging team and had championed me to win. The thought filled me with reassurance.

'Amber Clayton,' he said into the microphone. 'Congratulations on the success of your new business. Now the stage is all yours to tell this lovely audience what drove you to stand where you are right now.'

Passing the microphone to me, he stepped to one side, allowing me to take centre stage. I tried to seek out Jason and my friends in the crowd, but the spotlight shining on me was so bright that I could only look in the general direction that I knew I'd come from.

'Well,' I said, slightly startled as the sound of my voice filled the room. 'It all started when I accidently put a message in a group text including my boss instead of the friend it was intended for.' Laughter filled the room as I imagined Jason putting his head in his hands at my usual lack of a filter in an uncomfortable situation.

'After being told that my services were no longer required, a wonderful, wise friend reminded me that I was a strong, independent woman.' A few cheers erupted from the audience at this point as the women in the room registered their approval. 'And that I could embrace my love of writing, and create a company with the values I cherished. The belief that everyone's story deserved to be told and with my help, others would be able to listen.'

I was no longer nervous as I spoke into the microphone. I realised that I hadn't needed to plan a speech as it was the personal touch that made Autobiographies by Amber the success that it was becoming. There was nothing rehearsed or orchestrated about it. I told the story of people's lives as they shared it with me. Openly and honestly. And that is what my moment in the spotlight, *my Oscar moment*, was – pure and honest.

'Firstly, I would like to thank my friends, Shannon, Francesca, and Maddison, as had it not been for their sneaky application behind my back, the judges would probably never have heard of me. *Kayla's girls*, I love you all!'

The audience wouldn't have understood their nickname, but they would have done and that is all that mattered.

'I would like to thank Maria Denning and her daughter, Jenna,' I continued. 'For putting their trust in me to tell Maria's story, and allowing me to learn with them along the way so that I could approach future clients with Alzheimer's with the understanding and respect they deserve.'

A respectful clap arose from the audience at this point

337

as some people reflected on loved ones they may have had with dementia.

'I would like to thank my husband, Jason, for being the best husband and dad to our four boys I could ever ask for, even if he did boil peas in the kettle once – but that's another story!'

Whilst Jason undoubtedly cringed lower in his seat at my over-sharing revelation, I allowed the laughter at his expense to die down before thanking my last person.

'And finally, and most importantly, I would like to thank my friend, Kayla. I hadn't actually known Kayla for very long, but in that short time, she became very special to me. She was the one who pushed me to go it alone and start Autobiographies by Amber. Without her belief in me, and her ability to make me believe, none of this would have happened. I owe this all to her. They say that people come into your life for a reason, a season, or a lifetime. Well, Kayla came into mine for all three. She will be in my heart until the day our souls meet again, and I would like to dedicate this award to her precious memory.'

Holding up the award for everyone to see, I finished my speech with tears in my eyes. Tears of happiness, tears of sadness, tears of acceptance.

'This is for Kayla.'

Autobiographies by Amber…

Kerry Gibb was so inspired by the journey that she created for Amber with, Autobiographies by Amber, that she has actually set it up as a real-life venture. Creating the fictional joy that it brought to Maria Denning's family and then Kayla's family triggered an idea that she just couldn't let go of – if she could create such joy for her fictional characters, then imagine how amazing it would be to bring such emotion to every-day people. Find out more at www.autobiographiesbyamber.com

Other books by Kerry Gibb

If you enjoyed this, and you want your kids to
experience the same love of books, then please do
check out the It's A Kid's Life series for children aged
roughly seven to eleven. There are five in the series
which you can buy from the kerrygibb.com website,
Amazon, Waterstones, and all good bookshops. All
copies bought through the kerrygibb.com website can
also be personally signed to your child which really
does make the book special for them.

It's A Kid's Life

It's A Kid's Life – Arch-Enemies

It's A Kid's Life – Double Digits

It's A Kid's Life – Christmas Countdown

It's A Kid's Life – Camp Chaos

Acknowledgements

The first person that I need to thank here is the mum who contacted me to say how much she was loving reading It's A Kid's Life with her son and could I write one for the mums! This little seed of thought set in motion the wheels that quickly gained momentum to become Kayla's Girls.

Next, I would like to thank all of my readers for spending your precious 'me-time' with Kayla's Girls. Whether you are starting your journey in motherhood, a fully-fledged mum in the midst of it, or a grandmother who looks back with fond memories, I hope that this book resonated with you. One of my readers described it as 'getting a hug from a friend' when she finished the book which I absolutely loved. I felt like these characters were my friends when I wrote this and I hope they made you feel that way too.

Thank you to my wonderful friends, Gemma Stanton and Joanna Double, for reading the book during my time of self-doubt and giving me the kick up the backside that I needed to allow it to be read by others. Putting your creative side out there to be judged is a scary process, and having the support of friends like this in my life to achieve great things with is invaluable. Thank you also, Gemma, for happening to be an incredibly talented graphic designer and bringing my visions for my cover to life. Our psychological analysis of our different visions of the glass of wine spilling will always make me laugh!

Finally, thank you to my boys for accepting that this is one story that I couldn't read to them as I was writing it, but still giving me words of encouragement despite this. Their belief in me is what has made me the author I am today.

Writing this book has had me on a roller coaster journey of emotions but I have loved every second of it. I hope that you have enjoyed reading it as much as I enjoyed writing it. I love to hear from my readers, so please do get in touch via social media. Letting others know about a book means the world to authors like myself so please do tell your friends, shout about it on social media, and leave a lovely review – I do read each and every one of them.

Printed in Great Britain
by Amazon